Linda Lenhoff*

*Your Actual Life May Vary

A NOVEL

Copyright © Linda Lenhoff 2025
All rights reserved. No part of this book may be reproduced or transmitted in any form or by any means electronic or mechanical including photocopying recording or any information storage and retrieval system without permission in writing from the Publisher.

Library of Congress Cataloging-in-Publication Data
Names: Lenhoff, Linda, author.
Title: *Your actual life may vary / Linda Lenhoff.
Description: Santa Fe, NM: SFWP, 2025. | Summary: "In Linda Lenhoff's quirky comedy *Your Actual Life May Vary, faltering grad student Patty Grant escapes Southern California in search of a new place to live up north for herself and the young boy she has accidentally stolen. Instead, she finds a community where everyone has something to hide. She might just fit right in"—Provided by publisher.
Identifiers: LCCN 2024040143 (print) | LCCN 2024040144 (ebook) | ISBN 9781951631451 (trade paperback) | ISBN 9781951631468 (ebook)
Subjects: LCGFT: Humorous fiction. | Novels.
Classification: LCC PS3612.E53 Y68 2025 (print) | LCC PS3612.E53 (ebook) | DDC 813/.6—dc23/eng/20241210
LC record available at https://lccn.loc.gov/2024040143
LC ebook record available at https://lccn.loc.gov/2024040144

COVER ILLUSTRATION: Scott Baldwin
AUTHOR PHOTO: Haley Nelson

Published by SFWP
369 Montezuma Ave. #350
Santa Fe, NM 87501
www.sfwp.com

Contents

Chapter 1	Your Call Is Important	1
Chapter 2	Over the River	19
Chapter 3	The Color of My Parachute	43
Chapter 4	A Marshmallow World	65
Chapter 5	Over the River and Through the Woods	83
Chapter 6	Purple Mountain's Majesty	107
Chapter 7	Lost: Little Boy	127
Chapter 8	The Very Definition of Bereft	153
Chapter 9	The Best Possible World	169
Chapter 10	Safe Passage	179
Chapter 11	Day Is Done	195
Chapter 12	Visual Disturbances	213
Chapter 13	Purple Mountain's Majesty (Redux)	235
Chapter 14	Family, a Noun	255
Epilogue	My Actual Life May Vary	269

In memory of Patricia Everitt, for so many reasons.

It should be clear by now that the truth about the place is elusive, and must be tracked with caution.

—Joan Didion

Eureka, we have found it.

—California State Motto

Chapter 1

Your Call Is Important

Here's what I know, I tell myself each morning as I walk: There's a little boy four doors down chained to a doghouse in his backyard. There's a little boy chained up behind a house in my neighborhood. I let the sentences repeat in my mind as I take each step, the way children repeat rhymes as they jump to the next square in hopscotch. As if it will propel me forward. As if saying it does anything for anyone at all.

I start my walk to campus down a hill of broken sidewalk, a reminder that it's earthquake territory out here. I count the houses as a kind of mantra, one, two, three, then four, as if it will bring luck, which sometimes it does. Sometimes, I don't see him. I have to wonder, though, What do people in houses two and three think? What kind of comforting rhymes do they tell themselves?

House four: It's a sickly light green, shades always drawn, the dog run along the side leading no doubt to a back yard filled with overgrown weeds, mangled tree limbs, swirls of silt leading upward but not in an optimistic way. Sometimes I make out his little legs, ending in a pair of imitation Keds tennis shoes.

There's a little boy chained to a doghouse in my neighborhood. And I've done nothing about it, I whisper to the stop sign at the corner.

I'm the kind of person who's done nothing about it, I say silently to the crossing guard, who's too busy to notice me anyway.

But I'm pretty nearsighted. I once mistook this very stop sign for that very crossing guard, when some kids had put an orange jacket over it at Halloween. With my vision, he, she, it (how can I know)—the figment of my imagination on the dog chain could well be a German shepherd. A smallish one.

A German shepherd in imitation Keds. A German shepherd playing with imitation Keds. My imaginings do not soothe me.

Plus, there's this weather. San Diego choking smoggy mornings, afternoons that can heat up beyond expectation and reason. The dryness—it causes hallucinations, fantasies. Drought and destruction and cracked-up sidewalks. Face it, it's a desert, a mirage in itself.

That's right Patty (I say this to myself a lot, along with Wake up Patty, It's good for you Patty, and Just don't think about it Patty). That's right Patty: There's (maybe) a little boy chained to a dog run on the side of a house. In this heat. A little boy imagining mirages, dreaming something unimaginable, like trying to escape his leash in imitation Keds.

No wonder I'm always so sweaty by the time I reach school.

I'm sitting in my teaching cubicle—not an office, just a couple of closely placed partition walls, a desk, and a highly valued window—watching unexpected rain fill up the library pit. It's not really a library pit, of course, but a construction ditch for what's known as the new Library Center. No one's announced when it'll be finished, just as they haven't announced why it's called the Library Center instead of just Library, or even what was wrong with the old Library. As if every so often, every institution, every city, every town gets a new library, whether it needs it or not. The rain's sudden increase makes me wonder how weather can change so quickly, if we've done something indefensible to the environment, if we even have a chance. There's a sharp coolness in the air that wasn't there four hours ago, something not entirely unwelcome but still a little alarming. The steady raindrops tap against my window like a shy student wanting my attention but who's also afraid I'll notice how really badly he/she/they are doing in my class. This rain (and any rain is unexpected here), though I'm happy to see it, has begun to muddy most of the campus within my view. If it doesn't let up in a few hours, the streets will be flooded and traffic accidents will be in the double digits. You'll hear sirens from all directions. Plus, it's slowly, hypnotically, putting me to sleep.

I've fallen asleep before after teaching my back-to-back freshman English courses. Most of the graduate teachers come into our shared area all springy and wired, babbling of peer editing groups and issues debated, abortion, euthanasia, racial integration. The issues never change; they're in no way seasonal. As for me, well, I tend to go straight for my cubicle, look out the window at the pit, checking to make sure no progress has been made, as usual, and fall into dreamy sleep. I have probably failed to find my proper calling, and not for the first time. More than once, students have had to wake me to ask questions, but often they just leave little notes on my desk. "Came by to see you!" "Hope you feel better!" "Need help with essay when you're well!" I find it touching that they figure I'm sick. While sometimes I do have a headache, sleeping is just my natural reaction to teaching.

I am not very good at this.

But today I'm not just tired from classes, as I've gotten a memo that adds to the drowsiness, although you'd think it would get my heart pounding. It announces that the Samsons, both English teachers, both about sixty-five, with his and hers short gray haircuts (the kind of cut that's so short it looks prickly, like one of those things you wipe snowy boots on) have taken early retirement. The Samsons, my sometimes advisors (I never ask for much advice), my all-the-time landlords, have no doubt been forced out, as I can't imagine they'd ever voluntarily leave here. They love campus, decorating the place each Christmas with sprigs of fir, each Easter leaving little chocolate eggs for all their students. In the autumn they go out to the mountains and bring in fallen leaves, then scatter them through the halls for us to crunch our way through. They even clean up afterward.

I hold up my memo until the words start to blur. A voice wakes me.

"So much for Grandpa and Grandma," says a fellow graduate student, a dark, curly haired guy several years my junior (but aren't they all). I think his name is Mark, but for some reason, he's always referred to as Anti. He's part of the group known as neuropostmodernists around here. Their name for themselves, but many of us consider it a euphemism.

"I'm very fond of them," I say. "They've always been nice to me," which is true. They've hinted at wanting to sell me the house when I get a real teaching position, which they've hinted they'll make sure I get after earning my MFA. It's the most natural, familial gesture anyone's made to me in years.

"You're just buying into the sappiness of the status quo," the AntiMark says.

"You're just young and don't know anything," I think but don't say. Age is relative, of course, and I am old to be a graduate student, but I can't take seriously a twenty-two-year-old guy with neuropostmodernistic tendencies—whatever they may be, and I do have a feeling something sexual is involved—and sneakers that cost over two hundred dollars, although I'm estimating.

"I run toward sap," I say, turning away. The rain picks up outside, rattling the windows. I wonder if the neuropostmodernists have thought up some progressive, advanced way to get home in this rain without an umbrella, but I doubt it.

I walk home quickly, a *San Diego Union Tribune* over my head—I picked it since it's a little thicker than *USA Today*, which of course is also in color and might run onto my clothes. I pass by house number four without looking up, afraid of what I'll see, or what I might think I see. I do slow down though and listen (my hearing is far better than my eyesight anyhow), but all I hear is rain, drops hitting the ground, the deeper sound of drops hitting that doghouse. My grandmother used to say that not knowing was worse than knowing, and she may be right, unless what you find out is that there's a muddy boy in a splintering doghouse waiting for something else you can't imagine. I try to picture my grandmother's face, what she might say to this, but for some reason, she won't meet my eye.

Patty, you may need another nap.

But no, today something different is planned for me. I get home and change my wet clothes, then get in my car and head for the local Hilton hotel. I've never done this before, and I can't be sure why I agreed to do it now. Still.

You may already be a winner, Patty, I tell myself, driving carefully so that (a) I don't hit anyone and (b) the windshield wipers don't put me to sleep. I'm headed for a perfect rainy day activity, I tell myself, although I'd be embarrassed to tell anyone else.

The invitation came in a phone call, the kind you get at dinnertime, the kind you know better than to answer, but when you live alone, you don't always have your best interests at heart. Besides, I told myself, it's bad to eat dinner in front of the TV. Much better to eat while talking on the phone, which means you can talk to strangers with your mouth full, breaking two parental prohibitions at once. I surreptitiously took bites of chicken as the guy told me that I'd filled out an entry form to win a new Camaro, reminding me (of course) that I hadn't won the new Camaro but am a prizewinner nonetheless. Something electronic. Something electronic and new and free, if only I'd come to my choice of breakfast or late-afternoon lunch and listen to a presentation on a new planned community. Or a planned new community. I probably swallowed at this point and missed the real order, but it may not really matter. As any underpaid graduate student knows, the words *lunch is included* have a certain appeal.

The hall is warm and cozy at the Hilton, something I hadn't expected. It's the kind of room that's usually freezing with air conditioning, but somehow they've one-upped the weather, and this place is toasty without being too warm. I settle into an overly cushioned blue chair—there must be hundreds of them—and discover that it rocks slightly, not to mention that it's the kind of soft I must have always been looking for in a chair without even realizing it. I now know how Goldilocks must have felt.

I'm almost too comfortable to get up for the buffet, but the sweet smells of Danish, warmed turkey, mashed potatoes, and steaming chicken soup lure me. There's something to admire in a place that serves you chicken soup. Maybe they know more about me than I think. It's not even Campbell's, but something someone has chopped and stewed personally. The meal embraces me and those around me as we each eat in our slightly rocking seats, which have been pulled up to tables covered in deep blue cloth. The napkins are orange—real fabric, not paper. I realize that this moment is everything I've always wanted from Thanksgiving, as it's lacking only in family bickering and that disappointing cranberry sauce you slice out of a can. Whatever has led me here, I'm thankful.

I snap out of it only a little as the lights dim for the presentation. Somehow, I expected an old-fashioned slide show, someone clicking away at a rickety projector, the occasional slide turned upside-down. But welcome to the information age, Patty, where everything you need is digital. (Unless you're a graduate teacher—we have to bring our own laptops to class. But don't think about that now Patty.) No distracting clicking here, just the sounds of Windham Hill-like music behind a soothing woman's voice, the kind of voice that would anticipate your every need, offering you a second Danish before you'd finished the first. The kind of voice you'd want to accept from. Yes, thank you so much. I do want a second pastry, a warm cinnamon roll. I hadn't even realized how important one could be.

And I want to live in Santa Vallejo, I tell the voice, of course I do. The presentation brings to life all of our hopes and dreams: Not only does the room contain all the scents of home, the movie fills our eyes with visions of needs fulfilled, needs met by the new community of

Santa Vallejo. Parents hug little children and send them to play on the shiniest of swing sets. Grandparents cook up a stew in the kitchen of a house that could be yours (Patty), although it has clearly been cleaned by someone a little more attentive. In the kitchen's background I could swear I see the same pastries we've just consumed. Freshly baked. Smelling of cinnamon. Seconds and thirds. Back in the town center, low, tiled office buildings blend into the community. "Community," the woman's voice repeats at us, "community," although I'm not really registering the words as much as waiting for Grandma to reappear, waiting to see what lies beyond the next playground and the next, one tree-lined street after another, the houses with spaces between them large enough for another house. Teachers lead bands of children dressed in clean primary-colored clothing, some holding balloons. Malls greet you and fit into the architecture (of the community). Cleanliness. Godliness. All the comforts of home. Not too big, not too small. This place is just right.

After the show I find I've been asleep in my chair, the room quieted. Others are asleep, too, but not in any insulting way, not out of boredom. We've been rocked to sleep by the grannies of our dreams, by those with the power to say yes, yes you may. As I rise, a person hands me a brochure entitled *Santa Vallejo—the Promise of Community* and a small black-and-white traveling TV. I feel like I've been given an assignment, but then I remember that I was supposed to win a prize. For a brief moment I'm unsure which I value more, the TV or the brochure with its promise. It's a nice brochure, four color, thick, luxurious. With my arms and tummy full, I feel sated, as if I've gone home for a visit to a loving family (not mine) and they've loaded me up with homemade packages to take home. And promises they intend to keep.

The feeling lasts all the way home. I take my treasures into the house and find a note stuck under my door. It's from the Samsons, my somewhat adoptive family and sometime advisors, writing me a note, sharing their thoughts with me. They love me. I feel truly full, sated. I want to hug everything that is mine. Oh, the power of the written word, Patty. Savor it, Patty.

Dear Patty,
You've probably heard that we've accepted the Golden Handshake and are retiring. Well, life does hold its surprises. We've loved teaching and are so glad it has brought so many people into our lives, and we include you among our most treasured students. We're so sorry to say that we're going to need the house back. We'll have to consolidate our finances for our retirement, and we plan to move back into our small house that you've been so kind to care for. We've loved having you as a tenant and, we hope, as our friend. We wish you luck in every endeavor. Won't you please be out by the fifteenth?
Love, Elizabeth and George Samson

December fifteenth. Two days after the end of the semester. One week from yesterday. Seven whole days because they've loved knowing me. I think about all these numbers and passages of time as I go into the living room—with its nice old-fashioned moldings and working fireplace filled with wood. It's not really cold enough, but I don't care. I light the fireplace and watch the flames overcome the logs. On top of the fire, I place their letter. Warm as the room gets, I can't completely regain the feeling from this afternoon. But I still feel a little something hopeful. I can still picture the grandparents from the video, their arms open, offering sweets and something deeper, something true, something that's out there somewhere. They really look nothing like the Samsons.

In the morning, I stop at door number three. It's someone's dream house, the color of strawberry Haagen Daz, as clean and tidy and welcoming outside as the cottage Hansel and Gretel must have approached. The front door mat has bluebirds on it.

I knock softly, even though it's 8:45 and the neighborhood is up and hopping. I can hear that crossing guard down at the main intersection. She sings *Do Re Mi* today. Hearing it makes me glad I don't live nearer to the intersection. No one answers at the pink door, so I knock a little more forcefully, although I can't get the picture of Julie Andrews spinning around on that mountaintop out of my head. I know it's not even the right scene for the song. Finally, through a small square window centered high on the pink door, I see the top of a woman's head, an older woman. Many of my neighbors, I've been told, have lived in the area for years, lifetimes, which would explain the gray head top I see before me. *Doe, a deer, a female deer—*

"Yes," the gray top says through the door.

"Hi," I say, "I'm Patty Grant; I live in the Samson's house two doors down?" I point in my direction, then circle my hands around over my head as if describing my house as a large mushroom.

"Yes?"

"I'm your neighbor?" I wait. Nothing much happens. *Me, a name, I call myself.* "I was wondering if I could talk to you about the child next door?"

"Oh?"

"Could you open the door, just maybe a crack?"

"No, dear, we just don't do that."

Oh. "Well, have you noticed the child? Does it seem mistreated to you?" I lower my voice slightly at the word mistreated. I'm not sure if the whisper makes it through the door. *Far, a long, long way to run.*

"I'm sorry, dear, we really prefer not to buy anything door-to-door."

"I'm not selling anything." I raise my voice and stand on my tiptoes so I can see better into her small window. I can only make out to around her eyebrows. I've seen the woman before, of course, gardening. But she's never waved or greeted me. I don't know her name.

"The child next door?" I put my hand above my head and point in the doghouse's direction. "Have you seen one?"

She shakes her head. "Sorry dear. I can't say that I have." And she's gone. *Which will bring us back to Doe.*

All's quiet at house number four, but from the street I can see the thin chain that leads to the doghouse. Swaying. I cannot bring myself to knock at house number four's door, partly because I can't imagine what I'd say.

"Excuse me, is your child chained to the doghouse?" What if they answer Yes? What if they answer No?

Them: Yes, that's our [boy/girl] by the doghouse.

Me: Shall I come by after school and take him [her] for a walk?

No, of course I wouldn't say that.

Them: No, there's no child by our doghouse.

Me: Oh. (The door slams here.) Or....

Them: He's just playing. You know how children are. Or don't you have children? (Slightly accusatory voice here.)

Me: Playing with a leash on him?

Them: Safety first.

Me: What about the splintering wood, the rain?

Them: Children enjoy being outdoors. It's better for them than television. (The door slams here.)

None of the scenarios I can imagine makes any sense. I realize that this may not be my fault. But wouldn't a good neighbor find out more? Someone living in Santa Vallejo, say, in the midst of the closely knit community with its red-and-blue swing sets. Wouldn't a neighbor there be bound by some sort of community pledge to take matters into her own hands?

What if they don't open their door, Patty? What if they do?

When in doubt, consult a text. Like the good graduate student that I am, I head for the bookshelf in the TA offices. Actually, consulting the research librarian might be the thing to do. I approach her in my mind. "Hello, one of my neighbors has his or her child tied to a doghouse. Can you recommend a book or books to consult on this subject?"

Instead, I grab the aging phone books. Yellow or white? Is this a case for 911? Is it an out-and-out emergency? Is it a time-crucial matter? How could I explain that I'm calling only after noticing this for weeks, maybe longer, time flies on the semester system?

The White Pages. A to Z. I try the Easy Reference List at the beginning of the government pages. And it really is easy. I only have to go to the C's, Child Abuse Reporting, the county social services department. I flip the pages for the toll-free number (the department will be pleased there's no charge, since I'm using the school phone). I dial the 800 number and wait for the recorded message. The voice asks me to consider which button I want to push for which service. Please press one to report a probable case of child abuse in your area. That sounds like me. I press one, feeling a little guilty that I didn't listen to all the options.

Please hold, the voice says. On comes some music I used to work out to at aerobics, back when aerobics seemed necessary and wise. All she wants to do is dance, the music says, dance, dance. I'm not sure it's appropriate music, but it does have a strong bass.

Every few seconds I hear a click that sounds like someone's coming on the line. I get prepared to tell my story (should I mention the rain? The heat? The shoe?), but it's just another operator's voice telling me to (please) stay on the line and that my call is important. Your call is important, Patty. Finally, as the song plays for the second time—I'm not sure why they've only recorded the one song—I get transferred back to the main menu. I'm a little alarmed at this. If I want to report a probable case of child abuse, press one. If I want to inquire about adoptive services, press two. If I want information on an existing case, press three. To speak to a representative, press the star key. I press the star key.

Your call cannot be completed as dialed. Please try again.

Silence.

But I do try again because my call is important.

I press two this time, just because I haven't tried it before. I get the same song. I find it annoying that all she wants to do is dance, dance, dance. I put the phone down on my desk, where I can still hear the music, and try to read a student's paper about the similarities and differences between lesbianism and Judaism. The bass pounds. Toward the end of the song (it worries me a little that I can now tell when the song is going to end, that I know the song this well), I pick up the phone again. With the last beat, the recording hangs up on me. If a recording can do that.

I call a few more times, trying to keep track of which buttons I've pushed and which I haven't. The student paper has completely misrepresented Judaism, but all the words are spelled correctly. I dial 911. A real voice answers, surprising me, as I'm waiting for a recording to tell me which numbers to press.

"What is your emergency?"

"Yes, I'd like to report a possible case of child abuse in my neighborhood?" I've written the sentence down by now so I can just read it.

"You need to call child social services at 800-455-"

"Yes, I've tried, but their recording seems to be broken and won't transfer me to anyone."

"They might be busy and you have to be patient."

"I think the recording's broken, though."

"Then you can call the local office directly." She gives me the number.

Progress. I thank the real voice.

"Use 911 only for emergencies," the voice says, then hangs up, confirming my fear that a little boy in a doghouse is not considered an emergency.

I dial the new number. A different computer voice answers, instructing me to please wait and my call will be answered in order. It doesn't say in what kind of order. It doesn't mention that my call is at all important to them. A different song by the guy from the Eagles starts to play. It's slower and doesn't have anything to do with dancing, but it makes me wonder if someone got a Best of Eagles kind of CD on sale. Maybe each county agency takes one song. Still, I refuse to listen to the words—I don't want to memorize them inadvertently like I did the last song. So I stare at my watch and try to hum randomly, fill my ears with a kind of blurriness. The song plays four times for a total of fourteen and a half minutes. I start pushing buttons, which has no effect, but the push button sound does at least drown out the music. After the fifth version, I hang up.

I check the phone book for the downtown office address and get my papers together. I give the Judaism/lesbianism paper a C+. It does occur to me, looking around the office, that I wish I could confide in someone. I've seen other TAs gathered around one another, chatting about serial commas and boyfriends, and I've even joined into a few discussions on the values of plus and minus grades, whether a topic sentence is overrated, and how to properly tone down everyone's enthusiasm for the really cute boy students. But I don't feel I can confide something like this to any of them. This seems more the thing to tell a total stranger.

I leave campus and walk as quickly as possible back to my house for my car. The crossing guard (Is she there all day?) yells at me to slow up, although I think she means slow down. For some reason, I listen to her, as if she were really an authority figure instead of just a woman in orange. She has a forceful voice, I have to admit, even when she isn't singing show tunes. Once out of her sight, I run again, directly past house number four, and get my car going. I head in the direction of the local child abuse office. I will not be intimidated by any more answering machines. I prepare to be intimidated one-on-one.

But a sign on the door informs me that the office is closed until further notice. Other offices can be found in San Ysidro (this is far from here) and Riverside County (this is farther). Our local office may reopen if the new state budget is passed. It says this in professionally printed letters, as if trying to persuade me to take some political stance, some political action, which I might consider if I knew how I could possibly help. I try not to think about any of this.

On my way home I stop at Ralph's to get some good packing boxes, even though I still have a few in the garage, having moved too many times to admit to. I have boxes from my days in Mission Viejo working for the letters to the editor section of a horse magazine. I may even have a few boxes from old family days in Los Angeles, the brief visit to Orange County, the mistaken journey back to Los Angeles, although I don't always like to see the old markings. Kitchen, bedroom, living room. The words seem ambiguous enough, but they bring back memories. I prefer my boxes unmarked.

Next to the big trash bins behind the store I find some really good boxes—they're from canned goods, bottled water. No stains, no rips, no funny smells. I probably look a little odd standing there smelling boxes, but such things tend to be worthwhile. I pick up a nice smallish V8 box but something scurries out of it and runs behind the bin, startling me so that I throw the box back as fast as I can. It was something's home, I berate myself. I step back and feel a little dizzy.

Get a grip, Patty. Tell yourself what a nice set of boxes this is. Altogether I've got five good boxes, maybe more than I need given my previous collection, although you never know what will become of cardboard left too long in the garage. I fumble with the boxes, like a clown juggling items never intended by nature to be juggled, trying to load them into my car. My very old Toyota wagon, beige fading to a sickly skin color. I look up to see a woman in a shiny blue car slowly approaching me.

"You can ask for boxes inside!" she yells at me nastily. She gives me a sneer as I lift two of my boxes from the ground. The woman's about my age, although her car is much nicer and she's wearing noticeable makeup, pink lips and cheeks, although not the same shade.

Complementary shades, if you like pink. She drives away with this look of disgust, her car eerily making almost no noise at all. I guess that's an attractive quality in a car these days, stealthiness, but I find my thundering old Toyota comforting. I like to hear it roar as I press the gas, whether it's supposed to or not.

At home I find myself sorting and stacking belongings, unearthing long streams of dust-mite-ridden material. When it gets dark, I stand out in front of my house, looking out into the street, which is fairly still. The neighbors are all inside, so the only sounds I hear are cars from the distance, plus the rattling sounds of animals rustling through bushes. Occasionally, a skunk will come up to the backdoor, brave and fat, hunting around the garbage cans. Opossums are far less attractive—I tend to make a lot of noise in hopes they'll run off, but they're fearless and dumb. Creatures braver than I pad around through the trees as I examine my street, not looking in that certain direction of that certain green house. I turn back to the house I'll be leaving, wondering how long before the skunks need to move on, too. Something that lives out here ate my tomatoes right off the vines last summer, waiting until they were a perfectly deep, ripe red. I can't see the Samsons putting up with this, although there might have been a time when I'd have thought they would.

I spend the next days packing and grading final papers, writing little comments in the margin for the students who've been nice, turning in my grades, checking off all my things to do on some imaginary list in my mind. Taking breaks, I go room by room evaluating my belongings: Little of the furniture is mine, just books and blankets, mostly. Clothes, a few of my grandmother's pots and pans. The dishes belong to the Samsons, along with the silverware. Even the computer is one of theirs, old, the screen fading on one side, many pixels having bit the dust. I have my aging small TV (it's not cable ready) and its new little traveling TV offspring from the presentation, plus my tiny stereo. Folders and folders of schoolwork that I don't even want anymore. Old writing. Throwing things away at a time like this may come back and haunt me, I know. But I fill up several garbage bags anyhow. There's not even much in the fridge to part with. Living alone means I don't have much that's too heavy for me to carry by myself, that everything I have can be condensed enough to fit into a compact car. Even my TV seems oddly light, as if it were made out of Styrofoam like the fake display TVs you find at furniture stores.

When I'm through packing up the car, the house looks pretty much the same—lamps, pictures, sofas all the Samson's—enough so that I wonder whose life I've been living. I don't even like these pictures—flowers painted in periwinkle mostly, not even a real flower color. It makes me wonder if I've ever liked it here. I thought I did.

On the fourteenth I open my mail to find a package from the presentation. A full-color notebook filled with Santa Vallejo postcards, bumper stickers and a ten-page brochure. I go to put the original brochure from the presentation lunch inside this one, but find I've lost it in the mess of moving. It may be trapped inside a garbage bag, soon to be nibbled by skunks of various weight, heft, and aroma. It may turn up five years from now in a box with no markings whatsoever.

Late that night I stand outside again, since inside only feels like a house that I might have once lived in. The air feels as if it desperately needs to rain, but some other element won't let it. Something angry bites me, which somehow isn't surprising. I trip walking along the sidewalk as I have dozens of times—I've always thought that it's my nearsightedness that makes me trip, but these cracks are malevolent things. Tripping makes the right side of my head threaten to ache, just a stab, but it decides against it. I go up the street, but not with a great sense of purpose. It's a little surprising how purposeless I feel, unless I'm just hiding it from myself. I think back to Goldilocks for some reason—now, did she have a certain determination, looking from bowl to bowl, bed to bed? Was she actively pursuing that thing that would be just right? Or was she just wandering? No, Goldilocks was starving, exhausted, desperate, not just for food and sleep (she could get these) but for the right food and sleep. The loving sense of food and sleep, rest, warmth (*community*, the presentation's voice echoes in my mind, nodding, urging me on). But I'm not sure. Was she greedy or just in search of some much-needed and fulfilled promises?

Outside house number four I hear yelling. It's coming from way inside the house. A bathroom, maybe, because there's that funny reverberation you get from tile all around you. I can just picture the tiles—green with that bathroom mold and crud blackening the spaces between them. The porcelain tub with its orangey drippy-looking rust stains. I hear an odd woman's voice, slurring words, the way the parents on the Peanuts cartoons talk—just garbled sounds. The way dogs supposedly hear us. But these are angry sounds. Threatening. And outside, I see the chain leading into the doghouse.

Wake up, Patty.

It's after midnight. There's a little boy chained to a doghouse after midnight, bitten by angry insects, definitely without the right kind of food and sleep. I let myself into the dog run—it's locked, but the lock is so dilapidated it springs open in my hands. It's not much bigger than the cheap lock you keep on a diary—especially a diary you don't ever expect anyone to care enough to break into. I see an old dog bowl next to the house as I approach, and this bowl, with its dirty white outside and scratched up inside, this bowl is, I think, the worst thing I've ever seen. I once saw a woman with her head cracked open in a car accident (everyone was looking), but this is worse. This one ten-inch bowl is worse, and I want to tear it apart, bludgeon it with a hammer, just blast the hell out of it. But I can't move because this stupid bowl has me paralyzed.

I finally turn to look. A light from the side of the house shines directly into his eyes. What's around his neck isn't a dog collar, as I'd imagined, but a thick piece of rope, like a braided curtain sash, tied to the chain. Double-knotted. He looks at me sleepily, sucking on one hand, the other grasping one of those blankets people take to picnics or football games for their laps, only they wouldn't take this one. They wouldn't give this one to a dog, I think, a little afraid to approach, as if he were a scary stray dog. But he's a little boy, like I said, three or four, I can't tell. Curled up on an old pillow. This is a little boy, Patty. There's no such thing as a stray little boy.

Getting the rope off is hard—I finally have to cut at it with the small Swiss Army knife I have on my keychain. It has a dollsize, unreliable scissors, but I make them work this time. Although I worry briefly about him striking out, he stays amazingly still as the rope binds and pinches his skin. I hear a few sounds, squeaks that must come from him, but he continues only to grasp at the filthy blanket. When I take it from him I expect a little fight, but he lets go of it easily, as if he had no claim to it at all. I pull him out of the doghouse, his ripped imitation Keds half hanging off. He's so light. I carry him and try to figure out how heavy he is in comparison to other things, but I can't really imagine the weights of the usual standards. A sack of potatoes? I'm one person—I don't usually buy a whole sack. They'd go bad.

I'm not really surprised to find that he fits perfectly into the last free space in the car. I place him next to a soft, soft blanket (you have to have one when you live alone, or it's just too sad) and my unused guest pillow. The look on his face confirms for me what I already suspected, something about the vast difference between greed and desperation. He sinks into the thickness of the blanket and that plumpness I'd found so annoying in my extra pillow—I can tell they feel just right. I place the Santa Vallejo notebook between the front seats—there's a little map inside—and start driving my way out of this storybook.

Chapter 2

Over the River

We drive like bandits through the night. I picture myself this way while I dream and drive and worry my way along I-5. I see myself with a red bandana tied around my face, although even in my mind it clashes with my red hair. I wear it across my nose, my disguise, hiding those telltale freckles. I can hear my neighbors: *No officer, we don't remember anything about the nondescript woman who stole the boy, oh wait, yes, she had freckles. A grown woman with freckles* [they snicker here]. The boy wears a bandana, also (in my mind), his a light-blue to match his eyes, tied loosely so he can breathe, although it tends to fall down around his neck, hiding his own telltale signs.

You might need to stop for coffee, Patty.

Here is what I know: I have a little boy in my car. I've bungee corded him to the passenger seat, which I recognize may sound cruel, but actually it provides him with a bounciness he seems to like. I ascertain his approval despite the fact that he has not made much sound (but there's so little to comment on along I-5, Patty).

Start again, revise (revision is everything, Patty): I have a little boy bungee-corded to my passenger seat as we drive through the night in search of, well, I haven't gotten that far. I can barely imagine that part of the sentence, modifiers and adverbs, let alone the nouns. Am I in search of a town described in a brochure? It doesn't seem that crazy, this time of night. Right now, I'm somewhere in the neverland known in my mind as "above L.A.," as I always picture north as somehow above. I'm visual that way, my mind like a map that lacks all capitals and cities. Visual but nearsighted. He is very quiet, although is that such a bad thing? He has stayed quiet, snug on my spare pillow, bungee-corded to his seat (but in a good way, Patty), wrapped in a soft blanket. He has said only "oh" and "oon," but mostly when we hit a bump. I'm happy to hear any exclamations from his little voice (although happy may not be the right word), despite ages of telling composition students that exclamations are inappropriate. How wrong you've been, Patty.

I'm exhausted from driving in what I now recognize as the appropriately named dark of night (especially once you're beyond the lights of L.A.), as well as looking for flashing lights, waiting for that heart-stopping siren that means you (Patty) are about to be pulled over/arrested/humiliated/thrown in jail. The slammer. I say it to him.

"It's the slammer for me." I try it out. I can hear the thick metallic doors slam. Too much *Law and Order.* I turn up the radio. He's asleep anyway, having bounced in his cords for a while, most of the time tugging at the invisible rope around his neck, as I did of course remove it. I don't have a problem with imaginary annoyances, unrealistic phobias, and such, so his tugging doesn't upset me. It may be a perfectly reasonable response, to tug at something invisible that's scratching your neck when you are a small child who has been tied up for an undisclosed amount of time.

We stop at Carl's Junior, in the drive-through lane, after I've thrown the blanket over him. I try not to smother him, which could only bring more charges, plus of course, it isn't nice. (A spelling mnemonic goes through my mind—*there is a mother in smother*—but I let it go, fast.) I order us healthy chicken sandwiches (the authorities may look kindly on this) and French fries, but just small orders. I do not supersize. I have some judgment left, I like to think.

I wake him and we eat, him smelling each bite before eating (not too abnormal) and keeping two fingers at his neck. It's just two fingers, Patty. Not that much worse than sucking a thumb, right?

But then I notice his hand. This is my first chance to really look at him, and it occurs to me, sickeningly: Has something been biting his hand? An animal? An animal with small teeth?

My vision sparkles over, but it passes.

Just one hand, the right one. And as he rests from eating, I realize what it is. He has been gnawing on his hand. Knuckles, inside of the palm, cuticles. He's not fussy which part. I study him now: He bites a fry, he bites his hand. I look away. I feel ill.

He then removes the lettuce from his sandwich and throws it on the car floor. I'm relieved at the normalcy of it, a child indifferent to wilted vegetables. Please don't bite, I want to tell him. Just bite the sandwich, chew the hell out of it (how do people stop swearing around children? It must be like talking to freshmen), but I can't bring myself to mutter instructions at this moment. My teaching skills fail me yet again.

Instead, I remove the lettuce from my sandwich and toss it on the car floor, too. I model healthy behavior (sort of). I want him to feel accepted, bungee cord notwithstanding.

Biting yourself. There are worse things. There may have been worse things. Drive, Patty. Drive.

Between bouts of not being able to find anything decent on the radio, I begin to think of what I can say when pulled over by the black-and-white speeding police car I'm certain is somewhere just behind us. What could I say in response to the harshly threatening look the officer gives me once the siren frightens me to a stop?

Me: I'm sorry. It was an impulse.

Police guy: Step out of the car. (I do.)

Me: Can't you see how much happier he is? (We both look over to examine the boy bungee-corded to the seat. I can see how this might give the officer the wrong idea. He may draw a weapon here, if he hasn't already.)

Police guy: Step away from the child.

Me: Please, listen. There was a little boy on my street living in the doghouse. No one seemed to care. What would you do?

Police guy: We have authorities for that.

I realize here that I have never seen a gun up close before.

Me: But the phone lines were broken, and the office was shut down. The authorities were out of business.

Police guy: Are those *French fries* in his mouth?

Still, it's possible no one is following us at all. When I consider this, at a lull on the road (and there are many), wondering if anyone cares about the bungee-corded boy who is not mine, it makes me a little sad. In the scheme of things, although it wouldn't be good for me personally, someone with a clear and legally justifiable sense of right and wrong should be following us, shouldn't he (she or they)? Or have we passed beyond all sense of clear-cut right and wrong, left it behind us at sixty-five miles an hour somewhere along the highway, where your speed and who knows what else, really, are checked by radar? Maybe there is no radar, either, Patty. Maybe everything television has taught you about car chases is wrong, or at least dramatically altered.

Maybe no one cares. Or maybe you have crossed a line you can't even imagine the consequences for and are fooling yourself. Would it be the first time, Patty?

We exit the freeway at a sign that indicates Food Lodging, even though the sign doesn't use a comma or a conjunction. I would feel so comforted by a conjunction right now it's ridiculous.

I pass by the first hotel and chose one a little further on, figuring that at least it wouldn't be the first place someone might look for us. My mind tells me that if the people following me (the cops with guns, dogs, mace—their faces slightly blurred by the hour of the night, but always marked by expressions completely lacking in understanding), anyhow, if they didn't have to look all that hard, maybe I'd be in less trouble than, say, if I made them search through four motels. The things you tell yourself in the middle of the night.

I check in with no questions asked, as the check-in guy (he's about sophomore age) is half asleep, but then, who isn't. I wrap the little boy in his blanket (he's covered, not that anyone's watching, or are they?) and carry him into our room in motel number two. I will never be able to remember the motel's name.

I place him on the bed in the peppermint and vacuum cleaner-scented room. He watches me run a bath (it's a small room), and then I begin to do something I do not want to give much thought to. I take off his clothes. The Band-Aid question flashes through my mind: Should I rip them off quickly? Would that be less painful (for either of us) than to remove them slowly, and maybe in the process see something I long not to see—marks, welts, bruises, scars? Hints and indications?

Cigarette burns, Patty. You've read those books.

Ever ambivalent, I go for the in-between speed and remove his clothes as if it were the most normal thing in the world. He says nothing; as one hand goes to his mouth, the other one rubs at his neck. There's a moment of fear when I need to get his shirt over his head, but he moves his hands away pretty easily, as if free will has been lost to him for some time. Mine was a passing fear, which is a rare thing on a night like this.

I do not see that much. I had bruised knees all the time as a child, and what would that have said about me? There are assorted question marks, here and there. There is the sore, red area around his neck, where he rubs. Then the hand. I place him in the tub, and he sits calmly, sleepily. I get to work. I wish I were the kind of girl who traveled with lotion, for his neck. Or better yet, several lotions and a few antibiotic ointments. It's not the type of motel to provide them, and I'm not about to go back to the desk and ask. He chews slightly on his hand while I bathe him, and he makes a distracting humming sound every now and then. It's not entirely unpleasant. There's no one here right now who couldn't use a little distracting, after all.

I rinse out his clothes and place them over the heater (not much I can do about the cracked imitation Ked, as it looks as if it would disintegrate in water, which isn't the worst thing that could happen to it). I wrap him in an old T-shirt of mine, and he falls asleep, hand stuck to mouth. He is a small unknown boy in an undistinguished motel room. I don't have a firm grasp at all of who I am at the moment.

* * *

It is so quiet that I can only hear the familiar roar of my Toyota as we enter Santa Vallejo this morning. The morning after. We both awoke early and hit the road again. I stopped at a fast-food restaurant that looks just like all other fast-food restaurants for a breakfasty egg sandwich thing that he actually ate. It came in a box with smiley faces all over it, and I admit that's the reason I chose it from the drive thru menu. There was no clue that it was at all egg related, or fried, but some things I suppose you should just know by my age.

I have stolen a child and am clogging his arteries. I have to take the box away when he begins to chew on it, although it might be an improvement over his hand. I don't really have time to consider.

You did not sleep well, Patty.

But we are here. We pass by remarkably quiet street pavers crushing something blue-green on the road, smoothing it with a hypnotic rolling-pin-like back-and-forth motion. I'm mesmerized by Santa Vallejo, as is my passenger, who looks around, placing his hand against his mouth, where he sucks on a knuckle quietly.

The blue-green pebbles—surely it's not asphalt—lack that burning smell here, that odor that gets caught at the back of your throat, tickling you, but not in an amusing way. It's one of the first things I notice, that morning in Santa Vallejo smells nothing like home. Despite the freshly trimmed hedges and lawns, despite the trees that are in bloom in December, there's no aroma here whatsoever.

You may never need another nasal inhaler, Patty. You may be in the right place.

Still, the illegality of what I've done glimmers slightly in the corner of my eye as the sun comes through the windshield. I'm teased by the threat of an imposing migraine along with little pinpricks of recognition: Not only have I stolen a child, brought him many counties to the north (is it more of a crime the farther you go, or is distance not the issue?), but I don't even have him properly confined in a primary-colored car seat, as I see other children all around me in their families' brightly colored minivans. That alone, I know from my last test at the DMV, is a major traffic ticket item, although it's probably not my biggest worry here.

A living, breathing child, Patty. Imagine the fine.

The little boy, that's how I think of him. It's hard not knowing what to call him, and he doesn't have a word for himself. He hasn't cried at all, not that I would have thought less of him. I've been near tears many times, with one really tough stretch through Coalinga, when all the billboards seemed to show animals being led to slaughter, although these may have just been ads for truck stops. But that is far behind us. We have moved on.

"Pretty," I say, pointing at one especially happily blooming bush.

He nods and widens his eyes at me, which I translate to mean "impressive." I smile. We understand one another. I so rarely drive with anyone in the car. Agreement has a proud, comforting feel to it, almost as if I'd planted the flowers myself. And they'd thrived. Even if I'm making the whole thing up.

He goes back to biting his hand. I think I hear him whimper at the pain.

Please stop, I say softly to myself.

* * *

I may be lost, so when I see the great purple gas station, I pull in, despite that it is called the Proggleland Fill Me Up (no hyphens). I cover up the boy with his blanket—how quickly it has become his. I'd let him take it with him were he to be found by whoever might be looking for him (or should be looking for him), or if he were to suddenly disappear. Disappear again. Could that happen? Imagine that, Patty. What would you do then?

You need coffee, food, directions, Patty. The boy cuddles under his blanket, though I'm projecting. I lock the car door behind me.

I walk into the store to find an assortment of snack foods, including three rows of sweets shaped like snowballs. I buy two for my passenger because I think he'll enjoy the shape (if not the sugar), and because I always feel like I have to buy something when I ask for directions. The gas boy (I notice he isn't wearing a little patch on his shirt that says his name—Guy or Bud or Jim, it could be anything) rings up my purchase, then holds a snowball pack in his hands a moment before putting it into a bag, lingering over it with a smile that curves up half his face, as if he's too shy to smile with both sides. Maybe the snowballs are even better than I think.

I ask him about lodging, but it seems there isn't much in Santa Vallejo proper. He uses the word "proper," even as he holds the snowball. I don't remember this word from the brochure, not that I haven't had other things on my mind.

"You have to go just outside," he says, and I wonder what he means by outside.

"Outside?"

"On the other side of the SV River," he says, pointing over his head and to the left, with a gesture that reminds me of the stretches we used to do in aerobics. I imitate him, partially just to do a little stretching myself after so much driving. As I bend, I notice a mirror over the counter, one of those odd hubcap-like mirrors that makes you look elongated and pale. I clearly don't look my best here: I've got on an old pair of black-framed glasses for driving, and they seem to emphasize darkened circles under my eyes. My hair—which can best be described as dark red (darker than a fashionable light red or a trustworthy auburn) and straight—seems wrinkled. My bangs cling to the sides of my head, my hair parting somewhere left of center, but not in any stylish or attractive way. I look pretty distorted. I don't think it's just the hubcap's doing, either.

"We're not set up for overnight visitors yet," he tells me, "but just wait till we are. Once the amusement park catches on." He gives me this look of great expectation, great confidence. I smile, even though I'm clearly a visitor at the wrong time. I've caught the city unprepared, even though they already invited me in glossy four colors.

We start driving toward the river as I realize I forgot to buy a map. So it takes me a while to admit I've been driving in circles and to bravely take a new turn.

As I search for the river, I try, as I have off and on along the way, to call out popular boys' names to see if I can get a reaction from my passenger. Doesn't he need a name, or is it just a social convention? After all, he's been within arm's reach, and we've been fine. Beyond arm's reach, though, is what worries me. One of the things that worries me.

"Cody," I try. He holds a snowball in his left hand, squishing it gently, admiringly (I think) while chewing on his right. Now and then he'll stick a finger into the snowball and lick the frosting out. Like any small child.

"Sean," I say. "Jeremy. Jed." I'm trying to think trendy, what's hot in boy names. Is the bible in? "Noah. Samson." I get no response. "Jason" makes him scratch his ear, but it might be unrelated. I try the basics. "Bobby. Michael. David. Joey. Jeffrey. Steven. Peter. Mark." I think of boys on the playground who tormented me when I was little. "Ricky. Mitchell. Larry. Paul." When I stop and am finally quiet a few moments, he turns to me blankly. I wonder: When they wanted him, did they just yank the cord? The thought turns my hands cold and sweaty.

"Maybe we'll let you pick," I suggest, and he readjusts his body behind his bungee cord, as content as I've seen him. Maybe it's not so bad, his body language tells me. Then I see a thin almost inconspicuous line of blood flowing down his thumb, onto the snowball in his other hand. I try hard not to moan.

I grab a tissue from an old smashed-up box and reach over to dab at his hand. Then I breathe deeply.

We pass what looks like a lineup of nursery school children, and he lets out an *oh*.

I try to respond in a normal way to the child with a snowball in one hand and blood trickling down the other.

"They're going to school. Preschool, I guess. You can go, too, with other boys and girls your age." You can be normal, I tell him telepathically, happy, productive, safe. You can cross the street in a group, you can find someone to hold hands with, once yours has healed. A town can do that for you. I feel confident the brochure said so, the hand biting notwithstanding. Not that I read the fine print.

There are several things you need to do, Patty. Stop driving in circles. Get to the river. Find food, shelter. Settle in. To-do lists fill my head. He needs clothes. You need to look at some newspapers, see if you're the main story, or maybe just a blurb. Words appear banner style across my vision, although I do recognize this is not a safe way to drive. Still they come: *Patty Grant steals child. Graduate student kidnaps small boy from college neighborhood.* Then there's the smaller print. *Neighbors found her quiet and studious, although messy when lining up her trash cans for pickup. Department chairpersons call Grant nervous but nice, and an excellent grammarian. Her composition students describe her as exhausted and unsympathetic, but punctual. School crossing guard says the mousy Patty often crossed against the light.*

Turn to page A-3 for Grant's high school photograph.

Don't think about it, Patty.

We do get to the Santa Vallejo River, mostly I suspect by making wrong turns. I have to admit it isn't quite what I expected. It's more of a wash way than a river, but not like the wash ways of my Southern California youth. Clearly manmade (or as we say in my composition class's section on nonsexist language, constructed by humankind, or just plain unnatural), this river is bright turquoise. (L.A.'s river, as I recall, when there was any water at all, was the color of algae-infested mud.) A narrow park of small leafy trees and those ever-present pink blossoming bushes line the river. Little benches—they're turquoise too, and I have to admire a river that's color coordinated—pop up here and there throughout the park. I roll down the windows and notice the river makes a rumbling sound like you'd hear at a really active river, a sound that warns you not to jump in, that these are rough waters despite their glamorous appearance. There's some sort of deception to this river that moves stylishly toward its destination. It's the fashion model of rivers, proud, pouty, and utterly unreal. It's hard not to stare.

"Uh," my small passenger says, and I pretty much agree. This may well be his first river, and even though it's not what I've come to expect, it's an important milestone. Especially when your previous frame of reference regarding bodies of water is a half-empty, graying, filthy old doggie dish.

The bridge, plain, utilitarian, with no flowering bushes, leads my aging Toyota over the river and gives us a peek back at what might be called the highlands of Santa Vallejo. You'd know more if you had a map, Patty, I tell myself, but I try to go where the bridge takes me. There's no turnaround lane anyway. We go over the river.

At the bridge's end, we reach an area that feels familiar, lower, warmer even. I drive slowly, staking out the place. Buildings are older in these parts, but still tiled and stuccoed. Sidewalked streets only have trees here and there; lawns are turning brown. Plus, there's a scent of something slightly fertilizerish. Yes, over on this side, it looks a bit more like San Diego, like Orange County, like Los Angeles, like all the places I've lived in and left, although maybe a little more hopeful. For the first time since I got here, somebody honks at me to speed up. I'm not sure I'm in Santa Vallejo anymore.

When I get out of the car to stretch my legs, I trip on a crack in the sidewalk, and a sense of deja vu overtakes me.

I look over my shoulder for police cars, as if it matters anymore, then unstrap the boy and let him out his car door. He grabs the blanket, imitates my stretching then makes a little hop onto the sidewalk.

"Like a bunny," I say, but he looks at me oddly. "Hopping, like a bunny." I hop, bringing my hands forward like paws, and he imitates me, gripping the blanket. I realize a woman hopping with a child might draw extra attention, although perhaps not as much as a woman hopping without a child. *Yes, officer, we saw a woman with the child you describe hopping into that restaurant earlier.*

There was a time, oh, say, yesterday, when I would have avoided taking him into a restaurant at all, but today, in the light of a new town, I'm foolish, I'm hungry, I'm my own worst enemy. I am a felon, but I smell toast. We head to the order counter at a restaurant called The Toasted Loafer, although I believe that may be a mixed metaphor. But I'm in a new city, so I don't have to critique. The place looks from the woodsy sign over the counter and a few spilled sprouts by a table as if it serves health food, although I notice you can get extra fries with your sandwich, so I really have no problem. I order avocado sandwiches and take the boy to a booth as far from the door as possible, as if this would help us in our situation. We're still easily seen from the window—every booth is by a window, so this isn't exactly a place to hide, but it smells so nice here. It doesn't smell like fried food or impending jail time at all.

A waitress heads our way with a lime green booster seat that actually coordinates, somehow, with the turquoise booth.

"Hi," she says, lifting the boy and blanket into the seat without even asking and with a grace and swiftness I don't expect I'll ever have.

"There!" she says. "You can't beat that." She's a college-age young woman with wispy almost-white hair, wearing a long black T to her knees, and purple-and-green leggings beneath. She nearly flies back to the counter at the sound of ringing. Tinkerbell comes to mind, and I want to tell the boy, but he seems desperately unfamiliar with storybook icons. The boy looks surprised by his new height and even stops pawing at his neck, which he has done regularly all morning, trading off with chewing on his hand. I have not had the time to figure out which is worse.

He pulls the blanket almost completely over his head. I hear sucking noises. I pretend this is perfectly normal for a child. What do I know.

Our waitress skips back over to our table with sandwiches and smiles, neatly folds back the boy's blanket and ruffles his hair (it's sandy blondish, not in the slightest bit red, which makes me suddenly hopeful for him). I look at him as if for the first time. He's a cute little boy, the kind of child you might long for—curly blonde hair, blue eyes maybe turning a bit hazel, quiet and pleasant (his reddened neck hidden just beneath his now cleaner T-shirt). And you can't see the bad hand he keeps in his lap. At first look, you just wouldn't know.

I picture him in black and white, too. On the side of a milk carton, say.

I watch him eat fairly neatly, sniffing his food, taking little bites, then hiding under the blanket. Repeat. He pulls out sprouts and drops them on the floor. Maybe he's never seen sprouts before. Would I have been brave enough to try sprouts at his age? What is his age?

Just eat, Patty. Be thankful he's not fussy or noisy. It's just a few sprouts. I try not to think too hard about what lies ahead, but still it comes at me grocery list style. Get job, get apartment, get little boy clothes, get information on how much trouble you're in. Consider reordering list. Is it more important to get information or clean clothes? If you do one before the other, will it be the thing that sets your undoing in motion? Should you just find a way to get out of the situation entirely? Should you just exit, gracefully or otherwise?

And where would you leave him, Patty? And are you the kind of person who could do that? Maybe you should just stand up from the table right now and run like hell.

I realize that I may need a milk shake and order one, although the waitress already did shake up the boy's milk carton so it would be bubbly. (There was no missing face on the side—it was just one of those small cartons.)

I grab two newspapers stacked neatly at a back table, a larger *San Jose Mercury News,* and a smaller-town *Santa Vallejo Tattler.* I'm not sure I approve of the name, especially in my present circumstances, but I'm hopeful and suddenly ambitious. Avocado has that effect on me. Plus, I love a task.

I look through the big paper's classifieds first, but there seems to be no listing for Santa Vallejo, as if it doesn't exist. I grab the *Tattler,* squinting a little so that I don't have to see the actual word *Tattler.* Plus I've left my glasses in the car—I'm not good with keeping track of them. The "want" ads aren't lengthy, but clearly there is some wanting going on, albeit at a higher economic level than I can afford. I check housing first. (Do I want a job more or shelter more?) I see a few condos for rent in Santa Vallejo, way out of my price range, although they all seem to offer built-in tub Jacuzzis, which does sound like something worth aspiring to. I can't find any apartments for rent, but then I spot some under "outlying areas." A few possibilities. Children okay. Pets on approval. Better than vice versa.

Our waitress comes over with the shake, which she's split into a big glass for me and a little one for the boy. Her knowledge appears vast.

"Do you know where these outlying areas are?" I ask her. The boy peeks out from his blanket, mesmerized by her leggings, I notice.

"We are the outlying areas," she says, gesturing a little proudly. She shrugs. "I think it's somebody's idea of an insult."

"Is this Santa Vallejo?"

"Sure, technically. Some people," she says quietly, making clear that I probably want to stay away from these kind of people, "think that once you're over the river, you're out of the area. In a far away city or something. The Valley." She shrugs again.

"But you like it here?" I ask.

"Sure, well, plus I can afford it here." She whispers: "We're allowed to go over the river, too." With a laugh, she winks at the boy, who winks back with both eyes. More of a blink, but the effort's there.

* * *

The first apartment we see has three cats screaming at one another in the front yard. I like cats, I really do, but something about the three of them makes me back up, the boy too. We back up all the way to the car as they scream and yowl in an almost human way. *Flee,* they seem to tell me. *While you can.*

"I don't think so," I say to the boy, and he seems to agree. It wasn't like the place had a built-in tub Jacuzzi.

The second building is better. It's a low, detached cottage, like Hansel and Gretel might have lived in, although maybe it isn't a good sign that abused fairytale children have sprung to mind. Still, I like the place. It's got two small bedrooms. Mine has an alcove with a built-in desk and a matching bookcase. The boy's room has a low window seat that opens on top—a place for his toys. (Add toys to list.) Each room has a twin bed in it, topped with a thin white bedspread, which means someone has realized how chilling a naked mattress can look. The living room is small with one long window, the kitchen smaller and pretty basic. Appliances out of the sixties. A real Formica (forgive the oxymoron) table with metal chairs, the kind popular in diners, although not quite as pristine. Bits of furniture fill the place, which I can use at no charge. A couch, a few tables, all cast off but still good. Furnished or unfurnished—my options feel limitless.

"Your choice," says my impending landlord, pointing to his bits of furniture like a game show hostess, waiting to see if I'll choose the right prize.

"I could use some furniture," I say.

"Great!" he says, as if indicating that I am already a winner.

He's not old, which I thought when I'd called on the phone before. Maybe in his fifties. He introduced himself as John Johnson when I walked in, making me wonder if I should get myself an alias. Instead, I just gave him my name, Patty Grant. You're not very good at this, Patty.

"I manage the cottages here, plus a few places on Main and Bird streets, along with these on Ant Hill Road," he says. "Own them," he almost whispers.

"That's good," I say, and he seems relieved I feel this way. He seems to need a lot of encouragement for a real estate investor. I use my real name on the rental agreement, with a phony previous address. As reference and former landlord, I put the name of my Latin American literature professor, who did rent out a spare room to students. He also died last year.

Home. I survey my kitchen. These cupboards are mine. The boy climbs all the way into a low kitchen cupboard, but he only stays there a few minutes. It's not like he shut the door behind him in there, so I think it's normal curiosity on his part. I have to think this way.

After a little unpacking, the boy and I slump on the brown corduroy sofa, origins unknown. I bite at a cuticle. He gnaws on one of his own. It flashes through my mind, like an old-fashioned sign over the hearth: Home is where you chew on your hands. I dab a tissue at his bloody cuticles. You will need to carry tissues, Patty.

Check your list, Patty. I shut my eyes, and it begins to run for me teleprompter style. A job. Food. Day care. I hadn't thought of that before. Who put that on the list? Boy clothes. Boy toys, although not gender-exclusive. Boy names. I'm not sure if I can find these in the want ads. I'm not sure where else to look, but then all of a sudden I do, I know where to get information. I've always been a pretty good student.

Although we've really done just about enough today, somehow the idea of a trip to the library invigorates me. I pick up a map at a Qwick-Food (there doesn't seem to be any 7-Elevens here), and enough food to get us through a few days, especially if you like bread, peanut butter, and cheese. Basic supplies. The kind you'd keep in an emergency kit, were you smart enough to have a kit and recognize an emergency when you see it.

The library is back over the bridge. I'm not sure why we don't have one in our outlying valley, but just knowing there's one not too far away gives me hope and focus. I've bought us each a turkey dog to take our mind off things. It's very tasty, although it tastes nothing at all like a hot dog.

"Off to the library!" I tell him excitedly. He bites lightly at the hot dog in an all-too-familiar way.

There's a sign—it looks temporary, spray painted, even—that reads Santa Vallejo Library. We drive up a hill and we're there, and I have to admit I'm a little disappointed at what I see. Another library under construction, just like where I came from. It's blocked off by a large white-tented area, but I know a library-to-be when I see one. Not that I can quite see it.

Still, standing before the library-to-be is a long series of connected, skinny white trailers. After blinking a few times (where are your glasses, Patty?), I can see it's more like bungalows than trailers. It must be the temporary library, and I'm no snob. I take the boy's hand (the good one) and bounce it up and down enthusiastically.

Inside looks much the way you'd expect a long, narrow group of bungalows to look, although somehow, they've rigged up the fluorescent lights of my childhood, the classroom kind that stretch below ceiling tiles with little dots. It's also cramped, crowded with bookcases, small tables, and chairs, but that doesn't bother me in the slightest. And it smells like a library, that deep satisfying smell, a smell with answers to all your questions. I reach out and touch a few books, running my fingers down spines in psychology, history, science, makeshift sections stacked to the ceiling, but respectfully. The boy touches the books in the same way, and I'm so happy to have taught him this. Yes, you can touch the books I tell him telepathically.

It really is getting late, Patty. You'd better find the newspapers.

I take the boy to the temporary children's section. A few other kids sit quietly on a purple rug that features a little town you can trace with your finger, or maybe small cars, not that I approve of toys in a library. Such a place should be toy-free, but then you've never had children, have you Patty. A man about my age sits with a girl in his lap—and somehow I suspect he's the children's librarian. He waves at me in a children's librarian way, as does his daughter. (I'm assuming she's his daughter based on the shared waves, which surely you can pass on to your child as easily as eye color, can't you?) I sit the boy down on the rug with three Dr. Seuss books and something semihistorical, and watch as he turns the books over and over on the ground, using his good hand. I open one for him, and he closes it and pats it. Flipping books, that's a good enough start, I tell myself. I consider leaving him here in the safety of children's literature for a moment.

Or for longer, Patty?

Could there be a better, safer place for him, Patty? Is it time for you to go?

He grabs the skin around his knuckles with his teeth and bites down. My own hand begins to ache. Focus, Patty.

I lead him to a table where we sit side by side—I look at the newspapers, he examines Dr. Seuss, both of us a little mystified. His attention keeps shifting from the Grinch to the brightly colored *USA Today*, the spattering of color print in the *San Diego Union Tribune*. I must confess my own desire to sneak a peek at *The Cat in the Hat*, as I never really understood that story. I keep myself going out of a basic sense of fear that I'll see my own name in what used to be my local paper, balanced with the anxiety that I won't see my name. But there's no mention of me. No front page badly sketched mock-up assembled from statements provided by motel and Carl's Junior employees, sketches showing deeply ringed eyes and unusually straight hair, but not the kind people envy. No mention of a grad student fleeing with two small televisions and an unidentified little boy bungee corded to the front seat. No mention of the beige Toyota carrying felonious and probably previously abused cargo. No half-broken Keds. No missing children reported at all, nationwide, this holiday season. There's an article about it. It may be a first. It may be the happiest of holiday seasons ever.

"Maybe the Grinch will return Christmas," I say to him. He gives me a half smile, exposing a dimple I'll bet he doesn't even know he has. There is small gash by his third knuckle that I don't remember seeing before.

I must add bandages to the list. Children's Band-Aids with cartoon characters, puppet creatures, action heroes. Could they possibly be enough to heal him?

I select a few books and decide to get a library card before we leave. Live dangerously, Patty, I tell myself, pleased that I can still recognize irony. I show the library worker my rental agreement, real name and all. I'm leaving tracks, I think. *But no one has noticed we're gone yet,* the little boy's eyes tell me, as he holds on to his picture books and bites rabbit-like at his hand. *We need these books,* his eyes tell me. The library woman examines my rental agreement.

"I live here now," I say. "May I get a card?"

"Well, you're in the outlying valley," she says, turning the agreement over, although there's nothing on the reverse side, no mention of whether I'm responsible with library books despite living on the wrong side of the river, not to mention that I have potential kidnapping charges hanging over my head. "But you can get a card."

I've been approved by the city library system, and more so even than getting the apartment, I feel the first hint of relief, validation, permanence.

After a dinner of peanut butter sandwich for him—he seems to like it, and probably not just because it's really easy to make—and a cheese one I throw together for myself (peanut butter being something of a headache trigger), I put him to bed. It's my first official night of bedtime routine—motel rooms don't count to me. He looks exhausted after all we've accomplished. We have a home, we have books, we have peanut butter. I've put my old twin bed sheets on his bed, still bright yellow despite all the years. The pillowcases have orange butterflies on them, and he outlines them with his finger.

"This is your bed," I tell him, "in your room." I look around. It's small but warm. It has a real bed, with real blankets. After a bath, I've dressed him in another old T-shirt of mine, so he looks like an old-fashioned child in a long nightshirt. A character in a story, a character out of place and time. A nearly fictional boy.

"So you sleep here."

I try reading to him about the Grinch, but he really just wants to hold on to the closed book with his left hand. As I recognize that books have more than one purpose, this is fine with me.

He brings his right hand to his mouth, and I gently try to put it back to his side. He puts up no resistance at all, no cry or objection, but the moment I begin to leave, the sore hand returns to his mouth.

He makes a little sound of discomfort as he bites down, a kind of a verbal wince.

I make exactly the same sound.

A few minutes later, I look in on him to find him asleep in his bed. His mouth has relaxed around the hand, almost kissing it. I take my own books to bed and don't even read them. I know that late in the night, it's the weight of them on the bed that will help me the most.

* * *

I awake to the thud of a newspaper hitting the front door, although as I'm still somewhat asleep, it does remind me (again) of that *Law and Order* ever-closing jail cell sound. I have not had good dreams.

I open the door and grab the newspaper, although I don't know why it's been delivered here. But you have bigger problems, Patty. I turn to find the boy behind me, one hand holding his book, the other, well, in its usual place. It strikes me that this is a child who has not dreamt well, either. He seems too young to have dreams, let alone nightmares, and the unfairness of it all hits me hard.

"Cornflakes," I resolve, as I bought the especially sugary kind.

I glance through the paper. I am not this morning's news. No one misses me (us, Patty).

But I don't miss me, either. The girl I was. That girl skipped breakfast. That girl saved too many plastic bags under the sink, so that when you opened the cupboard, they'd fall out at you, making that deflated noise. Dead plastic bags. But don't think about it, Patty. Think about now, what's missing now. Make a jot list, an outline. A rough draft.

"You need a name," I tell him, as we pick at dry cornflakes in our bowls. I somehow just knew he'd want to eat them dry, just like me.

After eating, we pick up some boy clothes at the Kids Shop Here store. I'm pretty sure it used to be a Kmart or something, one of those huge warehouse-like stores with cement floors that can feel so cold even right through your shoes. Still, the boy clothes are sturdy and inexpensive. And real sneakers. These seem to impress him the most. He takes his hand out of his mouth to run his fingers across them, real red Keds.

You've done one thing right, Patty.

He practices his hopping in them in a little circle around me that makes me feel like an almost permanent fixture in his world.

We also become the owners of a primary-colored, plush car seat. With a cup holder. And a real water bottle for him (not a dingy bowl on the ground—ugh). The difference a couple of days makes. I place the plastic bottle in his (bad) hand. He switches it to his other hand, and hugs it to his chest. It costs less than four dollars.

We return to our cottage and spread ourselves out on the floor, arranging newspapers and his picture books, ready for a morning of study. He reaches for a book about the Trojan horse. I'm not sure if it's historically accurate, as the horse on the cover is soft and fluffy. And blue. I pat it myself a few times, fuzzy offbeat historical creature that it is.

"Okay. Now we need a name for you. Do you have one you like to be called?" I try to keep it light.

He just pats the horse.

"I'll start circling some possibilities." He nods and looks over at my newspaper. There's a picture of a war scene on the front page. I turn it quickly—who needs to be greeted with that in the morning edition? I'm not sure I've ever really understood journalism.

"Tad." I say. He returns to patting the horse. I don't blame him.

"I'll just call them out, see what you like."

"Jerry. Arthur. Mike." No response. "We could make it Mikey, or Michael. We can experiment," I suggest. None of the names I see seems worth circling.

Then he taps me and points to a word in his own book.

"Helen," I say. "That's her name. She's a girl, of course. Not that it isn't a good name." He turns the page and points again.

"Troy," I say. "It's a place. Although it's a name too," I say. I mean, I suggested Tad.

"Troy," I say. He smiles.

"We could call you Troy. Troy," I try it out. "Here's Troy."

I point to the city, then to him. I'm pleased, and not just because I realize he could have been looking through a Dr. Seuss book, where the choices might have been far scarier.

"Troy," I say. He leans back against our couch, and I pick up his storybook.

"Let's read this thing," I suggest. "Let's read about Troy." I point to him, and he strokes his neck, but gently. I turn the pages back to the beginning. He doesn't know where a book begins, where the story starts. And I wonder if they've improved upon the ending, but then it's a kids' book, and fuzzy, so I'm hopeful. I read some of the words, especially about the horse, and Helen, but I figure I'll have to make up a few things. I'll have to emphasize the positive, gloss over what's too painful to talk about. If it's even possible. After all, how can the story of Troy possibly have a happy ending?

Chapter 3
The Color of My Parachute

The woman answers the door while holding a child upside down by the ankles. What's stranger is that the child is laughing pretty loudly, though turning a slight bit more blue than might be a good idea, not that I'm in a position to judge anyone at the moment.

"Hi," the woman greets me, echoed by what I think is a gurgled hi from the little girl.

I assume that this is Larissa because the newspaper ad said Daycare by Larissa, which sounded a little bit trendy and designer-esque, but it was followed by Reasonable Rates, so I thought I'd stop by. And this Larissa is not the trendy representative I'd expected, not in her long hippylike skirt and loose T, both faded cotton but clean, two things I always appreciate in clothing. I can't imagine why I expected someone at day care to be dressed up, especially when they have reasonable rates.

"Come on in. I'm Larissa, in case you didn't guess," she says, easily taking the upside-down toddler back with her into the house. Larissa has long curly hair, a regular dark brown that a redheaded girl like me can only envy. Troy and I follow, Troy staring at the upside-down girl and quietly sucking on his hand, me intrigued by a scent I'm pretty sure is gingerbread.

"Did you just make gingerbread cookies?" I haven't made Troy anything more difficult than a peanut butter sandwich, so the scent makes me feel guilty.

Larissa looks at me. "You buy it in premade rolls, then slice." I nod, sensing she knows how much better this makes me feel. "It's all natural, of course, but there's no reason to go to extremes, like having to drag out the mix-master or anything," she says. We follow them into the kitchen. The little girl bites the head off a cookie, then offers the body to Troy. He takes it but looks a little appalled. Troy looks up at me as if questioning if something bad has just happened.

"He hasn't taken to the notion of irony yet," I say. "Let alone finishing someone else's food." I'm a bit of a germaphobe, although based on Troy's history, I'd wager he isn't. He may have eaten worse. Don't think about it, Patty.

"Plenty of time for that later," Larissa says. I introduce her to Troy, and to myself.

"Troy," Larissa begins, "there aren't too many limits here. I prefer that you don't throw up on me, or the furniture, if possible. Screaming gets to be a bit much at times; I'll let you know. We try to treat each other as we'd want to be treated in a perfect world."

"In a storybook," I say.

"Is a storybook a perfect world?" Larissa asks me, biting the fingernails of a gingerbread man. Troy leaves his cookie on the table and wanders off toward a slide in Larissa's yard, right behind the kitchen, where I can see him. I look back to the cookies. They're not all people, I notice. They're not all identifiable, either, although I think I see one shaped like a pancreas. I point at it, a question in my eyes and an odd queasiness in my stomach.

"The kids are always interested in anatomy," she says, eating a cookie shaped like a little ear.

"Anyway, I don't believe in fairy tales for children," Larissa says. "You should know this if you're going to leave Troy here."

"I don't believe in fairy tales for anyone."

"Ah, fairy tales are for people afraid to ask what they really believe in."

"Yeah, but what if I'm one of those people, only I don't even believe in fairy tales?"

"Then you have to wait a little longer for a happy ending," Larissa says to me. We toast one another with gingerbread pieces. I feel better here. It could be that I need day care myself.

"I'm not sure how well Troy will get along with others," I say. "He's kind of kept to himself over the years." An understatement, of course. Troy stands to the side, watching Larissa's three other preschoolers play on a small, cube-shaped, brightly colored climbing structure with a slide. I wonder where Larissa's gotten the sand, and how she's kept it out of the house. Respect for her takes over me. This is a woman who has control even over tiny particles, the clean (but not obsessively so) yard tells me.

"He seems a little cautious. I respect that in a child," Larissa says. "Could be he doesn't like slides. Why force him?"

A good philosophy, but of course, it could be Troy has never seen a slide, let alone gone down one on his back, feet first, to land in a pile of soft sand put there just for your benefit. He takes a tiny step back each time one of the others slides down. You might miss it, if you weren't watching him every second, waiting for him to explode.

"Could be he doesn't like sand," I say. Could be that we'll never really know, I think, but no sense telling Larissa everything. It might make her an accessory, and that's probably not worth the twenty dollars a day including lunch she charges.

A real mother would help her child have a new experience, Patty.

I go over and take Troy's hand. "Would you like to slide? We can do it together?" The second shouldn't be a question, but then maybe I shouldn't be a parent.

Troy remains glued to his spot, even when I try to lift him, and even though I know he weighs almost nothing, I'm hopeful the gingerbread will put a little weight on him, if I can find a cookie shape that doesn't frighten him.

"Or we don't have to slide," I say. It's not like I'm the decisive type anyhow.

Troy keeps his hand poised beside his lips, then steps forward and walks under the slide, into a shaded area made by the cube. He crawls in and picks up a little toy car with his (better) hand. Each hand is taken, for better or for worse.

Then Troy begins pushing sand into a mound with his head in an almost animalistic, clearly uncomfortable way. He makes those little humming sounds as he plays bulldozer, Troy style. My stomach flips, once.

I look at Larissa, hoping she'll know what to do.

"Okay, I'll say it," Larissa says. "That's using your head!"

I'm pretty sure I hear a deep sigh coming from him, from the depths of a little boy. I wouldn't have imagined a small child could have such depths, but then I have a lot to learn.

"He's fairly attached to his hand," I say to Larissa, as if it's not the first thing you notice.

"Not a big deal," Larissa says. "Everybody's got something they're dealing with." I nod. Oh yes.

"And he doesn't say a lot," I warn Larissa.

"That's highly underrated in a child, believe me," she says, and I can tell she means it, because she has to almost yell to be heard over the other three talking ones. It's more than a little possible that Larissa has a much better idea of what any child needs than I do, even a child like Troy.

Troy lies down, placing one cheek against the sand, as if listening for something, and begins to cover his hair with the mound of sand until the top of his head is somewhat covered. I stop myself from saying anything. Try not to be one of those mothers who worries that her child will get too dirty, Patty.

One of those mothers. It's something I haven't really considered. Am I somebody's mother? So far, I've just thought of myself as a woman with a child (okay, a stolen child) in the passenger seat. It's not enough to make you a mother, but it's a step, although probably not one advocated by many parenting books or magazines. Mine is not the kind of situation to find its way into *Parent* magazine's letters to the editor section, is it?

Dear Editor,
I have brought a child with me to a new town, or at least to the more affordable outlying area, which may or may not improve my situation in the eyes of the law. I'm exploring whether it's natural that this child would want to put his face in the sand, whether I should allow it, and what I should say if he decides to stick his whole head under. (I feel certain I wouldn't approve.) If I worry about the sand, does that make me a mother or just a natural worrier? Do you have a column or columns that address this sort of unexpected parenthood?
Yours, Patty [no last name given]

Troy lies peacefully under the climbing structure, his cheek against the sand, pushing a little truck around in front of him, making his little hum or buzz sound, his other hand at his mouth.

"Well, he's made his peace with sand," Larissa adds, as if saying, *See, he's perfectly normal. So what if he chews on himself and seems to want to be covered in dirt?*

One of the little girls stands next to Troy and yells, "Hello, hello," at him, not in the friendliest of ways. Then she sits down with her back toward him.

"Parallel play," Larissa says. "Appropriate at that age, or maybe any age."

What's left is for me to calm my stomach and get ready for my next task on my mental checklist of things to do after kidnapping a child. I'm a master at lists.

Chore one, get child care, check. Chore two, get job to pay for child care. I try not to worry that I've done them in the wrong order, and that this will affect us in ways we can't imagine. But the sand went okay, after all, and Troy didn't scream when a child handed him a gingerbread arm.

I tell Troy that I'll be back soon, worried about our first separation. Don't children cling at such times? But the yard is so cheerful, the smell of gingerbread body pieces wafting even out here. Troy is enthralled with the sand and seems less than concerned when I say good-bye.

"I'm going to leave for just a short while," I tell him. "Really short," I say, although I'm not certain that short is the proper adjective for the passage of time. And isn't time slower when you're four? (Or three, or five, how old is this child?)

There have been times in my life when a minute has not seemed short at all.

Troy rubs at his neck in a way that goes on a little too long.

I look at Larissa.

"It's okay," she tells me. She is all encouragement. She has no idea how much I need this, or what she's encouraging, of course.

I leave Larissa's and get into my skin-colored car, which is dusty from the drive up the highway that bisects California. I look at my passenger seat—he has left no indentation whatsoever—then at the car seat in back, which looks too bright and overwhelmingly empty, and for a moment I fear I've lost Troy somewhere. I feel something's missing. Where is that little tug on my leg, the warm but nearly silent presence by my side?

Troy is with Larissa, I tell myself, in a far, far better place, I suspect, than here with me. I probably don't even have the car seat in right.

I think about this. Should I start up the Toyota and just keep driving, abandoning all memories of my grandmother's sheets and a small passenger? Am I the kind of girl who could do that, and would it actually add to the number of felonious counts to have not only taken a child but then abandoned him?

Would there be a happy ending, Patty?

You should have taken more Philosophy classes. Or maybe fewer.

Maybe you just need coffee. Something warm and routine, not to mention legal. There is no offense related to purchasing a cup of coffee, especially after leaving one's (stolen) child safely in day care. Moms do it every day, stolen child part aside. Or maybe even including the stolen child part. Can I really be the only one who has done this?

I head back to the healthy Toasted Loafer restaurant with the turquoise booths, thinking this is no doubt a common (normal, Patty) place for a person to stop for a coffee after dropping her boy at day care, whether she intends to pick him up or not. A place to think, to wonder about what the child might be doing right now. What if he eats Colorforms, will that give me away? What if he doesn't eat Play-Doh and the other kids do, will that give me away?

What if he bites down too hard and bleeds all over the Play-Doh?

Work, Patty. You need a job to take your mind off your felonies. Worry about money instead (everyone else does, Patty). I settle into a soft padded booth. The waitress is once again wearing wide-striped leggings, although I'm not sure if the colors are the same. Maybe it's a thing with her.

"Hi, I'm Juliet," she says, approaching with one of those old-fashioned brown coffeepots like they used to leave at your table at the House of Pancakes.

"Hi, I'm Patty," I admit. Patty Grant, whereabouts unknown.

"I saw you yesterday with your little boy," Juliet says, "so I'm not saying Hi, I'm Juliet, because I'm your waitress, but more because I didn't really introduce myself yesterday."

"Oh, it's okay," I say.

"This isn't one of those places where anyone would make us introduce ourselves as your waitress," Juliet continues, looking around at the restaurant, which is homey despite the bright turquoise booths, which you probably wouldn't want in your own home. "Everyone assumes you can tell I'm the waitress—why else would I carry a coffeepot?"

"I don't usually go to the other kind of restaurants, anyhow," I tell her, and it's true. I'm uncomfortable with introductions in most situations, and I never know how to respond when a waiter or waitress tells me his or her name. But I feel comfortable around Juliet, maybe because she's constantly trying to blow the wisps of bangs out of her eyes. It's not a tic, or anything, more of a little game.

"Are you living in the Valley?" Juliet asks me.

"I'm going to," I say, as if telling myself something I really mean to do. "We rented a place on Ant Hill."

"Great," Juliet says, "I live on Bluebird myself."

"Would you happen to know if Ant Hill is named, well, appropriately? Should I load up on Raid or anything?" I ask.

Juliet looks around, over her shoulder, although I'm not sure who for. *The cops,* runs through my head, of course. Then she sits down next to me and looks into my eyes, an indication that a serious talk is ahead, if not a lecture. A lecture from a waitress in blue-and-purple striped leggings. Good former graduate student that I am, I lean in.

"We don't really like bug spray in the Valley," Juliet says simply.

"Oh," I say. "Well, me neither." I'm certain the smell alone could kill a bug, if not something larger.

Juliet looks so relieved. If there were another cup on the table, I think I'd offer it to her.

"Phew," she says, letting out a large breath. Juliet is young, probably 20 or 21, with her pale hair cut in what I think used to be called a Pixie cut, short and hanging mostly in front of her face into her eyes. Juliet is altogether slight and pixie-ish.

She rises from my booth. "Is your boy in day care?" she asks. I hesitate, at so many things, really, then decide to go for the simplified answer.

"Yes." We both nod easily. Just another customer with a child in day care. Nothing unusual here.

"I was a day-care child," Juliet says with a shrug. "Don't believe everything you read. I turned out fine." She blows at her hair again, and I believe her.

"So," she says with a nod. "Breakfast? Or just coffee on your way to work?"

"Coffee," I say, "and I need a place to go to work." And I guess I need someone to admit this to, because I seem to be doing just that. But a girl who doesn't use household ant spray seems so harmless to me, not the type to alert the local sheriff. I picture an old-west, small-town sheriff coming by for his own coffee. I wonder if he uses bug spray. I suspect he wouldn't. And wouldn't an officer of the law who won't harm defenseless creatures known for carrying their dead on their backs be less harsh on those of us who (impulsively, and once, only once), broke the law by removing a small child from a splintery doghouse? Is an environmentally pure community likely to look more favorably upon such a thing? Less favorably?

More coffee, Patty. There may be no correlation at all.

"Here," Juliet says, handing me the classifieds. I thank her and open to the employment ads, which are only three-quarters of a column long, in really large type.

"It's not a very big section," I say. Juliet nods, then gestures around her, saying in effect, *I know, I work here. Not that it isn't a nice restaurant.* I nod. I'm an overaged graduate student without the actual degree. I've worked in all kinds of places, of course, some of which I might have used as references, if I wanted anyone referring to me. The column looks daunting even given its limited size. Who do I want to be now?

"You may want a job out here in the Valley, rather than going into Santa Vallejo proper," she says. "Over the river," she says.

"Is that like over the river and through the woods?" I ask.

"No woods around there," Juliet says. "They're still developing, too. I just find it, well, easier, nicer here. I can't really explain. People ask fewer questions, or maybe just different ones," she says, raising an eyebrow, as if I know what she means. I might.

"Well, I don't want to be too far from Troy," I say.

Juliet nods. "Boy, have you come to the right place, Patty."

I settle into reading the paper, imagining myself in all sorts of employment opportunities necessary to our way of life, not one of which would require my knowing whether to add an apostrophe and s to a plural form of a word ending in x. I also consider how I couldn't possibly handle many of the positions necessary to our way of life, which strengthens my respect for other people. (A good essay for the freshman composition class—imagine yourself in a job you know you could not possibly do. A real growth exercise. Not that it matters anymore, Patty.) I could not, for example, get any of the jobs listed under automotive. I couldn't fix a car (hence my Toyota). I doubt I could sell cars, either. Who would buy a car from such a guilty-looking red-haired person? There are some administrative assistant positions, which may mean filing or answering phones, rather than really assisting anyone. I may have to come back to these.

My earlier jobs have been in publishing, at a horse magazine (*Horse Magazine*), and at a few lesser publications, a few of which dissolved and never paid me. I don't see any ads under editing, and I'm not even going to look under teaching. Not if I don't have to.

Juliet brings me more coffee. "Any luck?" she asks.

"Nothing has jumped out yet," I say.

"I once tossed a coin," Juliet says.

"You mean between two jobs?" I ask.

"No, no, tossed a penny onto the paper to see where it'd land. Bank teller," Juliet says, scrunching up her nose. "It didn't take."

I nod. I don't want to be a bank teller, plus there's probably background checks involved. And hidden cameras. Not a good fit, not with the color of my parachute.

"But I don't blame the actual toss or anything, if you want me to loan you a coin," Juliet says. She indicates a small jar on the counter. "We keep those just for such purposes."

"I thought they were for people who didn't have the right change," I say. I've never put a penny into one of those jars in all my thirty-one years. I feel guilty, now, wondering who has put the pennies in all the jars across California, if not nationwide. I'll let Troy drop one in, next time. Teach him something valuable, although pennies seem to be worth so little.

"No one ever takes them," she says. "We use them to balance short legs on the tables and to toss, to make decisions with. That's how I picked my hairdresser from the phonebook. She blows at her wispy hair again, and it's not really a bad cut, I notice.

"I'll consider it," I say. "But shouldn't I take more control of my life?" I'm not sure if I've said this last part out loud. Isn't there too much at stake for a coin toss?

"I think it adds an element of chance," says Juliet, "not that the element isn't there anyhow. Maybe this way we're acknowledging it." She looks so young.

"So, just close my eyes and make a wish?" I suggest.

Juliet shrugs. "Why not? Maybe it will take you somewhere unexpectedly wonderful. Like here," she says, gesturing, and it's as if the room becomes a little sparklier, in the best possible way.

Juliet walks off, leaving the jar behind, trusting me with its contents. Her trust may be what makes me put my hands around the jar and make a wish, a vague wish that I couldn't possibly put into words and probably shouldn't.

* * *

After reading through the ads twice (I can feel my right hand longing for a yellow highlighter, with its bad smell and that squeak it makes across the paper), I decide on the friendliest ad I see. Of course, it also has the best syntax and grammar, which still draw me in. Above all, the ad has a strong sense of voice and is truly compelling. (I'd give it an A.) The ad is simply for a helper, with a capital H, which I'll allow as it's at the start of the sentence:

Helper: *Come on over, as we can use your help. Bolts and Everything, 700 Main Street. We specialize in hardware and housewares, and everything in between. We've been here for years—why not come join us?*

I find that I want to join them, despite having no experience with hardware and generally not being a very good helper. (Patty is not a good helper, I can imagine my kindergarten report card saying; Ms. Grant is not helpful at all, I can imagine my students' reviews saying. And yes, I did sneak a look at them once, having accidentally found an envelope filled with them in my office mailbox. I took them into the bathroom and read them and cried. Lots of people cry in the bathrooms at the university. I doubt anyone noticed.)

I find Bolts and Everything on the town's Main Street, in a little old-fashioned storefront. My first thought was that I'd see something like Bed, Bath and Beyond (no serial comma, and I think somewhere along the way they may have dropped that first comma, but no way am I doing that). The huge store in San Diego had a strange scent wafting around—I could never tell from where, but I always felt there was something wrong with a place where the bakeware smelled like lavender. Bolts and Everything, a name that promises a lot, is a small store. It's mom-and-pop size, standing amongst a strip of stores, some of them closed, some of them needing new paint. I've never seen an actual old-fashioned Main Street in California, and I have moved around a bit. Bolts and Everything's building is an aged pink, with faded green awnings, not that it's going for shabby chic. It just happens to be pink—it's not trying to make a statement about it.

There is something peaceful about a hardware store, something orderly that appeals to the perennial student in me, the lover of libraries, details, and knowledge that is Patty. Despite the occasional sound of a drill revving, a hardware store is a place to study. Go and see for yourself: Watch visitors scouring the aisles in search of the smallest nail, the thinnest bolt, the most lightweight screwdriver. Tiny washers and the tiny tools with which to make the washers perform. Rows and rows of just the right wrench, the perfect size hammer. An entire bookshelf filled with bolts. Just bolts. A man in overalls stands before it, silently examining, considering, cataloguing. He weighs them with his hands. No conversation required. I like this place. It smells of seriousness, of study, of completion.

I walk to the front counter, where a man with soft-looking white eyebrows and only some white hair left on his head greets me. "What could I do for you today?" he asks me, although I think his use of the conditional is unnecessary, but maybe it's a generational thing.

"I saw the ad?" I ask, not really a question, although there's a question implied. Maybe more than one.

"Oh, a helper, yes," he says. "Boy, who couldn't use a little help?" I have to nod. No one I know.

"I'm Walter," says the white-haired man who really looks like a Walter in every way. He's thickening around the waist, probably late-sixties or seventies, wearing a denim work shirt and thinning denim pants.

"Hi, I'm Patty Grant," I say, implicating myself yet again, but who is more Patty Grant than I? "Is there an application I could fill in?" The English major in me starts to worry—is it fill in or fill out? Would it matter?

"Let's just pretend there's an application," Walter says happily. I'm not sure what he means, but okay.

"Okay," I say. Filling out paperwork makes me nervous anyhow, as I always seem to get confused about which line you're supposed to put your name on. Why is there an extra line at the top that you're not supposed to write in? I always have cross outs on my paperwork. I don't like what it says about me.

"I'll just be the questionnaire," Walter says. Walter's enjoying this. A couple of men in the store seem to listen in, smiling, but maybe they've just found bolts that they really, really like. Walter stands up straighter and clears his throat, pulls up his belt. I actually hear a man giggle behind me. I've never ever heard such a thing at a job interview before, but again, okay.

"Can you use a hammer," Walter says.

"Yes," I say. "I've hammered in all my own picture hangers for years. And I use the appropriate size picture hanger for the size of the frame."

"Not just a nail?" Walter asks. I practically hear guys lean in to hear.

"Not just a nail," I say. "It might not hold." I don't add how long I've lived alone. I also don't mention that I used to live where little earthquakes waited to shake the pictures off your walls, eager to toy with those foolish enough to use just a nail. But I don't want to admit to previous residences, to an instability of home addresses and single beds, plus I suspect I'm still in earthquake country. I haven't even left the state, after all, although that might have been a good idea, now that I think of it.

"Ever used a table saw?" Walter asks.

"No," I admit.

I think I hear all the men behind me hold their collective breath. "No problem," Walter says, "just wondering. Ever used a cash register?"

I worked once at the mall when I was a teenager, but I look at Walter's cash register with a mix of fear and awe.

"Wow," is all I can answer. This must be a cash register from the 1940s, maybe even before.

"It's been in my family for years," Walter says proudly. "Part of the store here. Original."

"It's impressive," I say. "Does it make a big *ka-ching* when you press down on the keys?" I'm not usually much into loud noises, but I'm curious, and I'd want to prepare myself for the sound. I'm a jumper.

"Come on back," Walter says, so I do, stepping behind an old-fashioned front desk that reaches nearly the whole width of the store. Behind it are neatly arranged catalogs, phone books, boxes, receipts. Nothing whatsoever smells of lavender. I think I even see a card catalog, and I have to work to calm down my heartbeat. "Press five dollars." But he doesn't tell me how.

I study the machine, which looks like a prop from an old movie. I press the dollar sign key, then the five, then the dot, then two zeros. It's a *ka-ching* all right, but a merry-go-round pleasant one.

"You're hired," says Walter, who closes the cash register door. I can feel the men around me happily going back to studying the shelves of building materials, household goods, plumbing supplies. There is a sense of fulfillment here I can't quite explain. "We'll get you a denim shirt," he says. "You can start tomorrow if you like."

"Thank you," I say for the job and the shirt. I've never had a uniform before and never imagined wanting one quite so much. Walter's says Bolts and Everything over his heart.

"The shirt's not mandatory, but it might help people get to know you," Walter says. "Or maybe they'll just feel like they know you."

"It's fine," I say, and mean it.

"They're organic cotton, too," he adds. I remember what the waitress Juliet said about the town's environmental bent and bug spray, and wonder if Bolts and Everything carries Raid, or maybe it should be *Bolts and Everything But Raid*. It's probably not worth changing the name of the store for.

* * *

Back at Larissa's, Play-Doh is in action—I can smell it before I see it. That sweetish smell of something almost like food. No wonder kids like it. It smells like dessert but offers so many more possibilities. I remember craving dessert as a child, then eating it, then craving the next night's dessert, in a vicious and unfulfilling cycle. Play-Doh is so much more available. All you have to do is turn over the little can, hit it, and listen as it makes an almost human gasp of release.

The four children sit at a faded but still colorful plastic table, the artificial dough spread out all around. There are cookie cutter shapes (I see that pancreas shape right there, and it still bothers me for some reason). Most of the kids are elbow deep in Play-Doh, really smashing away at it, one of them using a metal instrument of some kind. Larissa helps Troy, who sits with his left hand at his neck and his right one hanging by its skin from his mouth. He turns his head from side to side as he watches the frenetic activity known as child's play.

"He hasn't been all that into crafts, yet," I admit to Larissa. I was worried about his reaction to Play-Doh. Mother's intuition, Patty?

A small line of blood trails down the right hand, and I nearly hold my breath, then search myself for a tissue. What will Larissa think about a boy who makes himself bleed?

Larissa finds a tissue easily in her skirt pocket and wipes the blood away, humming nonchalantly. I'm humbled, my mouth opening slightly but no words, no words.

She picks up the discussion as if a child in her presence has not just bitten himself hard enough to bleed. "We all come to Play-Doh at different times in our lives. Some kids never go for it; some kids put it in their ears. Overall, I'd say his reaction is way on the plus side."

She tucks the tissue in a pocket and gives me a smile. I shrug back at her—I can't begin to explain, and she looks as if she's not really even asking why Troy bites himself, what's really going on here. Has she seen this before? Could she possibly know what to do?

If you ignore it, does it go away?

Her mother's intuition is obviously way stronger than mine, I realize.

Larissa places a little ball of Play-Doh in Troy's (bad) hand, then gives a piece to one of the girls.

Troy closely examines the little girl who was upside down earlier but is now right-side up, but with a leg tucked behind her in what looks like an uncomfortable position. Perhaps she'll be a gymnast—she looks double-jointed to me.

"What's this flattener?" I ask about the metal device. I don't remember anything like that from my childhood. We just used our hands. My brother used to flatten my dough for me, but not in a helpful way.

"Tortilla maker," Larissa says, and my estimation of her rises even higher. I wouldn't have thought of that. I wonder if they carry them at Bolts and Everything, as the implement seems not to be hazardous to insects, unless you stick one inside and smash. There's a boy at the end of the table who looks as if he might do something just like that, as I notice he keeps trying to grab a girl's finger and stick it in a smasher. She's not falling for it.

"Cecil, keep your hands to yourself, please," Larissa says, eyeing the same boy, "and leave Ella's hands to herself."

"The golden rule," Ella says snidely at Cecil, who seems to deserve it although may not deserve a name like Cecil. It makes me happy about Troy's name, which I hope will never cause him turmoil on playgrounds or Play-Doh sessions. Or later in life? Can I even have such a thought?

The gymnast girl manages to get both legs behind her and balance on the little chair as she leans on the table.

"How does she do that?" I whisper to Larissa, who is making a heart-shaped Play-Doh for Troy. He's watching carefully, nodding at imaginary steps. It's the regular heart shape, nothing aortic involved, for which I'm grateful.

"Gretel is our little acrobat," she says by way of introduction. Gretel smiles. She's probably four (like the others—they seem fourish, somewhere around Troy's age, though maybe the boy is older). They all keep busy. Not one of them appears to have ever been tied to a doghouse, although clearly not all signs are visible.

I pull up a chair to the colorful table and pick up a ball of bright pink dough. I'm not certain I care for Play-Doh as a grown-up—it doesn't feel right. It's not clay, it's not dough, it's not normal. But there is something to the idea of making a perfect ball that appeals to me. Something round, something smooth, albeit cakey. I show it to Ella.

'Round," she says flippantly, as if I'd been testing her.

"Show off," Cecil sort of sputters. His enunciation isn't as clear as Ella's, and I'll bet he knows it. Poor Cecil—bully that he is, I sort of feel for him. He reminds me a lot of the boys in freshman English, their bodies somehow too big for them, imperfect in their grammar and speech, lacking a tortilla press to make their point.

But Cecil looks somewhat unhealthy. I remove Troy's hand from his mouth (he brought it to his teeth when Cecil spoke) and roll my Play-Doh ball against it so he can feel it. Cecil snorts unhealthily, and I begin to worry. Doctors, I think. Troy will need a doctor, Patty, medical records, lists of immunizations, birth certificate with date of birth. The thought strikes me as insurmountable. The very plague of the situation, if not just the complete and total end of my story.

Maybe there's some counterculture, underground, a book for this, Patty. Sort of like, there are books that show you how to make a bomb. (Although with my math skills, it's unlikely I could follow along—I can't even get the proportions right for an angel food cake.) How to change your child's name, bad habits, memories of early physical and psychological abuse. For all I know, this could be a potential best-seller. A reference guide for the do gooders and the not-quite-so-good doers.

That's a sliding scale you've entirely fallen off, Patty. Focus on the boy. Parent (as a verb) Patty.

So, I shift my point of view at the sound of Cecil's heavy breathing: Is Troy healthy, in any sense of the word? I turn to Larissa. She's looking at Gretel's project, which may be an elephant. Larissa smiles. She's so nonjudgmental. She doesn't even tell Gretel that the trunk is in the wrong place. Art doesn't have to be just so. It's not a compare-and-contrast composition. Larissa and I rise from the table to let art be.

"I worry about Troy's health," I tell her softly. Who else am I going to tell?

Larissa feels his forehead, then shakes her head—he's fine.

"No, I mean, you know, development," I say. Not to mention the biting, which I can't bring myself to mention.

"Oh, parents worry all the time," Larissa says. "Look how many books have been written about it all. It's not like you're supposed to suddenly know how to be a parent."

"Books about it, yes," I say. I sincerely doubt they would include anything specific about Troy's previous history. Though even a generalization would be frightening enough.

"Come on," Larissa says. She checks the sliding back door, which is shut, then closes a little gate behind her, keeping the kids in the indoor Play-Doh area. I wonder if Troy will notice he's locked in, if he'll have any reaction to the idea of being trapped, but no, he holds his dough, watches as Cecil smashes Gretel's elephant with his fist. A noise escapes Troy's mouth, a puff of surprise, disapproval, artistic regret. Gretel screams. Ella smacks Cecil right on his forehead.

"Use your words, please," Larissa says back to them, leading me to a bookcase in the living room. There are books arranged by developmental age, *Your Child at One, Your Child at Two,* on up to twelve. Then another series called *Raising Your One-Year-Old,* etc., and that series goes up to twelve as well. I wonder what happens at twelve, if it's beyond common sense, unspeakable, something you can't even prepare for. Like adulthood.

"Feel free to borrow one anytime," Larissa says. "Some of the books are a little full of it, so you'll have to rely on what you truly believe is best," Larissa says, which worries me, as I'm probably not the poster girl for judgment skills. This makes me wonder if my face does actually appear on a poster of some kind, the word *wanted* stamped just below my chin, or maybe across my cheeks, covering up a few freckles that have never been proud points for me. Not the poster girl type at all.

"I say, if it seems helpful, use it," Larissa says, flipping through a book, then putting it back. "If it sounds like something someone wrote to get to three hundred pages, ignore it." Sounds like Larissa may have been an English major, too, but I don't ask.

"Do you suppose anyone reads all of these?" I ask her. It's not like you have to take notes on index cards or write a twenty-five-page report after reading them, but I still wonder. I am the type to take notes.

"You know," Larissa says, "it's really simple, I think. Now that Troy has started day care, which is really just the beginning of who knows how many years of school, your life is broken down in a much simpler way."

"It is?"

"Yes, your life is now run strictly by holidays," Larissa continues. "The only important times to remember are the beginning of the month, when your rent is due, and any holiday dates that fall within the month. The rest of the month is just laundry, vegetables disguised as cookies, and recognizing true calls for help. On holidays, you just add candy. Or take it away."

"I may have to get a calendar," I say.

"You definitely need one," Larissa says. "I have many, myself." Larissa lowers her voice, "See, I've been trying for the longest time—" she begins, but is interrupted by a large thud, followed by a cry, and an obnoxious and too nasal laugh by Cecil.

"Oops. Sometimes Gretel loses her balance," Larissa says as she runs back to them, and I imagine the gymnast tumbling off her delicately balanced perch. I wondered when that might happen.

Larissa rights Gretel with a quick upside down, cartwheel/reversing gesture Gretel seems to like, Larissa's easy way of putting the world right, I have to think, until I see a small pile of cookie mush exit Gretel's mouth on her way up. Cecil says Ha! emphatically and meanly, then chokes on the water he's trying to drink at the same time. All the other children stop and stare at him as he sputters, grabbing at air with almost swimlike gestures. Troy bites that fleshy part between thumb and forefinger; Ella watches him and says Ow. After four solid taps on the back from Larissa, Cecil begins to settle, to breathe more normally, if still noisily. What's normal for Cecil may be a definition Webster's hasn't thought of yet, but it still brings life back to the room.

I examine the shelf again. Should I read the one about three-year-olds? The one about four-year-olds? I don't know Troy's age. How could such a narrow book encompass all that is Cecil and all that is Troy, not even taking into account Ella and Gretel? I don't think it's possible, but having been forced to read some very objectionable postmodern fiction in my day, I don't see how these books could be any worse. Then a picture of Troy's hand flashes through my mind. I borrow a couple of books. I don't have any answers at all.

On the shelf below, I see something surprising: An entire row of books on how to become a parent. *Getting Pregnant When You Decide, You and Your Fertility, When Egg Meets Sperm and Other Bedtime Stories, Taking Control of Your Ovaries, Not My Eggs, Getting Pregnant This Time.* Pre-parenting. Bet they don't have one about your way, Patty.

The juxtaposition of the how-to parent books and the how-to-get-to-be-a-parent books seems surprising but also right, although I'd probably have put the pregnancy books on the shelf above the parenting books, chronological style. (First comes love, then comes marriage…I hear a nasty, sing-songy, vaguely ancestral voice say.) I can't help feeling a little relieved at not needing the pregnancy books, maybe even a little smug. *It really wasn't very hard at all.* I can hear myself explaining to a room full of women longing for a sweet blondish Troy of their own. *I barely gave it a moment's thought.*

Keep it way to yourself, Patty.

Chapter 4
A Marshmallow World

We take Larissa's advice along with a free wall calendar she got from her bank, which features outdoorsy photos. I realize that winter is here, although I don't think it will snow. It can't be that different a world from San Diego, can it? Troy will need warm things, still. A puffy coat, mittens—will he wear mittens? Will he find them itchy? Will they inflame his bad hand or soothe it in blanket-like warmth? Will he take them off along the side of some road, wandering, leaving them like crumbs to help find his way back? Stop, this is not a fairy tale, Patty. Stop thinking the worst. Look at the pretty pictures of snow instead.

The bank calendar also reminds me that maybe I should get a new bank account, having written my rent check on the old San Diego one. I am so easily traceable. What a bad criminal you are, Patty.

But at least I have a calendar, the first step in making a plan, if you believe Larissa, and I do. I feel somehow more officially a parent now, someone responsible, someone with a monthly planner, even though the calendar year doesn't begin for two weeks. I choose to think of the remainder of the year as a two-week free trial period, in part because I grew up watching too much television. In part because I could use a free trial period about now, the word trial not so much of course.

"It's a free trial period," I tell Troy, who looks at me funny. I don't imagine he's had a free trial for much of anything. "No obligation," I say just like the commercials, and even though he may be unaware of common TV ad jargon, I suspect he knows what I do: There's no such thing as no obligation.

Focus on the next two weeks, Patty. Focus on holidays, tradition. What do we choose to keep from our childhood and celebrate for the rest of our life? What do we leave by the side of some (dry, cracked, broken up) road. Given a chance to start fresh, what exactly is it that you want to celebrate? Do you want to open presents Christmas Eve or Christmas morning? Do you want to switch the holidays you celebrate now that Kwanza and Yule are printed on some calendars, as if they're not something you have to hide anymore? Shouldn't I do Hanukkah in some scheme of things like my Jewish family was supposed to do but must have stopped doing at some point? Where did my religion go? Have I no heritage at all?

What about dinner? Will you cook a festive meal with turkey that was raised in crowded, unthinkable conditions or opt for something healthier for all creatures involved, like a harmless rice-and-cheese dish? Shouldn't Troy experience the delirious wafting scent of a bird roasting for hours in a warm kitchen, even if everything else about the situation is morally repugnant? Is there a section (or sections) on this in one of the child-rearing books? Should I consult a website?

I want some sort of Christmas for Troy, that's all I know so far. No one could need it more.

"This date here," I point to the mini current year calendar on the first page, filled with a snowy winter wonderland far, far away, "is Christmas." Troy looks at me seriously. Maybe Santa Claus missed the smaller (dog) houses in the land.

"On Christmas, we celebrate," I say.

"Oh," Troy says. All of the kids say oh often at Larissa's, along with *no*, *stop*, and *ick*. So far, Troy's sticking mostly with oh, so maybe his "no" won't bother me as much as it does most people. Most parents, Patty. Parents who don't have to dream of the day when their boy can say no.

We eat a healthy dinner of French toast (because no one here would criticize me for serving breakfast at dinner and Troy of course barely speaks). I watch Troy eat. French toast, check, Patty, he likes it. I want Troy to have some happiness. I want to replace whatever memories he has that cause him to attack his own little hand, replace them with thoughts and tastes of something sweet, something mounds of sugar can provide to a child, at least till his baby teeth fall out. I wouldn't want to cause him any permanent harm.

While I am thirty-one years old and have obviously managed to survive every Christmas of my life, and a few Hanukkahs I can barely remember thrown in for tradition's sake, I still feel I need to do some research on what I really want the holiday season to be like. Can you have a happy Christmastime without being too materialistic, especially when there's only a certain amount of room in the car for possessions, should you need to make a quick getaway? Would eight nights of Hanukkah presents (and not just socks) increase or decrease your chance of being charged with more than one felony?

My research instinct kicks in, so Troy and I head back over the river to the library. The big tent behind the trailer looks somehow fuller, puffier, as if it has grown to resemble a giant marshmallow. Troy seems magically drawn to the library, which I think is a good thing for a child, even if the library isn't finished yet. I hope it maintains its allure once it no longer resembles a giant marshmallow, one that looks good enough to roast.

Troy and I enter the set of temporary bungalows that form the library-in-waiting. The ramp to the front door makes an extra deep banging sound when you walk on it, even for little Troy. He takes a few extra steps, a startled look on his face as his lightweight body makes big clomping noises. He runs to my side, pointing at the ramp as if it did something wrong.

"You made noise!" I say encouragingly. "It's good." Troy looks doubtful and bites at his sleeve. I hear a little ripping sound.

I let him. Another parent might not, I tell myself proudly, might tell him to stop ripping at his clothes, might yell and drag him inside the library, leaving emotional scars, fears, terrors. I can give him this calm, even if it means that I just stand here and do nothing. At least it's not his skin.

There's something about the quaintness of the temporary structure that reminds me of my local childhood library, a place I remember fondly despite a musty smell that stayed with me long after I left each Saturday afternoon. Like so much in Southern California, that library was just a bungalow, without promise or (even worse) air conditioning. I imagine it's still there, but I may be wrong. Maybe the whole block has been torn down and turned into a Whole Foods.

This set of bungalows feels toasty warm, as if a fireplace were going somewhere just to the left of Reference, maybe, although I suspect this would be a fire hazard in a place that holds numerous volumes of books.

We've arrived by chance on pajama night. Troy isn't wearing his pajamas, but many other kids are. We join a circle for story time. Other mothers and fathers (I'm assuming here) sit behind their child, with some children holding tightly to their parent and some parents holding tightly to their child. A girl in yellow footy pajamas—very clean yellow footy pajamas—hangs on to both a small square of what was probably a baby blanket and to her mother's right index finger. A boy wearing blue sweatpants that are frayed around the bottoms, the knees, and the seat (maybe it's in style) seems to be held in place by his mother, who has him by the waist as he twists around in an almost sixties-style dance, not that there's any music playing. Troy just sits quietly against my leg dressed in his brand-new clothes. Maybe I was supposed to wash them before he started wearing them. I may not know nearly enough about laundry to be a parent.

Do I blend in? I've got bags under my eyes, like everyone else. But I think theirs lack that certain expression of obvious guilt and an unthinkable future that I believe shows up around my mouth, which I fear may have opened into a permanent, shocked O. Not that anyone seems to notice.

At the pajama circle, I see the man we saw on our last visit, who must be the children's librarian, as he's carrying not only kids' books but a stuffed panda bear. He is accompanied again by a little girl of his own, or at least one he's responsible for, as I don't want to jump to conclusions. A largish man in all proportions, he bends in a manner that makes him less obtrusive in a circle of children. He has dark brown hair that goes straight for a while then gets very curly at the ends (I'm always jealous of curls), a brown beard, and dark, brown-framed glasses that are not quite square or round, that defy all geometrical terms and somehow just are. They look smooth to the touch and just heavy enough to be worth wearing. I am slightly nearsighted and usually lose my glasses when I bother buying them, as they just don't weigh much, it seems to me. His little girl reaches up to try to straighten his glasses with an expert's touch and an optician's seriousness.

"Hello everyone," he says quietly, waving the panda's arm at the group, then giving the bear to the little girl.

"Hi, Jake," everyone else says.

"He must be Jake," I whisper to Troy, who nods seriously, taking in the crowd. I try to take his hand from his mouth gently, and he lets me hold it for a while. His other hand stays at his neck, although he is not exactly rubbing. But he's ready. I have lotion in my purse. I've learned a few things.

I am lulled by the storyteller as he begins to set a scene filled with red ribbons, exotic white bird-like creatures, magical gifts wrapped in spun sugar. I become part of a Christmas tradition. The crackling sounds of the fireplace make me feel at home, despite my knowing there isn't a fireplace, and that it must be the popping sounds of the wind knocking against the big white tent just beyond the bungalows. Jake holds up a large, old-fashioned red book, a Christmas tale. Twelve days of Christmas, twelve days of Christmas gifts. I am behind: We have only seven days till Christmas. We're unlikely to find any swans singing here, and no geese-a-laying at all, although maybe I'm being too literal.

Jake reads the book, turning the pages to show full-color drawings. Rings hammered of gold, calling birds with golden feathers, swans with their bright orange beaks. I'm hoping Troy likes it. I clap his hands together for him lightly along with the other children, teaching him how to be a good member of an audience. Maybe it's okay. Maybe Troy doesn't realize Christmas is only a week away, that we've missed out on the anticipation. Swans are mean anyhow.

"This book is almost like magic but better because it's real," Jake says, revealing another red Christmas-y book. "This is *The Night Before Christmas,* and watch what it can do."

All of the kids lean in to look, and the parents lean in as well. Troy raises his hand to his mouth. I bite at my fingernail. We are all starved for someone to read to us, I guess. To hear a roomful of people breathing together in a small space as a voice tells us tales with happy endings. Please.

"Twas the night before Christmas," he says, showing us the book's magic. When Jake pulls a little tab, the black-and-white illustrations become brightly colored, red and green everywhere. I don't know how it works, but I know it isn't magic. More likely just a trick using a light gray plastic sheet to hide the truth from our gaze, as an innocuous looking piece of plastic can so often do. The children watch, entranced. I begin to register the importance of plastic in young people's lives.

I notice several kids hold little, fat, round plastic creatures, not the rubbery kind of Gumbys and Pokies of my childhood, although those were old-fashioned even then. These toys don't look as if you can bend them or do much of anything with them, but you can almost feel how tightly the children hold on to them, the rounded plastic sticking to their fingers in a way that must be familiar if not tingly, or maybe both to the right degree. The figures look warm, as if they've absorbed the children's heat. I wonder if Troy will want one, or many, collections of whatever's popular these days, small toys I'm bound to step on, stabbing my feet with their little hands. Small figures that will trip me up and be far more trouble than they're worth.

Maybe Troy won't want little plastic creatures to drag with him everywhere. My experience is limited with this kind of thing. My freshman English kids carried water bottles at all times. Were these just plastic substitutes for the Barbies and Ninja Turtles of their youth?

Jake completes the story about what's supposed to happen the night before Christmas, although my mind has wandered and now I have no idea whether the book included any useful tips I could borrow. All I remember from it is a mouse, which, stirring or not, I could do without. But I wouldn't mind other suggestions. Our first-ever night before Christmas. I may need help. I wonder if the reference librarian is working this late.

"Feel free to look around," Jake tells the kids somewhat needlessly, as they've begun to run though the children's area.

We'll have to get a Christmas tree. Real or fake? I am not up on trees, and I don't have any boxes marked XMAS ornaments or Treetop Angel. Not a candy cane to my name. If Santa did exist, would he suspect that I've been a bad girl in every sense? Would he skip our chimney altogether?

We don't have a chimney. I may be worrying for nothing.

Troy and I begin perusing the holiday books. Other children gorge on the sugary star-shaped cookies you can buy at the market this time of year that have pink frosting and sprinkles but relatively no taste, let alone nutritional value. But tis the season, Patty. Troy and I each take one. Mine actually does have a taste, but it's not really a cookie taste, more something semisweet but stale, like an old Danish that's been left out for a few days. Troy eats his slowly, letting pieces of it sit in his mouth and break down into cookie mush. He asks for a second by pointing at the cookies and raising one eyebrow, a characteristic that may one day serve him well. I let him have another, as it's hard for me to deny him such a simple pleasure. Has Troy never had a Christmas cookie? Even one that doesn't taste that good?

Although I do feel we're breaking the rules by having food in the library, I keep it to myself.

"Hi, I'm Jake Jones," says Jake Jones, the large librarian. He is accompanied by his little girl, who looks about Troy's age. Jake Jones, Patty Grant: Which sounds more like an alias?

"Hi," I say, "I'm Patty, and this is Troy." I feel as if I should hide my cookie from the authorities, not to mention hiding a few other things.

"Welcome to storytime," Jake says. "You must be new in town."

I nod. New girl in town, probably appearing on that *Most Wanted* television show as we speak. If they still have that show. I may be a little outdated.

"What can we help you find?" Jake asks. His girl nods and begins sharing a nondenominational-looking holiday book that's striped both blue and red with Troy. "This is my little girl, Dorothy, by the way," Jake says. "My assistant, I should say." Dorothy looks official, comfortable with her presence in the library, even this makeshift one. She doesn't really look like her father, with much lighter hair, blondish but not so blonde that people will think she's a silly girl. She looks a little like Troy, actually. I like her instantly.

"Hi, Dorothy," I say. "Troy is kind of quiet," I warn her, as he hasn't said hi or much of anything. He nods much like Dorothy just did, though, which I think is a great step forward from utter silence without notable motion. Nothing wrong with quiet, I remember Larissa saying, so maybe I don't need to apologize. *Sorry, my child is quiet.* It doesn't even sound right to me.

"I'm not quiet," Dorothy says. "But I don't smile."

"You don't?" I ask.

She shakes her head in a way that leaves no doubt.

"It's true, for now," Jake says. "Dorothy is my serious girl." He doesn't seem apologetic about it. More matter of fact. Take notes, Patty.

"I'm quiet in the library," she admits. "And," she says to Troy, "I know where all the good books are." Troy looks interested, although I have no idea how much he really understands when we talk to him. It could be her tone he's responding to, which seems expert and confident, but not braggy at all. I'd like to know where all the good books are located, too.

"Yes," Jake says, "you're both behaving wonderfully. All the kids are."

Of course, all the kids aren't. Some are starting to climb on tables. (One parent is yanking her child by his footed pj's to get him down, but not in a way you'd feel you need to report to the authorities.) Overall, it's a fairly wild crowd of pajama-clad children with pink icing on their faces. Some parents drag their kids from the bungalow; others sit on the large carpet reading classic tales of the season. I see little Cecil from day care in the corner, untended, striking a Santa-shaped punching bag. I wonder if he brought it with him. I wonder if it has been provided here just for him. It's taking a beating and seems to exhale a little squeak of exasperation when he lands a blow.

A few parents are turning their child's head the other way or blocking out the sight of Cecil's behavior entirely. When I realize I'm the only one staring, I do much the same and turn away quickly.

"Were you looking for something special?" Jake asks, as I turn my attention back to the holiday book display, no doubt a question on my face, something about what's wrong with that little boy, not to mention how to approach the holiday season when you have little experience with tradition, let alone happy holidays.

"I guess I need to brush up on my holiday stories," I say. Maybe I don't need to explain more.

"I know what you mean," Jake says, although I doubt it. "Sometimes you just need to get more in the spirit, reimagine what the holiday is supposed to be about."

"Yes. Maybe a fresh start," I say, although I'm providing more information than may be wise. *Patty Grant informed the librarian that she needed to make a fresh start, he said after she was apprehended.* Don't think about it, Patty.

Jake holds his hands far apart in a gesture that seems to agree with my very essence of being at the moment. "I think a lot of us go through that. New town, new ideas, new customs."

"And all in only seven days," I say.

"Some people believe you can create a whole world in seven days," says Jake. "If you watch those cable shows in the middle of the dial in the middle of the night." He looks a little skeptical, which is comforting, as I'm not in the mood to discuss religion, plus we don't even have cable. I know what he means, though. I used to zoom past those channels. I don't understand why those men (and they were always men) have to shout so loudly with their messages. If they really believed it, wouldn't they have the confidence to speak softly?

"Well," I say. "I'll settle for getting a little tree, a few presents, maybe figuring out something special to make for dinner. I like to start small." If not secular. I can't even imagine where to start with Troy about religion. How can a boy raised in a doghouse believe in much of anything?

Better to begin with greenery, sweet cookies, a few basic needs. Nothing too materialistic, just the smallest possessions that may hold some importance for someone raised with only torn imitation Keds to his name, whatever that name may have happened to be.

"Well, there's certainly a lot you don't need," Jake says. "Plus, you can check books out here, take them home. Borrowed presents. To be exchanged for new ones every fourteen days."

"And you can check out up to twenty," Dorothy says, flashing her ten fingers twice at Troy, which makes him reach for his neck.

"Maybe something about Santa," I suggest to Jake. Although what mom hasn't introduced Santa to a (probably) four-year-old by now? Jake doesn't question. He's a good librarian, nonjudgmental, noncritical. Good qualities in a therapist, too, although I tend to have had better results consulting with a librarian.

"We've got some great new ones about Santa," he says excitedly to Troy, who picks up on the excitement and begins patting a book about the big man that has a furry white beard (not unlike what some of us were told god looked like, come to think of it, but not now, Patty). This Santa has a beard that you can shape, which must have made it expensive to produce. But who can resist a style-able Santa?

"You get the last copy," Dorothy says to Troy, somewhat excitedly. But she's right, she's not exactly smiling.

You'd be so pretty if you'd smile more, I hear, although I'm not certain from where, but I could guess. I don't say it to her. I'd never say it.

"Oh," Troy says, patting away, then (I could swear) lifting Santa's beard to check Santa's neck. Troy looks at me. *No rope, no collar,* our eyes say. We're interrupted by some oohing from across the children's area. Thankfully.

"Oh well," Jake says, "they've found it," he says critically. Dorothy nods with a skeptical look on her face very similar to Jake's, so maybe they are related. I can think of a few traits of mine I'm glad Troy will never inherit. Being stolen may have some advantages after all. (But don't count on it, Patty.)

The four of us approach a makeshift crèche, something I've never really understood the purpose of, as it wasn't part of my religious education. (I had so little.) But this crèche defies convention, if not a clear and helpful description. We look at it, and Troy makes a sound that could be a gasp. Dorothy guffaws (without smiling), exhibiting an understanding of satire beyond her years.

Jake shakes his head. "Not my idea."

"What are they?" I ask.

Dorothy sighs. "Proggles, of course."

"Donated from Proggleland, of course," Jake says. "The amusement park."

"I don't know what they are," I admit.

"Proggles are everywhere." Dorothy shakes her head.

"Proggles will always be with us," Jake adds, "like the common cold." He picks one up and taps it. "Nearly indestructible plastic. Nonrecyclable no doubt."

Dorothy nods. "Bad."

The small figurines are like the ones the children around the room carry with them. They look like little robots, but rounded, with half grimaces on their faces that make them look not entirely beneficent. They're brightly colored, lightweight, and, indeed, plastic. They don't appear to do anything at all.

"Proggleland?" I ask.

"Okay, you are new in town," Jake says. I nod. "The developers in Santa Vallejo built the theme park, Proggleland, to attract people to the new town."

"I didn't know there was a theme park." I think back to the brochures. I remember only the grandmother, the town, the community, a warm and luring lunch.

"Well, it's there," he says, not that approvingly.

"Like Disneyland, you mean?"

"Well, there are some rides. Mostly it's built around the theme of the plastic proggles," Jake says. "A land where plastic roams freely."

Troy picks up another one. I suspect this crèche was created to be played with. There isn't a Do Not Touch sign. I almost wish there were.

"The park plays some fairly obnoxious music," Jake says, "so it might well remind you of Disneyland. Not to mention the endless merchandising of proggles, which you can also buy at toy stores and discount stores. Gas stations, too, although I don't understand why."

"You'll have to see Proggleland," Dorothy says to me and to Troy, but not that enthusiastically. More like someone would say You have to go the dentist. "People will come from all over. It's a little disappointing, though," she admits. Disappointing. A big word for a four-year-old to have mastered already.

"Sometimes they invite the locals for a special day," Jake concedes. I can tell it's not his favorite place. "More people will start coming soon," he says. "But at least it's over the river from where we live."

Troy suddenly puts a neon green proggle down and makes a face.

"I know," Dorothy says quietly. "They smell a little."

"Especially when they're new like this." Jake holds one up to my face. It's a funny smell, not terrible, kind of like a rubber raft but not as pleasing. A rubber raft made out of Vaporub, not that you'd seek out a raft like that.

"Vaporub?" I whisper.

"Sometimes I get that impression," Jake says. "Sometimes a combination of the old Head and Shoulders shampoo and WD 40."

"Not a good combination," I say.

"The smell wears away somewhat."

"I'd hope so."

"After a while," Dorothy says, "the proggles just sort of start to smell like whatever you had in your hand last."

"And it's an improvement," Jake says.

"Isn't that a little strange?"

"The place is expected to make a fortune," Jake says, unhappily. "I forgot to take business classes in school, so it's all beyond me." He just shrugs. I know how he feels, failed English graduate student that I am. At least he got his degree, I assume. I don't mention any of this, of course.

"Where do you go to preschool?" Dorothy asks Troy. Troy smells his hands after holding the proggle. He seems intrigued. Then he licks his hand.

"Troy, don't lick your hands," I say, an image of a dog licking its paws creeping into my mind, which I zap as quickly as I can. Troy practically shakes his whole body in response, then wipes his hand on my pants. He rubs at this neck. I put my arms around him hoping no one will notice anything unusual.

"Troy goes to Larissa's day care," I tell little Dorothy.

"Daycare by Larissa," she says. "Me, too."

"Dorothy likes to spend some days in the library with me," Jake answers.

"Wow, I would have liked that, I mean, as a kid," I say, stumbling over my words. "Staying in the library."

"Of course, there's arts and crafts at Larissa's," Jake says, trying to entice Dorothy into going a little more often, maybe.

"Oh," Troy adds, possibly in agreement. His right hand is in his mouth, but it isn't bleeding, so I don't bother him. After all, other kids have proggles hanging from their mouths and no one cares. And really, which is worse?

"Paints and what else?" Ask questions, the *You and Your Child* book suggests. It was a chapter title, that's why I caught it: Chapter 4, "Paints and What Else?"

"Play-doh, paints, crafts, glue sticks," Dorothy reads off from a mental list. "Cookies," she says, almost shyly. She pokes Troy in the elbow in a friendly gesture at the word cookies, as if only they could possibly know how much cookies mean to people their size, which may be true. Troy looks at his elbow that's been poked, examining it from different angles, although I don't see any harm done. Friendly pokes, though, seem beyond his ken.

"Sorry," Dorothy says in response to Troy's self-examination. Troy leans a little closer to me, but he smiles shyly at Dorothy, clearly having found no indication of injury on himself.

"Just a friendly poke," I say to Troy. I poke Jake. I wouldn't, normally, but it's a teaching device, modeling. I took Teaching 101. I did well in it, not that it worked in real academic life, if academic life can be considered real. Jake just smiles. He pokes Dorothy lightly.

Dorothy nods. She seems to get something about Troy without actual dialogue on any of our parts (especially Troy's). Just four people of various shapes and sizes standing around the library looking at festive books, gently poking one another in the elbow. Tis the season.

"You'll have to come to the tree lighting tonight," Jake says. "It's just after pajama time. You're in luck!" he tells me in a way that almost makes it sound true, and I do feel a hint of luck. This sounds exactly like what we should be doing to celebrate whatever we're going to celebrate in seven days' time.

"We have our own tree-lighting tomorrow in the valley, where there'll be singing and cocoa," Jake says in Dorothy's direction, as if trying to entice her mouth's muscles to turn upward in anticipation, even though he didn't seem judgmental about her seriousness. Still, a child who can't or won't smile. You'd have to think it's your fault, wouldn't you?

"Well, since we're here," I say. Troy's first tree-lighting ceremony, I think, in all likelihood. We might as well take advantage. Be a part of things, Patty. *Patty is antisocial,* wrote my kindergarten teacher, as if the label would do anyone any good.

"Let's go," I say to Troy.

"Oh!" Troy says. He says it almost like a normal child, at least one holding his hand right in front of his mouth. We are a normal pair, Patty and Troy, mother and child, or whatever, whoever.

"Let's go," I whisper. It says so much.

* * *

A small group gathers for the ceremony just outside the library, although I don't remember having seen a large tree earlier. But before us stands another tented thing, presumably a large oak or fir, whatever grows tall here in Northern California. I know so little about botany.

A few people pull away the giant tent, revealing the tree. Everyone applauds as if they don't even notice what I can't help but stare at.

"It's purple," I say. A large purple tree. The kind Charlie Brown would never have purchased from the shiny tree lot.

"Yep," Jake says.

"This isn't a surprise to you?" I ask, I guess it's a rhetorical question, although I usually avoid these.

"What's a town without a purple tree?" Jake asks, another rhetorical question, but he's smiling; he knows that one rhetorical question deserves another.

"It's something," Dorothy says.

"Oh," Troy exclaims. He seems a little afraid and steps back into my legs. I can hear him sucking a knuckle.

"They're not usually purple," I whisper to Troy. I want him to know. I don't want him to have unresolved fears that haunt him all his years, not about this, at least.

"It's more Christmas tree-like," Jake tells him.

"It makes a statement," I tell them. I'm trying to be positive. We all want to be, I can feel it, for Troy.

"Oh, yes," Jake says, trying hard. "You won't see one every day!"

"I'll see this one every day," Dorothy says. "But it's okay."

"It dares to be different," I say.

"But not in the way you'd hope," Jake whispers. I'm with him, but we don't want to be too cynical, of course. We're parents, or something.

Then it lights up.

"Oh!" Troy exclaims, holding my knee.

"That's a lot of lights," I say, although I'm not sure about my subject-verb agreement. Troy shades his eyes.

The group applauds lightly. Only a few more people have gathered since pajama time, which makes me feel a little bad for Jake, who seems to deserve a fuller crowd. But a tradition is a tradition, even if it's neither the right color nor well-attended. We applaud, too. We go with the crowd.

The four of us gravitate back toward the library, where I pick up some holiday books. I'd have thought they'd all be checked out, but I guess everyone has their favorites at home already, personal copies they drag down from the bookshelf each year. A family text, something to read from over and over, a heavy tome to cherish, whether it rhymes or not. Except I believe I'm mixing my holidays again, though maybe that's what parenting is really about. A meaningful possession is a rare thing for me, but it can happen with a book, I have to think. I look through the dark red volume, *The Night Before Christmas,* still six nights to go. I've crammed for finals in less time. I can do this. I turn the pages, Troy watching over my shoulder, as we absorb the details we can incorporate for ourselves: a teddy bear, stockings, lit candles. Although I've chosen a book without magic windows, it feels magical to me. Look how much we already have, the book tells us: birds outside in the trees, a child in his own bed, the moon outside your window. You have your answers right here, the red book tells me. Get books for Troy. They'll make perfect presents. I can stop at a bookstore for some we can keep, place on our shelves, consult, trust. But for tonight, nothing beats borrowing.

Chapter 5

Over the River and Through the Woods

The valley is gridlike and organized, starting at Main Street where I work, then stretching back in straight lines of roads and avenues, as if someone designed the place with an Etch a Sketch. The streets make it easy to walk from point A, Bolts and Everything, to point B, wherever it may be, usually Larissa's house. I have learned my way quickly, and although I always pride myself on getting around the new town of my choice easily, this one has taken me little effort and no leaving of bread crusts along the trail whatsoever, symbolically speaking, of course, as I'm not in a position to be wasting bread on my salary. I usually eat Troy's crusts. I suspect as a new parent that I am not alone in this.

Troy and I will set out for Larissa's after my Saturday morning work hours. At Bolts and Everything, Troy has been sitting on his own mini stool beside me as I unpack boxes. I stop every fifteen minutes to do jumping jacks with him, as I don't think a four year old should sit still for so long or want to. Customers sometimes join in.

Walter and his wife, Eva, fuss over Troy as we leave. "We are so glad you're here," Eva says to Troy, handing him a grape lollipop. Eva is all things large—as strong as Walter if not stronger, with matching short-cut gray hair. She's not the grandmother promised in the Santa Vallejo video—she's at least twice the size—but she looks like she could play any role you'd like her to. Troy smiles a little at Eva—he looks like any normal boy, quiet and sweet, but he examines the lollipop carefully from all angles. I've been lax in introducing him to candy, although a dentist might see it in a more positive light, might feel I've done something right, until informed otherwise.

Eva shifts her great self downward to hug Troy, which he just goes along with, still examining his lollipop while entrapped in Eva's arms. I wonder if I've given him enough physical affection. Hugging, Patty. It's called hugging. I know Troy likes to sit close to me, which I like, too. We touch knees a lot. We just haven't moved up to the arms that much. Still, I can almost feel him in Eva's arms. I may have been missing out. I add it to my mental list of things to do. Things it's okay to feel. It's becoming quite a list.

I notice Eva has no trouble hugging whatsoever and just puts Troy down lightly afterward.

What kind of mother doesn't hug her child, Patty? Though I know the answer to this. I know.

I carry a bagful of trash and take Troy through the store's back door, which leads to a little courtyard. It's a shady spot, the ground made of bricks with sprigs of grass peeking out, some small evergreens lining the area. Troy could play out here sometime, I find myself thinking. He would be safe, happy, untethered. A pretty ironwork fence encloses the area. Safety, it says, community. The trash bins hide beneath a branch-lined alcove, and I put my black bag down to try to figure out how to open the receptacle (large and green, marked with different sections for glass, cans, paper and, if you couldn't figure out how to recycle it, actual garbage). By the time I'm finished evaluating what goes where in the post-recyclable world, Troy is gone.

Troy is gone. I feel the emptiness at my right side, where my knee is unadorned by a small hand, where a small person no longer hides. There is only a vast empty space. Troy is gone, and a sudden pain shoots from the front of my stomach to the back, behind some vital internal organ I'd never recognized before, something large and deep, but without a specific job. It stabs at me in an accusatory fashion. What have you done now, Patty?

The world has gone brown and dotty, as if I've stared into a harsh sun, not the smiley kind from children's books. Not for you, Patty. As my vision begins to return, wavy like in a desert, I see Troy walking to the far reaches of the yard, slowly, approaching something that seems to my eyes like a mirage. I can't imagine what it might be in Troy's eyes.

"Troy," I say, and it comes out surprisingly low and authoritative, but he continues steadily, his hand climbing slowly toward his mouth.

"Troy," I say more gently, and I'm at his side in three giant steps that for some reason I have counted out loud. One, two, three, I've got him. "I'm here," I say. "I've got you."

Troy removes his hand from his mouth to point his reddened index finger. He is so clearly right-handed, I notice. He always uses (gnaws, bites) the right hand. My boy points at what stands before us, which is not a mirage and is all too real, and sickeningly familiar. We find an old, large shack in front of us. It's not a doghouse, although it looked like one from back at the trash receptacle to my nearsighted eyes with my sudden spotty blindness. This place is one step up from a doghouse but not a very big step. And it's occupied.

And Troy knows it. He drops his hand and stares blankly, unreadable to me at least. Then he touches the shack lightly.

"It's just a shack, a little storage shed," I tell Troy. "Lots of people keep them behind their shops to keep things in. Just things," I say, knowing well that I'm lying, or skimming across the truth dangerously. He just looks at me. He's not buying it.

Troy taps at the shed. It's almost a knock. It's close.

"It's a storage shed," I repeat. He's tapping the shed. I feel instantaneously sickened in an entirely different way, amazed at how many shades of nausea parenting can produce.

A figure appears from the darkened window (at least it has windows, darkened but not grimy, which is what I thought at first). Someone steps out from the shed. Troy and I each take one giant step back, but mine is bigger, and I try to drag him with me. I cannot seem to move him from his spot. I am a total failure as a parent at this particular moment.

Or maybe I need to trust Troy's instincts, which are unimaginable, especially at this particular moment.

"Hi," the guy says to Troy. He is a young man, about my students' age or so, I think. Or maybe early twenties. Straight, fine, light brown hair, honeybee colored. His glasses are small and silvery, dirty and crooked. He could be anyone.

"Oh," Troy says to him. Troy nods. The young man nods. I'm not breathing.

"I'm Patty," I say. "I work for Walter and Eva."

"I'm Will," he says. He rubs his right eye, then the whole right side of his face. "I have to get back to work," Will says. "I was reading."

"Oh," I say. He is so harmless. He's like a lump of grown little boy, elongated. Thin and scrawny, not having grown into himself. He is overwhelmingly sad.

Troy stares at me now. "We like to read," I say, moving Troy back incrementally yet still compelled by some force to be friendly. It's a contradiction I couldn't possibly explain, one that is making me feel as if my blood isn't circulating properly. Troy nods at the man enthusiastically, though, little reader that he is.

"You should read," he tells Troy.

"Oh," Troy says. I move him back a little more.

"You live, um, near here?" I ask. I feel the need for explanation, although most of me wants to run.

"I live here now," Will says. He's not very tall, and he slumps in a way his mother probably hated, if he had a mother. Even a boy in a shed had a mother, Patty. Any boy in a shed.

"We live near here now, I mean, not right here, but in the valley," I say. "We just moved here. We like it." I look at Troy, who nods. "This is Troy," I say, unsure if it's the right thing to do. I've just introduced my boy to a young man who lives in a shed. What kind of mother does such a thing? One without bias or prejudice? (I've lived in some tiny rundown apartments, after all.) One who is asking for trouble yet again?

Is a person living in a shed (it's not a doghouse Patty, not quite) necessarily dangerous or bad? Is he someone a four-year-old should know for any possible reason? Is he someone to avoid even if it means packing the Toyota again and taking to the road?

"We'd better go," I say. "Lunch," I say to Troy, then have this enormous guilty feeling. Does this young man have anything to eat? Should I not have reminded him about food?

"Bye," Will says, without a trace of envy or hunger or anything for that matter. He looks as if he's beyond hunger, beyond caring. Forlorn and lost, living in a shed, possibly by choice. I wonder if he has enough light to read by.

Troy waves his hand seriously, the bad hand. There aren't words to say anyway.

Troy and I totter off toward Larissa's, and I feel suddenly tired, as if each of my legs becomes more and more numb with every step. I can barely feel my torso at all.

"Let's go," I whisper to Troy, but I hold onto him tightly.

* * *

"I've just introduced Troy to a young man living in a run-down shack," I whisper to Larissa. "Behind the store. I don't think I can do this." I blurt it out—I can't help myself. "I make a terrible parent."

Larissa constructs peanut butter sandwiches, assembly style, and leaves my side to give one to Troy at the table. He eats as if he has never eaten before.

"You're probably just hungry," she says to me when she returns to the kitchen. I couldn't possibly eat, I want to tell her, but I have said way too much already. Watch it, Patty. Stick some peanut butter in your mouth. So what if it's a migraine trigger. Reconsider your priorities and shut up.

Still, I shake my head no when she offers me a sandwich, and I know I have a look on my face that indicates what she's offering me may be laced with poison. It's something left over from years of making really bad decisions, something that tastes gray and thick, the texture of mothballs.

"You're way overreacting," she says. She seats me beside Cecil, who smiles at me nonmenacingly, for Cecil, while he drools slightly on his food. Dorothy folds a napkin for me and pours me fruit juice, some of which spills, but Larissa doesn't say anything. Troy on my other side pats me on the leg and continues eating.

"Overreacting?" I ask Larissa. I wonder if we should be talking about this in front of the children.

"That's just Will," she says. "He lives behind Bolts and Everything," Larissa says.

"We noticed that," I say. "Maybe we should talk about this later?" I whisper.

"Oh, everybody knows Will," Larissa says, as if she were discussing some fact of life like lunar eclipses, something beyond the everyday person's control but completely nonthreatening. She joins the little table with her sandwich. We sit only about a foot off the ground. I cannot fall far from here. I hope.

"You kids all know Will," Larissa says calmly, in a teacher's tone, the tone you might take to introduce a new chapter on topic sentences, nothing too scary. They nod and drop food from their mouths. It's something of a domino effect, first one child does it, then the next.

"You don't have a protein," Ella tells me, putting half of a sandwich in front of me.

"Oh," I say. I wonder if Will has a protein in his shack.

"I'm surprised you saw him, though," Larissa says. "He doesn't come out that much in the daytime."

"Like a vampire," Cecil says.

"No, no," Larissa says. "Vampires aren't real."

"Why is he there, exactly?" I can't seem to stop myself from asking. It's a small shack. I think about Troy and his former place of residence. I'm not sure again that we should discuss this, but I'm not about to tell Larissa why.

Me: The thing is, my boy used to live in a shack.

Larissa: Sorry?

Me: A doghouse, actually.

Larissa: I don't understand.

Me: Before I stole him, he was tied to a doghouse. He lived down the street from me in a doghouse.

Larissa: He has excellent manners. You're doing a fine job. You just need a protein.

Try not to think about it, Patty.

"Will just lives there for now," Larissa says. "People live in different circumstances," she tells the kids. I already know this, of course, better than she can imagine. As does Troy.

* * *

Back in town, the tent that envelopes the new library seems engorged, as if it's about to pop. It's gone past the puffy marshmallow stage into something circus-y, something almost scary, foreboding. The tent billows in the January wind, which I've noticed feels stronger here, over the river, than in our little valley. Temperatures drop quickly here; the air goes suddenly cold. The wind batters the tent, slapping it around a little meanly. We are all here to watch the unveiling of the new Santa Vallejo Library. We wait, listening to the tent snapping and crackling as if it might explode any second.

A group of kids begins to pound on the tent as if it were a giant punching bag, which it sort of is, although I keep thinking someone should stop them.

"That looks like fun," Larissa says, clearly understanding appropriate children's aggression better than I do. "Do you think it will pop open, and then out will come the new library?"

"Kind of like the old Jiffy Pop," I say. I want it to pop open, too.

"Patty, this is Philip," Larissa says, "my partner in crime." I think she means husband, but I don't really ask. Philip is about Larissa's height—they're both a little taller than I am and meet each other at eye level. I like Philip instantly, in part because he wears what look like very outdated black glasses (Do all the men wear glasses around here?) and because, like me, he has red hair.

"Phillip's an information architect," Larissa says, using air quotes, as if she's not really sure what it entails.

"That sounds fun," I say. I like information, research, I mean, up to a point, especially if it doesn't involve looking for wanted pictures of myself.

"I just do what needs to be done, solve what needs to be solved," Philip says, lowering his voice. He looks down shyly.

"Philip makes solutions happen," Larissa adds. "It's printed on his business card."

"No one uses business cards anymore, but it's on my website," Philip admits. "I'll kind of miss the big tent. The element of surprise is disappearing far too much from our society."

"We've been wondering for so long," Larissa says. "How could any building live up to such anticipation?"

"How long have you been waiting for the new library?" I ask.

"About two years," Larissa says.

"Wow."

"We used to have our own library in the valley, of course," Larissa says. "Small but cozy, if you had the right frame of mind."

"The town brought all our books over here," Philip says, not happily.

"Not an entirely popular decision on all fronts," Larissa adds.

Troy tugs at my knee, looking afraid to go over and punch the tent. *Just because other kids are doing it,* echoes in my mind, and not in a good way, but I try to ignore such things. Maybe Troy could stand to be a little more aggressive. A little less like me.

"A library is a great thing," librarian Jake says, joining us.

"Have you taken a peek?" Larissa asks. He does work here after all.

"I haven't taken much," Jake says.

"Jake is not in favor of a new library," Larissa says for my benefit. Jake smiles and raises his hand.

"Voice of protest," Philip says.

"Pretty quiet voice," Larissa teases Jake.

"A librarian's is a don't ask, don't tell kind of existence," Jake says.

"Won't a new library be a good thing?" I ask. I don't know how I feel about it, having just moved here. I did question the need for a new library back at the university, as the old one seemed nice and broken in.

I see Jake's girl, Dorothy, go over to the tent and watch other kids pound on it. She stands back a little, as if evaluating. A quiet protest of her own. Jake looks on, and I sense he feels a little proud.

"There's Dorothy," I tell Troy, hoping he feels she's a friend. He seems to. "Go ahead and see the tent before it comes down," I say.

Troy hesitates, then joins Dorothy. I feel as if I'm walking with him even though I haven't moved. Together, they watch kids attack the tent. Little Cecil throws his whole body against it, then bounces back to his place.

"Should we stop them?" I ask.

"Seems safe enough," Larissa says, expert in child rearing that she is.

Troy approaches a part of the tent that's not being pummeled by anyone. He blows gently on it, causing maybe only the slightest of ripples. Dorothy joins him, then runs a hand down the smooth fiber of the tent. Troy runs his left hand down the tent, too, putting his other hand (the usual one, still red, though I have bought tons of lotion) to his mouth. He rubs the tent gently. I can almost feel the fabric under his hand.

Troy removes hand from mouth and blows lightly again on the tent. His blowing turns into the faintest whistle, surprising him. He jumps. Dorothy applauds, so Troy whistles softly again.

"He's a natural, that one," Larissa says to me. For which I plan to remain eternally grateful.

A man approaches the tent and begins to pull.

"Is it time?" Jake asks.

"No fanfare?" Philip asks.

"Troy!" I yell. I want him away from there, as the tarp looks large enough to swallow him up.

"Dorothy!" Jake yells to about the same effect, which isn't much.

"Kids!" Larissa yells, and it seems as if all the kids in the land turn at once and come back to their respective adults. Panels of the tent drop away, big sails of fabric flapping in the wind. I thought it was one giant marshmallow-y swath of material. I feel cheated. Then I notice the building.

We refocus. We outright stare. We don't know what to say.

"Abracadabra. There it is," Jake finally says.

"You must have gotten a look before," Larissa says, almost a question.

"We've been bringing books in a side entrance," Jake says. "It's been a little hard to figure out."

"It still is," Larissa says of the building.

I try to stay positive. It is a library, after all. "It's colorful," I say.

"It's Flinstonian," Philip says.

"It's purple," Dorothy says.

"Oh," Troy says.

"Good word," I tell him. Be supportive, Patty.

"The library of the future," Jake says, but not in a really good way.

"It's what's inside that counts," Larissa says.

"I hope so," Jake says.

The kids approach as if they can't help themselves, the library luring them closer and closer. Isn't that what we want from our community library, to attract children? Is this an ends-justifies-the-means situation? Or just a really bad design choice?

"Is that a slide on the building?" Larissa asks.

Jake exhales loudly.

The new Santa Vallejo Library is beyond cheerful, drenched in bright purple—with a richness that seems to exude from the building and that I can almost taste. Like grape. Like a lollipop. There's a slide that's pink, and another that's turquoise, both coming right out of the building and made from the same material. I've seen that blue before.

"Is it stucco?" I ask. I think of the architectures I've known. The Spanish styles of San Diego. The concrete and glass buildings of Los Angeles. The strip malls of Orange County. Not a happy architectural memory among them.

"Is it wood?" I ask.

"I suspect something slightly more manmade," Jake says.

"Humanmade, or manufactured," I say quietly, quoting the English department stylebook on nonsexist language. You're not supposed to say manmade anymore, although I don't think Jake means anything by it. "Artificial."

"All of them," he says, completely unoffended.

"Sorry," I say. "Former English instructor."

"Oh, I didn't know that," Larissa says, and I realize I've just revealed something about myself that makes me uncomfortable if not traceable, although there's a lot worse to reveal, of course.

Unveiled, the Santa Vallejo Library is a giant lollipop of a place. It must be the most playful library ever.

I've never dreamt of a purple library. And my dreams are vivid.

Inside we find four large rooms of books, divided into fiction, nonfiction, children's, and reference. There's a map of the place to help you through (if you're good with maps). Off to the side are puffy seats for your study or leisure time (and yes, they're turquoise and purple). A no-nonsense-looking young female librarian sits behind a reference desk. She looks up at me, and I nod at her seriously. She nods back, perhaps recognizing a fellow lifelong student in search. Hopefully having no idea, though, what I'm searching for, or what may be searching for me.

You should Google yourself Patty. You know you should.

The children's section is a vision, and you don't need a map to find it. The path to it is paved in a yellow brick pattern, the bricks having an odd bouncy give when you walk on them. Purple shelves match the outside of the building. Still, it's the children's section, and the shelves do look indestructible, the kind of structures that wouldn't be hurt by fire or flood, let alone crayons or the occasional kick of a child. (Cecil has started kicking them already.) Small turquoise tables wait with purple chairs for child-size patrons to be seated.

"Barney's castle," Larissa says.

"Barney, that's the dinosaur's name," I say mostly to myself. I have not gotten my cartoon characters straight, not that he's a cartoon, exactly. There's clearly something wrong about him, though.

"It's bright," Philip says. Jake just mumbles a little, making a path through the children's area. He lays out green lily pad mats on the purple carpet, as if trying to cover it up.

"I've never seen purple carpet," I say.

"Is this carpet?" Philip asks. We all lean down to touch it. It feels scratchy, like something you'd use to clean pots and pans, albeit slightly softer. It resembles purple artificial grass but not in the way I think artificial grass was intended.

"It's just stiff and new," Larissa says, removing her hand quickly from the flooring. Jake offers Dorothy a soft lily pad. Troy gets one and sits near Dorothy. He is sucking but not biting, which I feel is a step up. All the kids have come over and taken a pad, ready to be entertained in their new kingdom.

Jake pulls an old book from a shelf and begins to read, something about a frog who is a shoemaker (and looks happy about it, judging from the cover, although I know you're not supposed to judge from the cover). I guess the book goes with the lily pad motif. Jake seems good at what he does. I may appreciate a librarian more than most people, although I'm not sure what this says about me.

I notice Troy's wriggling his nose, then Dorothy begins to hold her nose. Funny how we didn't notice it so much when we walked in. Usually, when something smells bad, you are overcome by it at first, then adjust to it. But this smell has worked the other way around, almost insidiously, if a smell can have a motive.

"Now, now," Jake tells them. "The smell will go away."

"Proggles?" Dorothy asks.

"It does smell like those little dolls," I say to Larissa. She nods and looks to her husband, who shrugs.

"Something like proggles," Jake tells the kids. "And you like those." They all nod. It's kind of stinky in here, though, although the scent is somewhat changeable, a smell you can break down in your nose almost, one part tangy (a skunk comes to mind), two parts sweet (but not like a piece of pie or anything you'd long for). A pinch of something I don't really want to know about, although I guess it's part of my job as a parent to find out.

"Kind of like pesticide," Philip whispers very softly.

"Open a window, why don't we?" Larissa says, heading for the windows in the kids' area. For new windows, they're a bit wavy, as if you're looking into a house of mirrors. I don't like the library as funhouse motif at all.

You are so serious, Patty.

"They don't open," Jake tells her. Larissa gasps. She's into fresh air, I happen to know.

"I'll ask them to turn up the air conditioning," Philip tells Jake, then heads to the checkout desk in the distance.

"I hear there's automatic checkout," Larissa says, which makes me feel bad for the workers. I'll bet their pay scale goes down because of that, too. I don't want to be checked out automatically. Nodding at library workers while they check out my books is one of my few social skills.

Jake clears his throat, a professional librarian signal that we adults should be quiet (or better yet, leave the children's area), and that the kids should get ready for more story. It works on both counts.

Larissa and I meander, although I feel a little strange the farther I get from Troy. He is tucked beside Dorothy. I can still see him. But I have to let him go a little, don't I?

Stacks and stacks surround us, yet many of the shelves seem nearly empty. We pass by new tables and chairs. I run my hand across a table—it feels almost greasy, not quite dry. I look to see if there's anything on my fingers, not that I'm the kind of girl who usually checks.

"Feels funny," I say to Larissa.

"Everything new has its own scent and feel, of course," Larissa says. "Even new babies have a certain smell." I can tell I'm supposed to agree, having apparently had a new baby at some point.

Larissa takes out a marble from her purse and tries to roll it across the table. It doesn't roll, which is even more surprising than knowing that Larissa carries marbles around.

"Will you look at that," Larissa says, trying again with the marble, giving it a push, trying to propel it a little. "A table lacking any sense of play whatsoever."

"You can't roll pencils back and forth," I say a little disappointed. I spent much of my childhood in libraries, wishing someone would play this game with me. It is only marginally fun alone.

We walk around some more, Philip joining us. We can barely hear the children clapping for Jake from here. It's as if they're muffled in the distance, as if they're miles away, and I start to feel that sense of loss again, Troy too far from my side. A vast space silenced by unnatural carpet.

"Oh, there they are," Larissa says, pointing to a stack of books that seem not to have found their place yet.

"They used to be in our library, the one in the valley," Philip explains to me. "Local history."

"Well, this place is big enough," Larissa says. "Even if it smells like moldy Play-doh."

"It's starting to smell like a mud bath," Philip says. We look at him funny. "You know, those hot spring places. Not that I've had a mud bath, but I've driven by."

"Uh-huh," Larissa says. Philip's face turns a shade of red that only true redheads can turn. I feel for him. I'm hopeful the smell will go away soon, as a library is a vacation spot for me, a place to get away from my own thoughts and examine other (published, tenured, degreed) people's thoughts.

"It's starting to smell like ointment," I say to Larissa, although there's some kind of question involved, too.

"I was thinking Bactine," she says.

"Bactine," I say. "I haven't smelled that since childhood."

"It's almost nostalgic," Larissa agrees, "if it weren't just slightly nauseating, too."

"What do you suppose it will smell like by next week?" I ask.

The new library, clearly expensive to build (I read the paper, I see what buildings cost, especially in California, although I'm not sure why there should be geographical differences) is large enough to hold all the knowledge we small towners might need, but it lacks a quality that I want. It just doesn't smell like a library.

The group of children begins to break up. Kids rise from their cross-legged positions and scatter around the children's bookshelves (which are shorter than the adult stacks, but not in a condescending way) or hit one another with the lily pads, which Jake tries to gather from them. Dorothy helps collect them and places them next to Troy, who strokes each one.

Cecil chews on his lily pad mat until Jake can get it out of his mouth.

"Fresh air," is all Jake says when we join him, and we all seem to exit at once. Dorothy holds Troy's (unbitten) hand, making sure he leaves the library safely, it looks like, for which I'm grateful, although I miss the little pull of his hand on my leg. His other hand goes against his mouth, then flies out to wave at me, then goes back to his mouth. I consider catching up to him and taking his flyaway hand, but I let him have this moment to have and to hold onto someone new. It stings a little.

"Let's walk by the river," Philip says, joining us, his own hand holding Larissa's free one, I notice. I cannot remember the last time I held hands with anyone besides Troy. Holding a little boy's hand is different, more like holding an expensive little package, a box containing an expensive necklace, fragile and valuable, yet almost weightless. Something I can easily imagine losing.

We head for the Santa Vallejo River, also known as the SV. Or just *the river*, as it's the only one around here, although I don't think it's indigenous to the area. I suspect someone built it (manmade, inauthentic, false). Still, it makes for a nice place to walk. There's a tree-lined path just beside the river, the trees small and tied carefully to sticks. Silky green sashes accessorize each tree on its stick, making the trees look as if they're in a pageant, waiting to hear which one will be the winner.

We stroll with others from the library down what strikes me as a pebble-free path. I wonder if it gets slippery in the rain. Troy and Dorothy grab for the little trees and circle each of them as they go. The kids loop around Larissa, too, making her a part of the game. She takes it in stride, holding out her arms, a walking full-grown tree. Other children appear beside Troy and Dorothy—Cecil, Ella, Gretel, others I don't know yet. Some of the girls wear stockings with runs that go from heel to knee.

Now each child has his or her arms out, but they no longer seem like trees. Are they pretending to be birds? Troy is getting too far ahead (although with only one arm out) for me to ask him without drawing too much attention to myself, as I feel like the voice that would come out of my mouth would be too shrill, causing everyone to turn to me with questions and comments I can already hear: *Who is she, why is she yelling at her boy, who is that boy, funny they don't look alike, why isn't he dressed more warmly? Oh my god, his hand..."*

"You kids be careful," Larissa yells, not shrilly at all, not causing anyone the slightest alarm, in the most motherly tone possible. She puts her arms down. The kids are getting far ahead. I start to move faster. Larissa picks up her pace, her husband, Philip, by her side. Jake catches up to Dorothy and lifts her into the air then closer to his chest, allowing her to fly around him, absorbing any potential dangers into his large body.

The rest of the kids tear down the path, although Troy turns back to wait for Dorothy, and I catch him by one finger. I can't even tell which of his fingers I've got hold of, but it feels like enough, for now at least. We look ahead as the children race along, and they seem fine to me, now that I have Troy. But Cecil makes a poor choice, as the parenting books say. His wings take him too far, too fast. But then they weren't really wings at all.

"Ha-ha," Ella says meanly, watching Cecil trip and roll, an almost Laurel and Hardy pratfall, tumbling over and over himself. Little Gretel, a gymnast herself, applauds as he rolls further and further down the small artificial hillside.

Larissa gasps for us all.

Cecil turns and flails, and is gone.

"Bye, Cecil," Ella says, truly snidely for such a young child.

"He's in the river," says an adult voice, then the words echo around us in other voices. It's January and there's a boy in the river, I say to myself. The brief question—Can he swim?—works its way through the crowd. Cecil? Can such a clumsy, awkward boy swim? I can't hear anything else.

I hold Troy's entire hand now and tightly. Let people say what they want.

People run in a mass of coats and waving arms, but it's not that easy to walk from the path down the hill to the river. I don't know quite how Cecil did it. I can barely move my feet at all.

Jake, however, must have been a gymnast himself. Or maybe a track star. Or maybe athletic skill isn't at all what propels you through the air and down the hill. Whatever it is, speed, skill, happenstance, or some deeper need that drives him, it takes Jake straight into the water with no warning. He said nothing, just ran, tucked, rolled, jumped, seemingly effortlessly into the river. His head comes up with Cecil's head, Cecil's arms, Cecil's legs. The river, the turquoise and haughty SV River, really does have a current, and it takes them down with it toward the bridge that leads back to the valley. As if it knows where we live.

"I've got him," Jake says to no one in particular. I don't see Cecil's parents and realize I don't know if I've ever seen them. Still, wouldn't the parents in this situation be clear and easy to identify? Wouldn't you hear the mother exclaim? Wouldn't she be jumping up and down, trying hard to climb down the embankment herself, getting dirty and grimy without a care? Surely even odd Cecil deserves to have someone try desperately to save him, wouldn't you think?

I huddle with Larissa as we wait for Jake to pull Cecil from the swifter-than-anticipated river. They are soaked, which you'd pretty much have to expect. Cecil gurgles up water, his skin a cold blue beneath his shivering. They're worse than dirty. They're a little bit stained.

Jake pulls Cecil back up the path, climbing out by holding onto some tree supports, which are stronger than they look. Others help him, but it's all been so fast. I thought these kinds of things happened in slow motion, that you'd see the boy stumble, tumble in slo-mo, as if using the slow play button on the recording machine, then see the hero rip off his coat Superman-style (Jake wasn't wearing a coat, I think, just the big sweater), then ask the ladies to step aside, and then dive gracefully in, all of it taking about half an hour in your mind. But no, it really isn't like that. It's seemed about half a second. They stumble toward us, and a number of coats come flying to cover them. Dorothy tries to hand Cecil a mitten, but Cecil is too stunned and pale. Cecil is never all that healthy looking as it is.

"Were there fish?" Gretel asks Cecil. He does not respond. I don't think there are fish and can't imagine what color they'd be if there were, or maybe I can.

Jake says nothing, just leads Cecil and all of us to cars that have appeared by the walkway. Walter and Eva are in their van—a nononsense white industrial-looking one with Bolts and Everything painted on the outside. Jake gets in with Dorothy and Cecil, then the doors close and they speed off.

Philip finds us with Larissa's less industrial-looking van, although I don't know how he got back to the library and brought the car this quickly, but then this is a small town. A small community, where you can reach your car easily in times of trouble. Although there aren't supposed to be times of trouble, if you believe the literature.

I put Troy in a car seat, and he hugs his knees. I rub his head as we drive. Then I notice that he's gnawing on his knee through a rip in his pants, rocking in a way he seems to find comforting. I want to throw up but instead reach for tissue with one hand, continuing to pat his head as best I can with the other.

"It'll be okay," I tell him. I keep my voice quiet, hoping he will not notice that it is utterly unconvincing. I dab and pat, dab and pat.

* * *

Larissa's home has two bedrooms but three bathrooms, more than enough for both Jake and Cecil to bathe, cleanse themselves of the river, warm up, take on a rosier shade.

Jake sits under a blanket by the fire Philip has lit, Dorothy beside him quietly reading him a story, or at least reciting one, as I don't really know if she can read. The room has a great smell, aided by the fireplace, plus someone's thought to put a batch of brownies in the oven, and I see Eva in the kitchen, aproned and at work. It would almost be a party if there were something to celebrate. Or maybe there is.

Cecil comes in at last, wearing flannel pajamas. He has continued to cough since he got here. He seems the type of child who might cough most of the time (he constantly leaves his mouth hanging open just enough to make you feel that something is amiss with him). Jake coughs too, quieting himself, trying to seem as if he's just fine. Dorothy pats him on the back.

"Okay?" She has asked this five times, maybe more.

"Fine, no problem," says Jake again. Cecil coughs louder.

"Sit closer to the fire," Larissa says to Cecil. He gets a little too close, and about four of us reach over to pull him back. He is having trouble warming up. Larissa feeds him hot apple cider, which adds to the festive scents. His skin has turned from bluish to a definite cast of purple.

The brownies ding. I follow Larissa into the kitchen and lower my voice.

"Where are Cecil's parents?" I try not to sound too judgmental.

"Liv, his mom. She works quite a bit."

"We all work quite a bit," I say softly. "No dad?"

"No dad," she says. I shrug. Troy has no dad, either, that we can pinpoint, at least.

"I left a message for her," Larissa says, and now I hear judgment in her voice. I sense she feels you should be fiber-optically connected to your child at all times, for little crises, like falling into an unnaturally pretty river.

Larissa and I share a look.

"So he stays here sometimes?" I ask.

"Well at least that way I know he's cared for," Larissa answers succinctly. A definite yes.

"He's fine here," she says. "He's better here."

"Yes," I agree. He couldn't be in a better place, I suspect.

Larissa offers Jake a brownie, but he seems to be focused on warming up.

"Should we call a doctor?" I ask her. She's watching Jake. Everyone is, including Philip and Troy. Walter has appeared from somewhere and stands in the back of the room, but he's got his eyes in the same direction.

"Probably," Larissa says. "Maybe."

"I'm fine," Jake says, as clearly jumping into the river has not affected his hearing.

We turn to Cecil, who has fallen asleep with a brownie in his mouth, but is otherwise quieter, at least.

"Everyone stays here," Philip says, and Larissa nods.

"Yay," Dorothy says, but not extravagantly, not with an exclamation mark. More with a sense of relief I would not normally associate with a four-year-old. What could she have gone through to make her understand the concept of relief? Shouldn't all of life have been fine up till four years old?

Troy looks sleepy, having decided he's through licking his apple cider (he would not sip, would only lick at it in his cup, but we did not criticize). This home is nonjudgmental about eating. It is a relief in every way.

"We'll get going," I say quietly, but Dorothy shrieks, "Stay home!" and grabs Troy's leg, startling him, as he was nearly dozing.

Troy proceeds to close his eyes. The child can sleep anywhere, though I don't tell them this. He's sucking on his pinky, but that's an improvement. I wonder if his bitten knee, now bandaged, hurts, a throbbing reminder of whatever horrid thoughts go through his mind.

"I'm going to set up the back room for Cecil," Larissa says. "It's time." I go with her into a small bedroom in the back of the house, decorated, well, unusually.

"I've been meaning to take all this stuff down, anyway," Larissa says.

"Wow," I say, staring at the charts on the wall, wondering if someone's been tracking something. Movements of stars? Changes in weather patterns? Stock market highs and lows? Mathematical graphs line the walls, carefully drawn, carefully taped up.

"I don't know what these are," I say, feeling somehow that I should.

"Basal charts," Larissa says with a shrug. "I got carried away, but we had the room, and this way I could see them all." They stretch across each of the four walls in a fairly decorative manner, despite that there's something postmodern if not plain old *Twilight Zone* about them.

"They're kind of pretty," I say after a moment. And they are. Carefully done on strong white paper with printed purple lines.

"Yeah, I liked them, too. I figured while I was doing them, no harm in making them nice," Larissa says.

"I don't know much about basal charts," I say.

"Ah, you must have gotten Troy the old-fashioned way," Larissa says. I do not contradict her. I certainly never charted it out.

"Some women are just lucky," Larissa tells me. "No fuss, no years of worry and hope, just, Hey, there's your boy. All yours."

"Something like that," I say. There he was.

"And for others," her voice trails off a little as she carefully removes charts from the wall, then nods to me that I can take them down, too. I treat them as valuable, necessary art. I do not bend the corners. "Well," she continues, "some of us have to try different things."

I look around the room, all the walls. There are years' worth of charts here. I don't say anything. I've spent years studying language, rules, commas. But not this, not close to this.

"I'm sorry," I say.

"Oh, well," she says. "You still never know."

"That's true." I can say for a fact.

"I think I'll stop with the charts, though, especially since we need the room for Cecil. Maybe go back to a more relaxed approach. You can only predict so much."

"True," I tell her. "I didn't always think so, but I do now." Have I become a fatalist? Or just a parent?

The rest of us camp out in the living room, the fire in the hearth burning lower, a campfire minus the marshmallows. Within seconds, the children are asleep, Larissa by Dorothy, then Troy then me. Dorothy snores, which I find sweet. I like a child who makes a little noise so you know she's asleep. Alive, I mean. I often feel a stab of fear when I look at Troy sleeping—is he breathing? What would I do if for some reason he wasn't? Which direction would I go then?

Troy rolls, head moving to where feet once were, somehow untucking himself from a zipped up sleeping bag. I could watch him all night, as the fire dims, as another child coughs in the distance, a strange child in every way. My child turns like a starfish in this cider-scented room. Your child is safe, Patty. It may be okay to close your eyes.

Chapter 6
Purple Mountain's Majesty

It's as if we're about to embark on a field trip from our youth, but without the yellow busses, their sticky seats, and deceptively freeing lack of seat belts. We meet at Larissa's house, where we'll prepare the kids for the trip over the river, to a not-so-faraway land. It will be Troy's first trip to an amusement park, and I don't know how either of us will feel by day's end.

Troy seems excited about today's trip, although he can have no idea what he's in for. Every now and then, he takes a little bite at his fingertips. I'm less excited, but then I guess I was never the Mickey Mouse type, and I really couldn't figure out Minnie at all. I'm a Southern California girl who's seen her share of amusement parks. But don't think about it, Patty, because today is Community Open House Day at Proggleland, when admission is free for locals, even those of us in the outlying areas. Rain or shine, and it is far from shining today.

"What do you suppose is the derivation of Proggleland," I ask Philip, who works to get raincoats on the kids. Philip, a pure computer science guy, seems to like the logical progression of inserting arms, securing buttons, battening down Velcro. The raincoats squeak once they find their way onto the kids, as if they're arguing with one another, prepared to battle it out till they successfully cover their victims.

"Hmm, Proggleland," Philip says. "It sounds Swiss. Maybe Danish." I think he's joking.

"And what is 'proggle'—noun, adjective, verb? He proggles, they proggle, we all proggle?" I ask. Philip brings out a comfort level in me that's familial, but in a good way. We could be siblings, from the look of us. I notice his red hair is flyaway like mine today.

"Please," Philip says, "there are children here."

"You don't know, either," I suggest.

"In my line of work, most words are made up. As long as they sound fancy, they don't need to have any meaning. Many of them just came from someone's idea of a joke."

"He said *proggily*," I add.

"Or something drug induced." Philip says.

"Really?"

"Only geeky drugs," he says, "Mostly over-the-counter nasal sprays."

"I find those little proggle toys kind of disgusting," I say. "Or maybe I just don't get them."

"Boy stuff," Philip says. "But girls like them too, if the colors are pretty. I suppose you didn't get Barbie either?"

"Barbie was human-colored plastic, or is it rubber?"

"You're asking the wrong guy," Philip says. "Computer geeks have always been Barbie-phobic. It's not a concept we can handle."

"Interesting," I say. I had a brother, but I don't know what his opinion of Barbie was. He never much talked to me. He wasn't a redhead but instead had bold blond hair, another species entirely. I was the only redhead in the immediate family. It think it explains some things. I look at Troy's light sandy colored hair and am relieved for him. He can so easily fit into just about any family.

"Do you have to capitalize proggle?" I ask. Philip just laughs, but I don't think it's a proper noun in any way.

"Ready?" Larissa asks, bringing me back from questions of conjugation and capitalization, the kind of things I do in my spare time. The kids jump up and down in squawking raingear, then move themselves outdoors where it's misting. Troy opens his mouth to get some mist to drink, although he's bound to be disappointed.

"I'm coming too," says waitress Juliet, who looks barely older than the children with her wispy hair and striped leggings—they're purple and blue, the official colors of Proggleland.

Juliet takes hold of Troy and whirls him around airplane style, which makes his mouth open into a small O, even if little to no sound escapes.

"I'm driving," Larissa says, and the kids cheer. Her aging van looks as if it may have once been used by a touring company, or maybe an old folks' home—the kind of van with lots of windows. I like its practicality and its sparkly dark green finish.

"I can drive, but I just have the little car," I say, pointing to the pale Toyota.

"Oh, that's your car," Juliet says. "I've never seen a car that color." She's not being critical, just honest. I've never seen another flesh-colored car, either.

"It looks naked," little Ella says, plenty of criticism in her voice.

"I think it's a nice neutral color," Larissa says. "I'd buy a car that color."

"Me too," admits Jake, who will be joining us and whose car is actually pink.

"Jake's car is pi-ink," singsong Ella and Gretel.

"I like to think of it as rose-colored," Jake says. "And Dorothy picked it out." Dorothy looks proudly at the car. She who watches the world through rose-colored windows and yet still does not smile.

"Maybe you want to drive, then," I say to Jake. His car seems remarkably free of markings—I can't tell if it's a Ford or something foreign, but it has good seating in the back. I don't mind traveling in a pink car, although it's kind of noticeable for my needs these days.

"I don't particularly want to drive anyone," Jake says, and Philip rushes over to interrupt.

"I'm driving," Philip says. His car is a midsize gray, older, yet very utilitarian looking vehicle, a car designed to hold however many people you need it to hold. I suspect it's a Volvo, but an old one, which makes it okay.

"How can someone who has a pink car not like to drive?" I ask Jake, who smiles a little sadly then heads off for Philip's car. I'm being rallied into Larissa's van, which I like the idea of. A field trip deserves a van, no offense to the Volvo.

"Maybe we should paint our Toyota pink?" I say to Troy, although I don't think I would. It could use a paint job, though, for several reasons.

We head over the river, Larissa driving, me in the copilot seat, the other adults in the more serious Volvo. Larissa puts on a tape of children's music. My car's tape deck and CD player are broken, so I'm not surprised to see that Larissa's CD player has something that looks like a badly made crisscross potholder sticking out of it. It's like we're a club, the two of us with our old reliable cars and broken-down CD players. I fit right in.

The music clatters with too much tambourine, interrupting my thoughts. I can almost feel the instrument clanging sharply in one spot of my brain, way above my right ear, down deep. Such sensitivities are never a good sign.

I adjust the car's sun visor and notice it has a small tag that reads, "Death or serious injury can occur...." I stop reading it and flip up the visor. As if I don't worry enough.

Ella teases Cecil in the back of the van. I hear her ordering, "Sit still, sit still," to Cecil, who clearly is having trouble getting comfortable. (Could the tambourine be bothering him, too?) He's also struggling to walk and talk well, so I hope this day isn't too much for him. He coughs along with the music, a strange type of harmonizing. I find the tambourine more annoying than the coughing, so either Cecil's improving or I'm getting used to him.

The kids mostly sing along, except for Troy, who watches out the window. He taps a finger to the beat, a good sign.

As we cross the bridge, I begin to feel happy that I've left the flesh-colored Toyota at home. Not only do the cars become more brightly colored, but we seem to be surrounded by red Hummers and other huge vehicles, which makes me wonder if there's some kind of military activity over the river, although red, I suspect, isn't a government-issued color.

"Big cars," I announce to Larissa.

"The tanks?" she asks.

"Yeah, I guess they are tanks. Look there's another," I say, pointing to a black one.

"Watch, they're carrying one driver only, those big cars," Larissa says. I look and notice that she's right—there aren't kids in the backseats (or soldiers), and even the passenger seats are empty.

"Maybe they're carrying ammo in the back," I whisper to her. Oddly enough, the tanks seem to be driven by women who look much like Larissa or me (not redheads, though). But our age. They keep one hand on the wheel, the other gesturing wildly. The music is really bothering me, children chattering like chipmunks on the tape. Cecil's singing along badly, as if things could get worse.

I look far off on the hillside and after a quick flash of possible migraine ahead, I see a house slide down the hill and disappear. I turn in my seat to try to see more, then look to Troy. He makes that O with his mouth again and looks to me, but neither of us can say anything. No one else in the car seems to have noticed. Troy struggles to look behind him at the hillside. He has stopped tapping to the music.

Just face front, Patty. This is supposed to be an adventure.

* * *

Proggleland announces itself with garbled, weird music, the words and instruments behind them completely unidentifiable, and about as soothing as the gnashing garbage trucks that used to wake me up in San Diego. I feel rattled by the music. And we're only in the parking lot.

"Kind of loud," I say to Larissa.

"Just wait," she says.

"I'm not sure about this," I tell her. I certainly don't recognize the music, which seems made up of voices, not children's exactly, but maybe adult voices synthesized to sound higher. They're not singing in English. As a former English instructor, I feel I'm competent in saying this, although I've no idea what language it is, or if we're hearing many languages, one synthesized on top of the other. I have never liked amusement parks.

"I'm not sure about a place that plays music out in the parking lot. Where's it coming from, anyway?" I ask Larissa.

"Proggleland is a land of wonder," she says, but not all that approvingly.

It's certainly a purple mountain's majesty if there ever was one. Like the color of the new Santa Vallejo library, Proggleland is a huge, imposing combination of Swiss Alps and Matterhorn, in a deep and yet unsettling purple. Like Disneyland splattered with Welch's. It seems to be neither steel nor wood, neither too hard nor too soft. It's not quite real and not quite fake. It doesn't look right to me at all.

"Purple is big around here," I say to Larissa.

"Like it was on sale or something," she says.

The fake mountain sprawls across a large expanse of soft dirt that looks as if it's been tapped down recently, smoothed with a giant shovel, the way you would make a nice flat surface of beach sand, given a long afternoon, the proper tools, friends to help pave, and a few gallons of sunscreen. Back and forth, someone has gone across this place, leaving plenty of room for parking and, no doubt, snack stands. And who knows what else. Santa Vallejo proper appears vast out here, lying in wait. Waiting for us. To do what, though?

We make our way through the rain, which is heavier now. The purple mountain seems too bright and shiny for a winter day. As if it's just trying too hard. Troy holds my hand under our umbrella—he wears a deep green coat and is one of few kids not wearing a yellow or purple one. At least I'd be able to pick him out of the crowd if I needed to, I think. Not that I plan on letting go of him.

"Cool," says Cecil in awe. I notice he's limping badly.

"Let's go!" says Ella.

Gretel does a cartwheel.

Dorothy takes Troy's other hand, for which I'm grateful. The rest of our group has caught up with us, and we stand in front of Proggleland, waiting to be let in, shielded by our many umbrellas, along with our hopes and dreams, which no doubt vary and will be of little help by the end of the day. As these things tend to go.

Perk up, Patty.

"Is it covered inside?" I ask.

"Sort of," Jake says, appearing to Dorothy's right, so that we're a single line of valley folk. "But the kids tend not to notice the weather when they get in."

"Are there rides?" I ask. I should have gotten a brochure. I should have prepared Troy better. I don't suspect he'll do all that well on rollercoasters, although he did somewhat enjoy being bungee corded to his seat, once upon a time.

"It'll be fun," Jake says encouragingly to Dorothy, who looks skeptical.

"You've been here before?" I ask Dorothy.

"Yes," Dorothy says.

"And it was fun, right?" Jake asks. "Interesting, at least? For a short period of time?" I can tell he's trying his best. Proggleland looks as if it might be fun, but it looks as if it might just as easily make some of us cry in a few hours, if not all of us.

"What's that language?" I ask Jake. He's a librarian, after all. He must know.

"Something Scandinavian. Actually, they combine several languages."

"Just to confuse you?" Really, I don't think it's linguistically correct to do such a thing, not that I've ever met a linguistics professor you'd really want anything to do with.

"One of life's mysteries," Jake answers.

The gates open, and they let us in, or closer at least. We approach the purple mountain's cavernous insides. Something tells me this isn't the Matterhorn at all. It certainly doesn't smell like the Matterhorn. I could swear the music intensifies. Troy covers his ears, making me feel at a loss as now I can't hold his hand. Maybe I can cover his ears for him. It seems like something a mother should be able to do.

We walk that way for a moment, me juggling the umbrella and covering Troy's ears for him. He begins to gnaw on his hand, but just lightly, I can tell.

"Earmuffs next time," Larissa suggests, and Philip snorts "next time" in a way that suggests we may not return to our local tourist trap, which today is dedicated just to us local folks. I try to see if I can tell the valley folks from Santa Vallejo proper folks. (I refuse to capitalize *proper*, although I've seen it that way. I believe Webster's would not approve or at least should not approve. And I don't think you need to have completed the actual graduate degree to feel this way.) I can't help myself, though—I compare and contrast: Do the townspeople seem more eager? Aren't their clothes brighter, and aren't they wearing purple scarves more than we are? Fashionably tied twice around the neck, rather than, say, dangling carelessly, ready to fall to the ground? (Cecil's brown scarf looks as if it will easily drop behind us somewhere, forgotten, lost.) Are their children the ones butting into the front of the lines, despite that I really don't know what we're lining up for?

"What are we lining up for?" I ask.

"Not sure," Gretel says, edging Cecil out of place. Troy takes Dorothy's hand. They don't look miserable, exactly, but neither is smiling, but then Dorothy wouldn't. I feel sorry for Jake, who's watching his girl with such an expression of hope. How it must trouble him not to be able to make her smile. You'd have to take it personally as a parent, even in a long line on a gray and drizzly day. You'd have to feel it's all your fault.

"It's the line for a ride," Larissa says.

"Rollercoaster?" I ask.

"No, they're just kiddie rides through displays of proggles," she says.

"Will someone please tell me what a proggle does and why it exists?" I ask. We're in line with nothing to do, stuck in a huge purple mountain with a familiar yet irritating new car/Shout stain remover smell. The rain seems to be blowing at us despite that we're officially inside the mountain.

"I'll try," Philip says.

"In twenty-five words or less," I say.

"Oh, okay," he continues. "Proggles are these made-up creatures from some other country, a faraway plastic land where natural resources must be scarce. They're very popular despite having no purpose we can determine. You can't exactly bend them, but you can collect them if you're so inclined."

"You're over twenty-five words," Jake says. "And it's still not exactly going to make sense."

"Do they talk?" I ask.

"No and that's probably for the best," Larissa says, waving her arm out toward the chatty music.

I notice many kids holding their little proggle figures, kind of round, plastic, and not all that friendly looking. I don't get it.

"Do you like the proggles?" I bend down to ask Troy.

"Oh?" he says, a question really. He looks to Dorothy.

Dorothy shrugs. "They're everywhere," she says, a four-year-old fatalist.

"Later they'll be all over the ground," Larissa says. "They don't break when you step on them."

"It's part of the magic," Philip tells me. "A force of sheer numbers and survivability."

"So everyone's got them, but there's not really that much to be done with them, and therein lies some kind of appeal?" I ask.

"It's kind of fun to stomp on them," Gretel says.

"Yeah," Cecil snorts. And those two so rarely agree on anything.

"It's a psychosocial phenomenon," Philip says with a shrug.

"It says so in the brochure," Jake says. He shows me the brochure, and it really does say this, and I doubt you'd find any such description at the Magic Kingdom, which brings me a new-found respect for a place I used to throw up at on every visit as a child.

"Wow," I say.

"It says it in several languages," Jake says, indicating the back of the brochure, where sure enough there are several languages I cannot understand, typed in varying shades of purple. I lean in closer to him, which is surprisingly not that bad a feeling. He's large and does exude warmth, which makes my face feel hot for a moment.

"People pay a lot to come here, except on locals' day," says Larissa. "It costs thirty-five per person."

"Oh my god," I say. That's a lot of money to me. Santa Vallejo valley is fairly reasonable in rent and food costs, and we can both eat for a week on a little more than that, and sometimes less, since Troy likes peanut butter so much and no one is around who would tell him not to eat it several times a day.

"Even the little kids cost thirty-five?" I ask. I would never pay that to take Troy anywhere so smelly. He likes to play in the storeroom at work, stacking small cardboard boxes for free, which, as the commercial says, is priceless.

"Yes, but under one month old is free," Philip says sarcastically. He seems to be telling the truth, though.

"So, enjoy," Larissa says. "It's bargain fun day."

"I usually like to stay home when it's raining," I whisper to her.

"We could be having hot chocolate at home, where it smells like cinnamon," she whispers back to me in agreement.

"We know better, but we do it anyway," Philip says softly.

Still, we look to the kids, Larissa turning to Cecil, who for the time being is her responsibility, not that she's said anything, but I get the implication without more explanation. Though I suspect we'll all keep an eye on him—it's hard not to stare sometimes. The day holds some hope, as Cecil (like Troy I have to wonder?) seems to know little happiness. Cecil chews on something almost compulsively, and I don't think anyone has given him any food, and I know Larissa does not approve of gum. Plus he's drooling. Poor Cecil, I think. Larissa and I sigh deeply and fold up our umbrellas, bracing ourselves against the slight mist in our faces and the illusion of happiness all around us.

We get to the front of the line and are now safely tucked within a Proggleland exhibit. Inside the great mountain we find separate theme areas, each one featuring a ride, each one aided (if you're feeling positive) by a variation in the music. Maybe we're supposed to assume it's the proggles singing—those little plastic almost-people shaped blobs. What could they be saying?

Calm down, Patty. You know you're not good at waiting in line.

It's warmer in the mountain, and we begin taking off our coats and tying them around our waists, around the children's waists, although the coats have been misted on and are slippery.

"Are we having fun yet?" Philip whispers.

"The music is giving me a headache," I say. "Not to mention that it smells funny in here."

"Like the library," Dorothy says, holding her nose.

"U," Troy says.

"It's P-U," says Ella bossily.

"Does the library still smell?" I ask Jake. We have been lax in visiting. I have a strong sense of smell and sometimes wonder if the world smells the same way to anyone else. I'm not in the normal range. Super smeller, they call it with an enormous amount of judgement.

"Yes, it still smells," Jake says. "It's in the walls," he leans over to tap a Proggleland wall beside us. It doesn't sound like something constructed from the materials you'd use to build a shed, say, which is the first thing that comes to mind. No one would live in a shed made of this, but then we're not supposed to be living in sheds, Patty. Or purple mountain's majesties.

"You can make decks out of this stuff," Philip says, knocking on a wall. "They last forever, supposedly."

"But has this place been here a while?" I ask.

"Over a year now," Jake says, tapping the walls again, which makes all the kids lean over and start tapping, producing a series of dull thuds. Not the secure sound you want from a building, although this place is starting to seem more like a cave the further we go. The word *spelunking* comes to mind, but not in a good way.

"Can you hammer this stuff?" I say, tapping too. People are looking at us, but what else are you supposed to do when standing in line in an artificial purple cave? The tapping drowns out the music a little, so it's dual-purposed.

"Is it me," Philip leans over, "or is it starting to look like we're going down someone's throat?"

"Someone with a very bad cold," Larissa says.

"Someone who's been sucking on a grape lollipop," Philip suggests.

And finally, it is our turn. (I think there are about twenty rides, so it could be a long day, especially if the kids know there are twenty rides and insist on riding all of them.) Our group gets into a small vehicle that is a cross between a tram and a boat.

"Who wants to sit in front with me?" asks Juliet, who has been busy trying to keep Ella and Gretel from twisting one another's scarves too tightly around each other's neck. Both girls attach themselves to her sides. She now wears both of their scarves, a good solution, and they go fine with her striped leggings, although she must be warm.

Troy stays close to me. Dorothy follows us with Jake, the four of us in the second row, although I'm not sure it's really designed for four. Jake is hardly small, being something of a bear-like human.

"I'm in the front!" Juliet says excitedly, putting her arms around Ella and Gretel at her sides. Poor Cecil is tucked behind us with Larissa and Philip. I can hear him breathing heavily, as if it takes all his energy just to get air, and it might, as it's fairly clammy in here.

"Don't you always get wet in the front row?" I ask.

"Ah, a theme park aficionado," Jake says to me.

"Well," I say. I don't want to explain. I'm from Los Angeles. I've been to theme parks, often not of my own volition. Kind of like today.

"There's no water in this one, you're safe," Jake says. "I know what you mean, though."

Troy looks at me, concerned. He's not a great lover of water and doesn't seem all that pleased with our surroundings, but then neither do I. I still can't get the word *spelunking* out of my head. *He spelunks, we spelunk, they spelunk.* Or is it only a noun? I don't want to make a verb out of a noun without a good reason.

"Splashing, hah," Cecil nearly spits out. Larissa pats him, but no one else pays much attention.

"We won't get wet," Dorothy says to Troy. "It's just a ride."

"It's Troy's first ride," I say, proudly, as if Troy should be excited.

"That's great, Troy," Jake says, trying to help, which I so appreciate. It may indeed take a village with Troy or maybe a valley.

"Rides are supposed to be fun," Dorothy explains to him seriously, the most skeptical four-year-old in the world, I suspect. Jake looks at me and shakes his head a little. We both sigh.

"A little enthusiasm, please!" Jake announces.

"A little sunshine might have helped," I suggest, "although we are in a cave." I turn to Troy. "It's kind of exciting." I try.

"Oh," he says agreeably, sweet child that he is. And we're off.

It's not Pirates of the Caribbean, although I don't remember being frightened by that as a child, just more concerned at the way the boat went this way and that with no discernable driver.

We go this way and that, a little sickeningly, along with the "It's a Small World"-wannabe music in the background. The boat/tram (Jake's right, there's no water) takes us through a land filled with proggles—maybe even more than one land. We see proggles positioned in little vignettes. One set of proggles appears to be caring for proggle-y misshapen animals. Purple ones.

"Aww," Larissa says, trying to encourage the children. Juliet responds, "Aww," and I think she really means it. It's a cute scenario, although the proggles don't all have hands, exactly, and I'm not sure how they feed their animals, let alone milk them. Not that plastic characters necessarily have such issues, especially Scandinavian ones.

We zig and zag in the boat mildly, but the kids hold on to us, and to each other. Troy looks up at me.

"It's fun," I tell him. He begins to relax and watch the proggles. They are somewhat animated, parts of them moving up and down or side to side to the ever-present music, but not really doing anything you could put a name to. I think they're supposed to be singing, but there are no openings where mouths should be.

"They don't have a lot of expression," I whisper, leaning back toward Larissa, who's behind me to the right. Cecil is directly behind me, leaning over the side a little to see, as we're on the left side of the boat/tram. It's not like we can fall out, so kids can sit on the sides, not that I'd let my child sit there.

"Fairly expressionless manmade nonhumans," Philip says. I didn't realize he heard me, but his description fits.

"Such good singers!" Jake says. It's the children's librarian in him taking over. He wants these kids to have a good time even if he has to narrate the day himself. I decide to have a better time, or at least act as if I am. I do respect librarians.

"You know, it's starting to be a catchy tune," I say to the kids. I bounce my head along with the song like one of those little statues of a dog with a bobbling head. Troy giggles at me.

"Funny," I say. "Look at that one," I say, pointing to a proggle. I think it's actually shaped like the Liberty Bell, but I can't begin to explain this to Troy. "Funny," I say again, nodding. Just keep nodding, Patty. Just keep nodding.

Jake laughs. "I like that one," he says. "History buff," he whispers.

"Ah hah," I say at Jake's revelation of personal information.

"It's cracked," Dorothy comments.

"I'll tell you about it later," he says to her, enticing her with history, a child in need of knowledge. This seems to make Jake happy.

We zag into a little gulch and Troy slides forward slightly into Gretel, Gretel letting loose with an "ouch" and nearly punching him back into place. We settle everyone down and it seems okay, I think, until I look behind me in response to a certain sound that I suspect more seasoned parents know, especially judging by Jake's uttered uh-oh. Behind me, Cecil leans over the side of the tram and throws up.

"Now it's really starting to feel like a theme park," I say to no one in particular, but Larissa, Philip, and Jake all have looks on their faces that say they agree.

We enjoy, or maybe just endure, another half dozen rides of similar style and noise level. The kids are relatively appeased, the music goes on and on, as if propelling me through the day (like really bad coffee would, or someone pushing you annoyingly from behind), but no one throws up for the rest of the morning. You could call it a success or at least not a disaster, so far.

At lunchtime, Philip runs out to the car and brings us our lunches and a basket Larissa has prepared. We find a courtyard area with deep green grass just beyond the mountain in the flatlands (and no, it's not real grass) and some small blue molded seats that look uncomfortable.

"You're only allowed to bring food in on locals' day," Larissa tells me. "Otherwise, you have to buy it here, and it's mostly overpriced cheese-based products and small dried fish that look bitter."

"Maybe they're plastic fish," I suggest, but they just nod. They've no doubt already thought of this.

I munch on apples and bread, a prisoner's lunch, although I do think the apples are organic. The kids eat peanut butter sandwiches, Dorothy and Troy politely, carefully, inspecting their sandwiches for I don't know what. Cecil shoves a huge amount in his mouth and chews as best he can—peanut butter doesn't lend itself well to gorging, and I feel for him, but not enough to, say, stick my hands in and pull the sandwich out. The kids take their uneaten portions with them and wander over to a large playground made up of structures you can climb and swing on, which look surprisingly dry for the weather. It's not sunny out, but it's not misting as much as earlier.

"The exercise will do them good," Larissa says knowledgeably.

"This is fun," says Juliet, who looks inclined to go on the blue molded swings but sits with the grown-ups, instead. She's eating a peanut butter sandwich in a way that suggests she has had one every day for twenty-one years, by choice. She's a fan. I don't really miss peanut butter, but I do miss the jelly, and as a grown-up it's very hard to justify a jelly sandwich to anyone, let alone yourself.

"They can wear themselves out, then we can get them back in the car," Jake says.

"And go home," I say. "Have you ever been anyplace that made you want to go home so much?" I ask Larissa.

"It's as if we're not learning from our mistakes," Larissa says, "because I felt exactly the same on our visit last year."

"It's as if this place makes you forget what you're supposed to remember," says Philip. "Maybe it's the annoying color scheme."

"Not to mention that music that won't stop," I add. A painful combination. I can barely think straight and wonder if I'm coming down with something.

"We're not exactly the right audience," Jake says. "We'd have to ask the kids if it makes them want to come back."

"Oh, let's not ask," Larissa says.

The kids play by a large, immobile proggle-like structure. Cecil punches and kicks it. Dorothy watches, munching her sandwich and helping Cecil up after each punch, as he keeps falling over. "I think I won't bother asking Dorothy," Jake says.

"Or Troy," I add.

"Or Cecil," Larissa says. He's fallen three times that I've noticed, which is making him angrier and angrier, as he rises then attacks the proggle with more and more force. Although I do believe the proggle had it coming. (I'm not sympathetic to proggles at all.) Cecil's nearly beating himself up, though. It is hard to look away but feels well worth it when I do.

We're quiet a moment. Our children are not normal, would not make a good Nielsen audience, for example. No one would want them to take a follow-up Twitter survey. At any moment, I keep expecting a ride attendant to walk up to us and demand that Dorothy smile, or that we take her away. I feel as if people have been watching us, and that they are not pleased by our attendance, free or otherwise. Other kids do appear happier than our group, although I feel Troy is giving it his best.

"They're selling those bizarre dried fish over there," Philip says. I think he's interested.

"Is that a traditional dish, either in Scandinavia or in the plastic food world?" I ask.

"Not in any universe I know of," Jake says.

"I think it's from the south," says Juliet, our local waitress and food expert.

"Philip wants some," Larissa teases him.

"It's a delicacy in the land of Proggles," he says. "When in Scandinavia, or wherever we are," he says. He goes off to get some dried fish.

"How do you dry small fish?" I ask.

"And why?" Larissa adds.

Jake chuckles.

"Food snob," Juliet kids him. "You should see the stuff he orders." Jake shrugs it off. He doesn't eat his crusts, I notice. I point to them.

"I thought all boys ate crusts," I say.

"Most boys," Juliet says. Jake wraps up his crusts in a napkin.

"Birds would eat those," Juliet says. Jake hands them to her.

"Go find some little bluebirds and make them happy," he says. Juliet actually takes the crusts and walks off. She's the kind of girl you can easily imagine handing scraps to little birds that flock to her gently, feeding from her hands. She's the kind of girl who looks as if she'd attract little bluebirds even without bread scraps in her hands.

Philip returns with dried fish. There are several small longish grayish fish that look as if they should be fed to something else, but not necessarily us.

"At least they're not purple," Jake says. He seems to be enjoying himself, in a way. I think he's made two jokes. For a children's librarian, he's usually awfully serious. I find myself sticking near him, but of course we're a small group in a crowded park, so we're all pretty close together.

Philip takes a bite. "They don't taste like plastic!" he says excitedly. He offers them around, but none of us takes one. We really are food snobs, I guess, if you consider peanut butter a snobby food. It is compared to dried fish, in our minds, at least.

"We may have trouble gathering the kids," says Larissa, examining the growing group of children.

"And Juliet," says Jake. Juliet has some children around her, and they are feeding blue jays, which approach the children a little menacingly. I don't care for birds.

"Juliet feeds the birds," Philip names the scene for us. I'm glad Troy's not in the little group, as I don't want him touching birds, or birds touching him, although maybe I'm being overprotective. Or worse. But then something gives me a chill.

"Where's Troy?" I say, scanning the playground.

"They were torturing that proggle a minute ago," Jake says proudly. He really doesn't much like this place.

"Proggles are useful for relieving aggression," Larissa adds.

I stand up to get a better view. There are lots of proggle statues for kids to climb, many of them with ladders on the hidden side, so kids can go up a little ways, but not that high. Some of the proggle structures have towers.

"Where's Troy?" I ask again, and Larissa and Jake rise beside me. I don't see Troy. We move in a small mass, a circle of arms and legs propelled toward the playground. I do not see Troy. But he could be anywhere. He could be in the tower; he could be in that little area by the proggle Merry Go Round, where three proggles are joined at the arms (no fingers—why don't proggles have fingers?) and little kids can hop on and spin around. He could be under that plastic-looking bridge. I get to the edge of the playground, and I suddenly can't distinguish one child from another, or a proggle from a child. It is all a blur of bright purple, bright blues and reds, colors that are too intense for winter and that would be blinding in summer. It is all a blob of plastic out here, and it smells, and it's raining slightly, the kind of splintery thin drops that sting your eyes.

"Where is Troy?" I ask, but I don't know if I'm speaking out loud or if anyone stands beside me, and I cannot see Troy. I couldn't tell you if he's here or not, or what he's wearing. (That green coat—has he taken it off, is it around his waist, did someone take it back to the car, has it fallen behind a swing?) Where is Troy, Patty, Did you lose Troy, Patty?

What have you done now, Patty?

Juliet is beside me—I can sense her striped legs, feel her light fingers on my shoulder, her very fairy presence, her whitish blonde hair. I feel calmed a moment by her touch, just for the strangest quietest moment, as all sound stops. There is no noise, only the light touch on my shoulder, and I know, with that touch. I know that I will not see him here, not in any primary color, not with mist in his hair or peanut butter on his fingers. And when I know that he's gone, that Troy is gone (he's gone, Patty, Troy is gone), then all sound returns slowly, as if someone were turning up the volume on the TV bar by bar, and then brightness comes in, bit by bit, the contrast going completely out of control, overcoming me so that I have to squint. It becomes too bright. And I just make out Jake through the migraine. He's glowing, with a purple aura.

"We'll find him," Jake says. I look at him. He is bright and shiny and serious, his edges sparkling. He's a large angelic force, looking my way.

I can't say anything, and the pressure on my shoulder stops as I hear shouting, Jake's voice, commanding. I know this even though I can no longer focus, even though the voice begins to fade into the distance and the colors turn less vibrant. I know without looking at anything before me, and I'm flooded by all the things I can't really begin to see or even think about but know are true at this moment. Patty, I hear a voice say. Oh, Patty, it says critically, over and over, accusing, blaming, and right about all of it. Oh Patty, the voice says, shaking the head I don't even need to see. My eyes close, and the sound turns off. I can't see and I can't hear, but it doesn't matter because I know. Troy is gone.

Chapter 7

Lost: Little Boy

What brings my mind back to this nightmare I'm in is the nearly heart-stopping sound of a piercing alarm, the kind of signal that makes you think that either the sky is falling or that nuclear destruction is here at last—or maybe both. It's clearly the end of the world as you know it, Patty. This alarm freezes you in your place. It is a metallic-sounding old-firehouse-type bell that means stop what you're doing and start doing something else, and do it fast. I just stand still, terrified. I'm nobody's idea of an authority figure.

We all cover our ears and turn to one another, our mouths all about equally agape. The alarm in no way tells us which way to run or where the immediate danger lies, but then, how can an alarm know such a thing? How can an alarm know more than we do? Yet somehow, I need it to. I want an all-knowing distress signal, something watching over me to say Patty, if you'd just run to your left, your problems would be over. I want more than a harsh warning. I want a high-tech security system. I want, for the first time, someone or -thing to have been watching and recording my every move. I no longer have anything to hide.

Thoughts come at me quickly. Should a theme park even have such an alarm? And what happened to the music? I want a voice on the loudspeaker, in English, not an operator's voice but something more grandmotherly, giving soothing instructions, offering comfort. The alarm stops abruptly, and we all breathe in, but then it blares again.

"Make it stop," begs Cecil in a screech that I can hear even though I have my hands fitted over my ears as tightly as possible. Larissa takes her hands from her ears to cover Cecil's. She is all generosity and goodness, and I'm a girl whose feet are glued to the ground.

"What is it?" I ask.

"It's an alarm," screams Dorothy. I don't bother to tell her I know that much. Or that I know more. It is the siren call of a missing child. A lost child. A stolen child. I should hear it in my dreams.

This is not just a drill, Patty.

We huddle against one another at the side of the mountain, not so much for warmth but as protection from something so horrible that a shrieking alarm has been sounded that should be reserved for incoming missiles. It's the kind of sound that reaches into your body and attempts to move your organs around somewhat vindictively, and it feels as if it's working. It is ripping my heart out.

The alarm stops again suddenly, and the annoying music takes its place. I guess someone considers this calming, the norm, just another day in the park. Maybe it is. Jake comes running over, although I hadn't realized he was gone. I am clutching Juliet and Dorothy. Dorothy says, "finally," as the alarm stops, but I'm afraid she's jumping to conclusions, and it will start again. Then I'm afraid that it won't. What does it say about Troy if the alarm does not sound again? Is it good news or bad?

"They've closed off the park," Jake says in my direction. "They'll let people out one at a time. We'll find him," Jake says. He's still all glittery around the edges, although some of it could be from the misting.

"Jake's good in a crisis," Larissa whispers to me. I'd be glad to hear this if only I could start breathing properly.

"Do you have a picture in your wallet?" Jake asks me. He and Philip have surrounded me. The kids sit on the ground practically under Larissa, playing rock, paper, scissors, a cruel game of loss. Troy doesn't care for the game, as he always wants to be paper, which seems never the right choice. He loves paper, any color. I admire his loyalty.

Where is Troy, Patty, where is Troy?

I remember the stories I read in San Diego, where they used to kidnap kids at the Wal-Mart, drag them into the bathroom, chloroform them (although that idea's from old noir movies, and maybe they use something else now, a different chemical compound that no doubt gives you cancer when you grow up, if you grow up), dye their hair black (funny, Patty, how you never would have thought of such a thing), and put them into a large drawstring trash bag before rushing them away in the back of an unmarked van. Is Troy in a bag? Is he still a little blonde-haired boy but in a black trash bag? A little blonde-haired boy struggling for air, drugged in a black trash bag?

"What?" I ask.

"Picture, we need a photo of Troy," Philip says.

"I don't have a photo," I say.

"On your phone?" Jake asks.

"No," I say, then it hits me. "I don't have a photo." Anything more could be used against me in a court of law, but then I have it coming. "I don't have any photos."

It must sound bizarre, inexplicable. What kind of mother are you, Patty, not to have a picture of your child smiling, a picture of him hugging a tree, cradling his first puppy, taking his first step? No photo of him on a bike, flying a kite, asleep under his favorite blanket.

"I don't," I say.

"Birth certificate?" Philip asks very quietly.

I just look at him in the least self-incriminating way I know how, although I'm sure I look as guilty as I am.

"The move," Jake says. "Did it all get lost in the move?" I just stare at him. He is nodding. He shares a look with Philip that somehow explains something I have yet to say, as I wouldn't know where to begin. They seem to know that I don't have a birth certificate and also still seem not to be judging me. That much I can tell despite my guilt at the moment, and most of the time.

"I've got photos at home—I forgot my phone," Larissa says. "The kids playing in the backyard. Let's go."

"I can't go," I say.

"They've probably already gone," Philip says quietly.

"Who?" I ask, but I know who. The people with the trash bag. A heavy-duty one, like you'd use for the leaves you rake up in the fall, if you had a garden, some land, a place for your child to run around and jump in a pile of leaves, if you lived in a place that had trees that shed leaves in the autumn. If your child weren't at this moment trapped in a bag (maybe). I start to groan. I can hear the sickly squeaking sound the garbage bag makes when you rub at it with your hand, fighting to get out (if you're still conscious). Your small hand with the bite wounds on it, reopening. I can sense how hard it would be to breathe inside it, the slick feel of it against your face. Gasping. You're not supposed to put a bag over your head, for so many good, good reasons. The sound of it alone would be unbearable, plus that plastic smell, the slimy, filmy touch. I don't feel well, and Troy's little face is inside a bag (maybe). How can either of us breathe?

Larissa leads us all to the front of the theme park, Juliet somehow managing to hold each child's hand even though there are four children—Cecil, Gretel, Ella, Dorothy. There is no fifth. Who is holding his hand? Who let go of his hand?

You know the answer to that one, Patty.

Dorothy touches the small of my back. I feel her little palm, bigger than Troy's. His is a really little hand. I don't need a photo to know this.

"The police want to talk to you here," Philip says to me. The police want me. He has no idea how long I've been expecting to hear this, how in the end, I'm not surprised at all.

"The police want me," I find I have to say out loud to Larissa. She nods and gestures to Juliet, who herds the kids around us in a circle, as if protecting me. Dorothy gives me a solid, secure nod. She clearly does not envision Troy in a garbage bag, although she is not without imagination, I've found. Perhaps she's just decided to keep it to herself.

The police officer introduces himself, but I can barely recognize the words he says. Officer something. From Santa Vallejo proper. I catch the word *proper* but find it's completely unnecessary to the situation here, and if he's the kind of guy who's going to waste time on useless adjectives, then I am in trouble. More trouble. Black garbage bag—now *black* is an adjective essential to the moment, but I don't have the words to convey this right now. I don't even have a photo. Just an image.

"You don't have a photo?" he asks me. *Bad mommy.* He wants to say it.

"We have them at home," Larissa answers for me. Clearly, I'm beside myself, and it occurs to me that I probably look perfectly correct for someone whose child has just been stolen, removed from a theme park against his or her will. I am disheveled and speechless, needing to scream, needing to run in all directions and no doubt comb my limp and hopeless hair. It occurs to me that perhaps they see this every day. A woman, unable to speak, who's forgotten to put a picture in her wallet (it's just a hemp wallet, very light, no room for photos, but they can't know that), not that I have a picture anyway, but I don't need to say this. And not a single shot on my phone, which I have also forgotten. Bad mommy alright.

"Okay," the guy says. He's very young. Would an older one ask better questions or just more questions I couldn't answer?

Focus on Troy, Patty. Your life as you know it is over anyway.

And so the truth sets me free, as those history books like to say, despite that I took as few history courses as necessary.

"His name is Troy," I say. "He's a little sandy-blond-haired boy, four years old. Blue eyes. He may be wearing a green parka, kind of a raincoat, medium thick. Under it he wore [is wearing, Patty, use the present tense, be a little optimistic] a blue shirt. Blue pants, not jeans. He doesn't like jeans."

"He likes blue," Gretel adds, a positive note.

"The shirt's got a big picture of the Earth on it," Dorothy adds. "One of those decal kinds that peel a little when you pick at it."

"He picks at it," Cecil adds accusingly.

"He's this tall," I say, pointing to the spot on my leg where Troy reaches. The officer actually takes out a measuring tape in a bright yellow plastic packet. (They're called Bright Measure, and they sell for three ninety-nine at the store; you can attach them to your key ring or belt, not that they're stylish.)

"Twenty-six inches," the officer says, writing it down.

"He's shrimpy," Ella says, and Cecil hits her in the arm. Juliet tries to separate them.

"It's called short stature," Dorothy tells both Cecil and the officer. "And it doesn't mean anything."

"He doesn't talk a lot," I tell the officer.

"He doesn't cry, either," Larissa adds, and I realize this is true. Cecil, though, is crying now. (Ella hit him back, which he seems in no shape for.)

"No, he doesn't cry," I say. He doesn't scream, even when you'd think he'd need to most, although I don't tell them this. I know this about him, though. I cannot picture him calling out for help in a situation endangering his life. It's not like he hasn't had the opportunity before. I can see him right now, and he's quiet. Quiet, bagged, and drugged or not. *You wouldn't have needed to drug him,* I silently tell someone out there, *but I bet you didn't realize that, did you?*

Jake approaches us. He looks serious, determined, but there is something on his face that I cannot read, something devastating. Then I see that he's carrying the coat, Troy's coat. The green one that may not be warm enough for the weather but is definitely not warm enough at the moment, as it's nowhere near Troy. Troy is cold, I start repeating in my mind. Troy is cold.

And I do not remember the last time, if ever, that I cried like this, loudly and, as the chorus director used to say, with feeling. I sense the group around me take one step closer to me, although I would have thought they'd go the opposite direction. I grab the green coat and hug it to my knee. It's cold, but I need it there just the same, I need to warm it with my body weight. When the officer takes it away from me, I feel that I might kill him in what's referred to by journalists as a sudden rage. Dorothy reaches for the coat from the officer and tugs it to her face, then takes a small bite, all of which I completely understand. I can taste it, too, soft and slightly sweet.

I could swallow it whole.

* * *

Newspeople line up outside Larissa's house. I hear a constant beeping, trucks backing up, people yelling to get out of the way. Crowds of people I've never seen before look on, but whether they're watching the house or watching the news crew I'm not really sure. At times, just for an extra surreal effect, we turn on the TV to see the people watching the house, but then Cecil or Dorothy catches a glimpse of it, and we snap it off. There is no news anyway, really, just a constant repetition of what some people believe to be facts. Temporary facts, an oxymoron of the information age. One that I've never found the least bit entertaining.

I'm wrapped in several throws—Larissa claims to have one for every holiday or occasion, although I'm hopeful she has never thought of this one. I can't know for certain. Newspapers are full of this sort of thing, after all, except when you're looking for it.

Dorothy has put on a nurse's outfit. She comes in the room to adjust the blankets, fluff up the pillows. She's good at this.

I hear Cecil coughing badly from the back room—he's had some sort of attack.

"Is Cecil all right?" I ask Larissa, who has come out to search the room for something, gone back, and then come out again.

"It's subsiding," Larissa says, sitting next to me and covering herself with another blanket. We are all pitiful in this house, I think, or maybe it's just me. And Cecil. We're not a very useful team. Neither of us would pick the other for a team sport. We would be the last ones left standing, morosely, an asset to no one.

"How are you?" Larissa asks.

"I want to do something," I say. "But I also want to disappear into the couch."

"The guys are working on it," Larissa says. "Let them." Philip has disappeared into his improvised office (also the laundry room, but I don't think he's doing laundry). Jake is still at Proggleland at a makeshift lookout post the police put together. (It's really just the main entrance, but Jake reported to Larissa that there are donuts and other foods now that aren't cheese based or fried but still reek of emergency.) Dorothy brings cups of peppermint tea that are not hot at all, as she's not allowed to use the stove. But they smell nice.

Dorothy leaves again, and Larissa sneaks on the TV. We keep the volume low. I find I really want it on, too.

"We're standing outside the home of a friend of Patty Grant's, the woman whose child, Troy Grant, is missing from Proggleland."

And there it is, and I can barely look at it, despite that I have been waiting to see it all along. It's my high school picture, up on the screen, and I only wish that Larissa didn't have such a large TV.

"Shouldn't they be showing the photo of Troy?" Larissa asks. "It's not like you're missing, or a criminal, or anything." She doesn't comment on my bad hairstyle in the photo, but then I am not the story, as far as she knows.

"Did we give them Troy's picture?" I ask. I've been sort of out of it. I'm not good at this, the newscasters' looks indicate when they sneer and say "Patty Grant remains secluded," as I haven't come out of the house to cry and beg for my child. Punishment only begins with the high school photo, their look indicates. It's an unflattering shot, but their tone implies I don't deserve any better. And they're right.

"Yes, we gave them the one of him at the Christmas party," Larissa says. "Also one of him smiling, one on the slide, one making cookies in the kitchen." I try to remember these times, what the photos might have looked like. Larissa brings over a photo album, where she has pictures of all the kids in day care, and I see Troy in a variety of activities: in the sand (he does like it); making snowmen, or snowshapes at least, out of marshmallows. With Dorothy, with Cecil. Cecil does look worse these days, I realize, noticeably so. But my boy is in these books, he's all around, and I realize I didn't know what activities he did every day, which ones may have made him laugh. What few syllables he might have pronounced when I wasn't here. What have I missed?

"Has he been happy here, in day care?" I ask.

Larissa looks at me, not as if she's offended (I didn't mean it that way) but with more empathy than I deserve. "Troy loves it here," she says. "He's very happy."

"I haven't been very good for him," I say.

"Every parent feels that way sometimes, but it certainly isn't true in your case," she says. "Troy adores you." I wonder about this. How does she know? Because he eats and follows directions? (Okay, he only eats a little.) Because he doesn't complain? Oh, the things Troy has never complained about. The photos make him seem far away, which I don't think is their purpose at all. He's moving fast, in the opposite direction from me. With every photo, he's easily another mile away.

"I don't think we'll see him again," I say. "I think he's been taken for good." I don't add *this time*.

"I don't believe in pessimism," Larissa says. "It's unfounded and unproductive."

"Maybe there's a reason for this," I say.

"I don't go in for that kind of stuff either," Larissa says.

"I don't mean religious," I say. "I don't know." And I don't. I haven't a clue, really, and no one to ask. I can't imagine that consulting a reference librarian would help.

Excuse me, my child has just been taken by a person or persons from a purple theme park made of manmade materials. Do you have a book (and/or research article within a book) that I could consult? Did I mention this sort of thing has happened to him before, but that I was the one who kidnapped him? Do you think that, given the odds, he will turn out okay, what with this being the second time (that we know of)?

Don't mention that, Patty.

And there on the TV we see the picture of Troy in his blue shirt, the one with the Earth on it, the one he's wearing, as if somehow Larissa knew all along to snap a picture of him in this shirt, as if she knew the shirt would be important. (He really doesn't have that many shirts—we're on a budget, and blue is his favorite, as even little Dorothy well knows.)

"Troy Grant is four years old and was last seen wearing a blue shirt much like this one," says the newsgirl.

"He *is* wearing that shirt," both Larissa and I say. She looks at me. "Maybe I'll go yell it out the door," she says. Larissa would do this.

"He was last seen at Proggleland in the play structure area," the newsgirl says, although I believe just the words "play structure" are all you need to say. "At the time, he may have been wearing a green windbreaker, but the coat has been located."

"It's a parka," I say defensively. "And it's scotch-guarded against rain."

"It's a perfectly good coat," Larissa yells at the television. They show a phone number to call at the bottom of the screen if you've seen Troy.

"The boy was seemingly unsupervised at the time," she adds.

"Hey," Larissa yells at the screen.

"Seemingly unsupervised?" I ask. Her comment is accusatory and redundant, and I don't know where to begin to complain, even though I also believe it's true.

You looked away, Patty. All the books say not to.

"Police are asking viewers to contact them with any information, and to remember that the boy's looks might have undergone some changes."

I feel sickened by this thought, and not for the first time. From the back of the house we hear Cecil coughing somewhat compulsively. We turn the sound down, although the two are probably not related.

"Should I go out there?" I ask. Philip joins us and sits on the arm of the couch next to Larissa.

"I gave them a copy of a birth certificate and the photo," Philip says. "I'm not sure you have to go out there, yet."

"Birth certificate," I say quietly, not exactly a question, because there would be so many questions, and not a decent legal answer in the bunch. There must be a birth certificate of some sorts, right?

He wasn't part of a litter, Patty.

But there's no birth certificate for who he is now. Nothing verifiable. Only vague imaginings and some pretty harsh reality on top of it. There is just Troy, somewhere, totally undocumented, almost nonexistent.

"It's a copy," Philip says, showing us a black-and-white sheet of paper filled with both facts and suggestions, carefully created, official looking to me at least. It burns my hands a little as I take it. Warm from the printer; hotter than hell, it occurs to me, though I rarely swear.

Utterly manufactured and manmade.

"Troy Grant," I say. That's what they said on the news—that's who he is now. Or was an hour or so ago, at least.

The information age, Patty. The information age in the DIY world. What information can't you create? What can't you change, revise. Revision—isn't it essential, Patty, failed writing teacher that you are? Isn't revising where the real shape of the story takes place, where the future becomes a possibility? Don't we use the saying Revise, Revise, Revise for a reason? Have you really learned nothing at all?

The word hacker comes to me, but I've never met one before. I think of a movie with a creepy girl hacker that I had to turn off at one point. But Philip has red hair and freckles. Maybe there's more than one definition of hacker in Merriam Webster's. It's not like I've memorized the thing.

"No middle initial," Philip says. I hadn't bothered to come up with a middle name, either. What these people don't know about me, I think, looking from Larissa to Philip. I am in their home, plastered across their TV screen, my hair a faded red in the old high school photo, as the lighting was really bad. There's nothing in my high school photo that would inspire pity, that would make anyone want to help me. I look almost black and white, but Troy—Troy looks healthy, normal, a little boy in blue. A little missing boy in blue. A boy you'd want to find. A boy we've all come to know and (just say it, Patty), love.

But who is he missing from, and what will happen to him next?

Philip looks completely innocent or at least justifiably confident and competent in all ways. But I know there's no official birth certificate to make a copy of, just as I know there's no middle initial. He's right about that.

Never undervalue the tech guy. That much I have learned. Let me tell you.

"Philip helps people out," Larissa says to me. "We help each other," she says.

You really have come to the right place, Patty. I'm stunned, I'm deeply moved, I'm indebted in a way I feel completely committed to, completely ready for. But I'm far from off the hook. It's just a copy. But this is where my next chapter has brought me.

"Where is Troy?" I ask them softly. Philip puts a hand on my arm. He must have looked just like me in his own high school photo, faded red hair in bad lighting, acne against that white skin. Why senior photos were printed in color I never understood. Black and white would have been so much kinder. Where's Troy?

The TV picture switches to the front entrance at Proggleland, which is dripping wet in the rain. The storm has picked up (and Troy is no longer scotch-guarded, it occurs to me). Still, *wrapped in plastic* comes to mind. We see the officer in charge again, who looks even younger with his hair all wet. We see Jake scoot behind him on the screen, talking on his cellphone in the rain.

"Jake's there," I say.

"On the scene," Philip says.

"Why?" I ask. Philip and Larissa look at each other.

"He likes to help, too," Philip says.

"He pulled Cecil out of the river," I say.

"He's good in a crisis," Larissa says. "Valuable quality."

"We're here at Proggleland," says another newscaster from the screen, this one a guy—he's young too (is everyone suddenly younger than I am?)—who's dressed in a puffy blue coat with a hood. "Behind us the officers in charge are searching for the boy in question, four-year-old valley resident Troy Grant, last seen just seconds from this spot. The park has been evacuated and several road stops have been set up by the river and at other points in town."

"Should they be saying that?" Larissa says. "Won't someone just go a different way?" Philip shushes her a little.

"Wouldn't it be too late?" I ask. "They must be long gone." They, them, more than one? A man? A woman? They always think it's a man. But they're not always right.

I envision a man, too. It's a prejudice, I tell myself, habit. The man's face is fuzzy, as if I'm imagining him without putting on my glasses, which I've left home yet again. Actually, I think I've lost my glasses, too, along with everything else. I may be a total loss.

The man does not have red hair. Though it's just a guess at this point.

"Let's talk to the officer in charge. Are they looking for a particular vehicle?" asks the puffy newsman.

"That information is not available," the officer replies, wiping his mouth in a way that makes me think he's just eaten something, although I don't see crumbs or anything. I feel inflamed that he's eating right now.

"What do we know?" the newscaster asks.

"Any information on sightings would be appreciated, anyone who saw the boy in the park, anyone who might have seen him leave the park," says the officer.

"They don't know," I say.

Philip grumbles. He doesn't like the guy, either. We see Jake walk by again, still glued to his phone, heading away from the entrance. He looks into the camera for a second, just a second. He looks right at me, and for a moment we're both lost, too. It makes sense. If your child is lost, how could you be anything but lost as well? We have only the look between us to our names. Then it's gone, too.

"He's gone," I whisper to Jake.

Dorothy has snuck up behind the couch. "Hi, Dad," she says softly. We try to shoo her away, but she's not having it and settles next to Philip.

"He'll find him," Dorothy says, and I don't think it's for the first time. *He won't,* I don't tell her, but it's what I believe. He won't find him.

But you're always wrong, Patty, aren't you?

* * *

It's dinnertime when I finally make my appearance in front of the house, the news folks having convinced Philip that everyone's watching now, sitting at dinner, listening to local news' tales of traffic accidents, number of dead soldiers, violent storms, missing children. Sports and weather for dessert. We don't watch dinnertime news, but I admit to having done so in what seems like a previous lifetime. I lived alone. I understand the allure of the local broadcast—that need to hear about people in worse situations than your own. Knowing this about myself in no way makes me feel better.

I have never had a microphone jabbed in my face, let alone five of them. In Los Angeles, it probably would be more like thirty. Which is more knowledge that does not make me feel any better at all.

"Please, if anyone knows anything about Troy, where he is now, please tell the police," I begin. I can't think straight but try to say please more often than usual. "He doesn't deserve any of this. He's such a good little boy." I don't know what else to say. I put my hand at my leg again and let it out: "He comes up to here, he's just little, so little." I become an idiot. I think of my student evaluations: Patty Grant is not a good public speaker. I never realized the importance.

I want to tell them it's my fault, but certainly they can all tell that by looking at me. It's implied by my standing here in the rain, a thirty-one-year old woman with mussed red hair, nose dripping, childless by fate or fortune. My words lack emphasis and succinctness, not to mention persuasiveness. Is there anyone out there who wouldn't accuse me at the moment, if they're paying the slightest attention and haven't decided to look away entirely? I can almost hear people passing the mashed potatoes judgmentally, clucking their tongues harshly, then clicking off the TV.

And who would notice Troy's missing? Who has ever noticed?

This also runs through my mind: Who wouldn't take a perfect little boy such as Troy? I almost ask it but thankfully stop myself. I know I don't necessarily think like the next person, but this would be taking it all too far. I'm on to me. I will get no sympathy whatsoever, especially if I keep talking.

The *Law and Order* door slams with a serious if not deadly bang again somewhere off to my right.

Back inside the house, we wait. Dorothy and Larissa cook dinner between the times Cecil needs Larissa, with his attacks of coughing and agonizing breathing, worse than I've heard before.

"Stress makes him worse," Larissa tells me, after giving Cecil what she calls a breathing treatment, a procedure I walked in on and found so disgusting that I was glad the news crew couldn't film it. It's not appropriate dinnertime viewing, for certain. Even a body bag is less heartrending than a child struggling so. Even when it's a child like Cecil.

"The treatment will help him," she continues back in the kitchen, although I didn't know Cecil required medical treatments, devices, prescriptions—while not even in his own home. With Larissa in control. But who else is there, and it's not even a question.

Larissa's putting dots of butter on baked potatoes that I don't imagine anyone can eat right now, although we should. What could Troy be having for dinner? Will Troy have another meal? Is he long gone from here, black-haired, not smiling, belted into a car? (They probably used a real seat belt—not everyone has bungee cords handy, Patty, though the thought disgusts me.)

Is Troy hungry, or worse? Has someone, well, has someone harmed him in a way that is unspeakable and unimaginable, but that once you get it into your mind you can't help seeing over and over, the boy's mouth in a little O? Has someone hurt the little blonde perfect quiet boy known as Troy? Is hunger the furthest thing from his mind?

I sit dizzily at the table, so far from hungry that I don't even know an antonym that would be appropriate. I could not eat a baked potato, even if I could somehow, magically, eat one for Troy, so that he could get through what has become this horror show. I am not a good mother. I do not believe that I could save him, even in this little, tiny way, even if it were possible to make some kind of deal with a godlike creature that actually cares about little children. Larissa puts a plate in front of me and sits down beside me. She puts napkins in each of our laps and picks up her fork. She nods at Dorothy to do the same. The three of us look at one another, and both of them take little bites. Larissa stares at me—she will not let up. Tears run down my face, but she stares me down, putting delicate bits of buttered baked potato into her mouth. (There's also broccoli on each plate—I glimpse a tiny floret of it in my peripheral vision before it blurs into a green blob.) She hands me my fork. I can barely see it, as I think there are tears now pouring out of my face from a variety of places, which may not be physically possible but is true nonetheless. They run down my hand, down the fork. They salt the potato. Larissa looks on. She is unwavering. I begin to eat, trying harder not to choke than I've ever tried to do anything in my life.

Troy likes baked potato. I swallow.

* * *

I hear them even though I am almost asleep. Philip and Larissa sink into the loveseat together, TV turned down low, Philip with remote in hand, where he likes it. He's a lefty, but then so am I.

"There are thirty-four registered pedophiles in Santa Vallejo County," he tells her. I so wish I really was asleep. This is not the stuff of dreams.

"Shh," she says.

"There's a website now, you can check. You can put your house number in, and they draw you a map around it. Little arrows light up."

"How is this helpful?" Larissa asks him. "How is this a responsible use of the Internet? What good does it do a sane person?"

"Wouldn't you want to know?" he says.

"I'm not sure it tells us anything much," she says.

"They're not that far away, the ones we know of, of course," he says. "Websites being out of date and all. Still, it's a lot of arrows."

"So, what, you're going to go check out their streets?" Larissa asks.

"They give exact addresses," Philip says. "I certainly expect the police have checked."

"Exact addresses," Larissa says. "Please don't show me the map. I'll never be able to leave home."

"They list exact offenses, too," he says even more softly. "Convictions, counts." I have pictured many of these in my mind and do not really need to know the precise legal terminology for such felonious images. I will not be looking them up in reference materials. I will not require a trip to the library or an online search. I forfeit certain understanding. I do not want to know.

He's mine, he could have been mine, he was seemingly mine. I could have figured it out better, taken better care of him. I only needed time, know-how, experience to have been somebody better, smarter, a parent even. I will not be receiving an A. Maybe there is no end to what I might have needed to learn, judging from our unusual beginning, although it's come to seem more and more natural to me, whatever it was that brought Troy and I together, although this does wreak of passive tense. Lack of active voice and failure of the subject to take responsibility for her actions. But then, that's what passive tense is good for.

You still don't get an A, Patty. Not without active verbs.

It all becomes clearer and clearer yet dizzier and dizzier. It's not like someone is going to bring him back. I feel fairly certain that this kind of thing does not happen, the bringing back part.

You could have returned him, too Patty. Anytime. Any old time.

The thought had crossed my mind. *Here, I thought you might like your child back, perhaps you can keep him indoors now,* I might have said. Or left a note. I'm better in writing, especially in Times Roman.

Troy must be sleeping now. It's unthinkable that he isn't. But he sleeps so quietly, so still. Sometimes I have to get up close. Picturing him right now, I can't tell whether he is breathing or not.

* * *

It's morning and quiet as I wake up on Larissa's couch, for a moment hopeful and warm, until I realize why I am here. The thought of where Troy might be waking up (if he's waking up, but don't think about it,

Patty) makes me want to cover my head with any of the number of blankets Larissa has placed on me, not one of which I deserve. I should have gone cold.

I drag myself out of the blankets, and because my legs are asleep, I have to pound on the pins and needles, causing myself even more pain. Larissa and Philip, already awake, watch me from the kitchen, and I realize I've just been standing here for a moment or two, unsure which direction to take, hitting myself frantically. The flesh-colored Toyota is right in front of the house; I could get to it easily. It's right by the sleeping news truck, its generator finally turned off late last night. Where would you go this time Patty? Would you be headed to find something or to leave something behind?

"Breakfast," Larissa says, and although I can still feel the five bites of baked potato sitting in my stomach from last night, I follow her lead. Dorothy and Cecil sit at the table already, surprisingly, Cecil pale and wheezing, Dorothy having slept in her paper nurse's cap so that it is crumpled and in no way regulation. They drink from little juice glasses filled with pulpless orange juice. There's a third glass untouched, and Dorothy catches my eye after I see it. She looks bold and fearless, as if she were daring me to say something about it, object to its very presence. I could take a lesson from Dorothy, maybe more than one. No one here is to touch this glassful, her glance tells me. It is not symbolic, not the glass for some spirit who may or may not come through the door at the end of the meal, Dorothy's look challenges me. It is real and purposeful (and don't even think of smiling at it, her face indicates). It's a lot to take in at seven in the morning, even on a good day, which is more than any of us could hope for, except maybe Dorothy. It's a lot to hope for from a glass of juice.

Larissa makes breakfast, taking out cereal and milk, bananas, eggs, bread, bacon. A large bowl that I know will be for dipping bread in to make French toast. There's actually no telling how much breakfast she's about to make. Survival skills are taking over. Breakfast will be served. I hope she's not feeding the news crew, as I'd prefer they go away hungry, or at least go away to eat. I can't imagine Juliet being very nice to them at the diner despite that it's in her true nature.

But if they go away, Patty, then what? Would their leaving mean it's over? If there's no news crew to cover it, can there be news, let alone good news?

I will help with breakfast, I tell myself, because I want to be the kind of person who would do that. Be helpful. Be ambulatory. Take care of those who need tending, Patty. (Dorothy seems not to have slept well, her face lined with little creases that make her look as though she's slept on a Christmas tree.) She does not complain. How Troy-like, I think. She also does not smile. French toast isn't going to fix anything, but she's not going to tell us that. She and Larissa seem to see eye to eye.

"We're not mentioning that no one's supposed to eat bacon anymore," Larissa quietly tells me as I whip eggs.

We are surrounded by food when Jake arrives. Dorothy does not jump up to greet him, although I sense that she would if she thought it was in any way appropriate for a serious four-year-old whose friend has disappeared from a local theme park. Dorothy knows more about propriety at four than I ever will, but I don't know how she's come by the knowledge. As far as I know, she only reads storybooks about animals (she has not touched the bacon), but then perhaps she has her secrets, too.

We greet Jake quietly, although I feel the need to get closer to him, to see if he's somehow physically hiding some knowledge behind his bulk.

"How's it going?" Philip asks him, which is vague and general enough so that we all know just what he means.

My eyes meet Jake's, and he tells me that he is not finished. I am almost hopeful and truly thankful for the feeling, fleeting though it is.

Jake looks behind him and makes a gesture I don't completely understand, as if trying to coax forward a reluctant spirit. The spirit that appears is not very clean, but not as dirty as I always suspect, and alive, although ghostly in his way. It's Will, from the shack, or from the former shack. It collapsed in a storm; Jake, I know has had a hand in starting to build a new and improved one. Dorothy shields her extra juice glass from Will. He's not who she had in mind, either.

"Boy, do we have food," Larissa says. Will looks at the table full of breakfast items, a little horrified. I'd have thought he might be thrilled by it, but I'm so bad a judge of character.

"Will has something to tell us," Jake says to all of us. Philip sort of nods him on.

"You have Troy," I say, rising, not even a question. A mother should know these things. Why add a question mark?

"No," Jake says loudly but calmly at me, and it's as if several hands (it would have to be more than one person) have grabbed me at once, pulling me down into an empty chair. This is the chair Troy sits on. This is Troy's place. It's as if the chair is still warm, although it's been many, many hours since Troy's little body could have sat here.

"No, no," Will says, and I am humbled at what a prejudiced person I am. Just because he's homeless, or shackless. Of course he wouldn't have Troy. But you can't always tell by looking at a person, I want to tell them. Some of us fit right in, somehow hide in normalcy despite red hair and not being normal at all. And Will sticks out, despite regular brown hair. He looks far guiltier than I do.

"No, I just know about Proggleland," Will says.

"Right," Jake says. He points to large rolls of paper Will holds.

"Right," Philip says as well. "Let's take a look, Will. It's okay." They lay out the papers on another nearby table. Larissa has lots of large tables, crafts being essential in her profession.

Seeing the paper unrolled, Cecil grabs at a crayon and starts to head over, but Larissa puts both hands on his shoulders and says, "Just eat now." He puts the crayon in his mouth before Larissa can stop him.

The men look through the papers. Larissa joins them, watching over their shoulders. Cecil sucks on bacon noisily. Dorothy guards the juice glass while managing to keep her eyes on Jake the entire time, as if afraid he might get lost, too. She looks as if she wants to join him at his table, but she can't give up on her juice glass. She must keep watch. I take one of her hands (the one not guarding the juice). We look at one another, understanding, as I can't move from the table, either. I am glued to Troy's chair, suddenly overwhelmed by the idea that I cannot let it go empty.

"It's Proggleland," Larissa says. She looks at me, calling me over with her eyes. I force myself to leave Dorothy. It hurts, a sharp, brief pain to the abdomen.

"Why do you have maps?" I ask Will.

"These aren't maps," Philip says. "They're plans. They show the whole place."

"Why do you have them?" I ask again. I'm sorry for what I said before, and I know I didn't apologize, but there is still something untrustworthy going on. I should know.

"They outline the entire area, including the old unused spaces a mile or so beyond the amusement structure. There are paths, places to hide," Will says. He takes a red crayon from the floor. (I think someone has stepped on it, as it's a little flat, plus it has teeth marks, but Will seems not to mind, and I don't think he even has children.) He starts drawing circles, perfectly round ones that I thought only math teachers could make. Will's are flawless, even with a rough and scraggly crayon.

"Who are you?" I say to Will. He just looks at me. I realize I should have some pity for him, as the others do, or at least a gentleness toward him, but I don't, and I want to know. I might usually be reluctant to answer the same question, it occurs to me, but a little boy is lost, my little boy, and I'd tell anyone anything right now.

"I was an architect," Will says. "I've been keeping these."

"You built Proggleland?" I ask. I mean, he doesn't look like much of a person, let alone a professional, although I'm probably being politically incorrect about this. Just a whisp of a guy ready to disappear.

Will rubs his eyes beneath his dirty glasses. "Yes. I designed Proggleland."

"Why do you need these?" I ask.

"I don't need them," Will says. "But you do. There are still unused areas. Places to hide; places people have to live," he says. "Leftover places no one would stay in unless they had to."

There are people who live under the subways in major cities, I know, on some dimly lit underground level that no doubt smells of damp, foul substances. Could there be something beneath the majestic purple Proggleland, something smelly, greasy, dark, unknown? Could such knowledge make you become a young man/failed architect who lives in a shack? He is quiet and calm, older somehow today. He says "I was an architect" the way someone else might say "I was a kidnapper," a person who shouldn't be trusted, a guilty person of little worth. We watch as he finishes making his perfect circles, then connects them with a neat little line, forming paths, passageways that may very well smell of rotting dried fish and splashes of dried purple paint. I can't imagine, except I can't stop imagining. Just try it sometime when your own child is involved.

"Let's go, then," Philip says, looking at the carefully placed circles.

Dorothy hides behind Jake, looking on. She hands the juice glass to Will, but he shakes his head no. She nods him on, and at last he drinks. Jake scoops her up with a whoosh of a hug so strong that it almost takes me with it. He places a hand on my arm, and I can feel it down to the bottom of my feet.

"Okie-dokey," Philip says and claps his hands.

As if some kind of alarm clock has gone off in the house, we jump up and gather our things. Coats fly from one place to another. Hands grab for bacon, French toast. (It isn't buttered or syrupy, so you really could grab it with your hands, but I don't, I couldn't.) We're leaving the children here, the remaining children, under the watch of Juliet, who has arrived silently. Juliet isn't serving the newspeople after all—maybe she has standards. Her leggings are striped again today, but they look faded, pale white and gray, leggings that cry out in some sort of mourning.

Juliet stands in the kitchen rearranging food under the direction of my large boss Eva, who somehow is also here, cleaning pans, making lists, tossing coats overhand in a practiced, perfect way. Eva pats us all on the back, buttoning our coats as if we were four-year-olds, and Juliet hands out napkins, toast, bacon.

"It's the waitress in me," she says, pushing into my hands a cinnamon roll wrapped in a napkin, which I will have to stash in my coat pocket. I didn't know anyone made cinnamon rolls this morning, where anyone found the time or inclination. Troy loves them. Troy.

Larissa packs us into her van, me in front with her in the driver's seat, Jake and Philip in the row behind, Will in the way-back part, next to an empty car seat, where he pages through his sketches. He speaks to himself. His voice is small, questioning, weighing. I catch his eye in the sun visor's little mirror, which I suspect most people use to apply makeup. He looks away quickly. I'm watching you, I tell him in the mirror. It doesn't matter if you look up. It doesn't matter that you have an advanced degree.

The visor reminds me that Death or Injury May Occur. Would it be better or worse it if said death *and* injury? Is it too late for conjunctions to make a difference?

The reporters' van is still asleep. Larissa looks at it, then at me, then starts the engine quietly (it's an old van, but she tries). The rain has stopped, and the sun is just breaking through the clouds, ready to lead us back over the river, to the scene of the crime, or one of the crimes, anyway. Larissa's car smells of cinnamon, bacon, and the scents of a robust feast no one has really eaten. Dorothy watches us leave from the front window. She looks right at me, but she does not wave. I can't bring myself to wave, either, as if the simple gesture might imply more than I could handle right now. We don't have a wave left between us.

We drive off, onto the little highway, behind us a just awakened caravan of reporters. I am being followed. It bothers me in ways even I hadn't imagined.

Chapter 8
The Very Definition of Bereft

Will glares at the mountain of Proggleland, kind of how I tend to glare at him. The place stares him down but looks as if it's got something to hide. Or someone. Although I could be projecting. But there really isn't time for such thoughts. It is absurdly quiet here without the startling music. I propel Will forward with the force of my mind. Or maybe he just moves by himself. I have not slept well.

It's just our little group here except for the police, who seem both too jolly and too young today. We find ourselves at the brink of a childhood fantasy—a whole amusement park to ourselves, no lines, no waiting, no fighting with your brother. This place is ours, but we don't want it. What Will thinks may be more pessimistic than I could bear to know. I imagine paths, walkways, claustrophobic tunnels leading downward into utter despair. Does Will's mind follow these paths down, beyond, to a place I can't imagine but perhaps Troy can? Can Troy see? Is he blinded by a plastic bag or is that part long behind him? Has the bag been thrown aside, no longer needed, left to decay for however many years it takes a bag to decay, someone keeps changing the estimate for this? I try to sense it, envision Troy, feel what he feels, be wherever he is. I just see everything fading, dripping, darkening. I smell plastic bags even though there aren't any in sight. I may always smell them from here on. Will stops again, and Jake pulls him through the park. I'll bet Will was one of those children who didn't enjoy theme parks at all. No one would have offered him a free return visit.

But you didn't enjoy theme parks either, Patty. Not that this matters now. It's not about you anymore, Patty. I touch my knee, where no little hand waits for mine. Larissa grabs my arm with purpose and sympathy, but I can't meet her eye.

I imagine for a moment what the place might be like on a good day, a sunny day. Our children deserved sunshine yesterday, I can't help but think, as if sun might have made all the difference. Wouldn't a brilliant blue day have forced me to watch Troy more carefully, to be sure he had enough sunscreen, a hat, a sippy bottle of cold water at all times? Instead, I let the mist lull me into mindlessness, numb my usual sense of nervousness, and lose track of him completely. I am not above blaming the weather, at least momentarily, but I won't be able to blame it for long. It would never hold up in court, say. I know who is to blame.

"Where could he be?" I ask Will, who studies the circles on his plans. Jake and Philip have been speaking to the officer. Officer Loop? I still cannot remember his name and cannot focus on his badge—it's just a blur for some reason, fear of authority, maybe, or nearsightedness, or something ancestral in me, maybe, who can say. The few police officers around us all shake their heads at what Jake and Philip tell them. They don't believe us.

"We've searched the entire usable area," Officer Loop says. I suddenly like him even less than I like Will and realize I'm thinking like a three-year-old. I don't like you; I don't like you (and I'm not too thrilled with myself). Larissa puts her arms all the way around me.

"We're here to help," says Jake, clearly implying that he has no intention of leaving.

Will looks up from his trance. "That way," he says, and we follow. Officer Loop comes along, although he does not look as if he'll be much help and has a slight air about him indicating he'd like us to be wrong. He also looks ill-prepared. Shouldn't he have one of those sticks? A gun? I don't see one. Weapons, I think, we don't have weapons. We don't even carry bottles of spring water, and everyone these days carries those. We are utterly empty-handed.

We follow Will to the park-like area behind the purple structure, where we ate our lunches. It appears sunnier and friendlier today than it did yesterday, all innocent and beneficent. I'm not about to fall for it twice, though. Will leads us out a side exit I don't remember seeing, where we encounter a path that takes us slightly downward, then up, then twists and turns in the small hills, becoming dustier and dirtier in a not very yellow-brick-road way at all.

"This just leads to an old maintenance area, nothing out there," says the young cop.

"Keep going," Will says.

"Just half torn down shacks," says the officer, as if he had no idea how much shacks mean to some people.

"You've searched it?" Jake asks him, towering over him. Jake's body looks armed, whether he is or not.

"Well," says the officer. We don't know whether he's using the word as an adverb or as an excuse, or whether he knows the difference.

"Where are we going?" I whine. The path goes on and on. I'm not much of hiker, so it feels like miles to me but is probably only minutes, in the scheme of things, if you're not looking for your lost child, say. The path gets dustier, rockier, more broken up, and is lined in trash. Empty Popsicle wrappers, small pieces of foil. Bits of dried fish. The stink of used food surrounds us.

Can Troy smell? Is he beyond inhaling?

Pieces of clothing and odd shoes lay scattered here and there, as you'd find on the freeway, not that I've ever figured out how people lose one shoe or shirt on the freeway. These are unloved shoes abandoned behind a theme park. Pink ballerina slippers. A clog. A boy's black boot. I look up and can't see where they could have fallen from, as above there's just blue sky. Today.

We follow the path till I trip over something metal. Jake catches me and somehow rights me so fast, no sound even comes out of my mouth. It is ghostly quiet out here.

"Old water mains," he says, pointing to the pipes.

"Something wicked this way comes," Philip says quietly. But then we know that.

"Why are there shoes?" Larissa asks the unanswerable.

"Shh," Philip says, but I want to know, too. Or maybe I don't.

We all stop, everyone for a moment looking at me, and then of course, of course, I see them: Troy's shoes. His new real red Keds, not imitation brand, not cracked. (He takes good care of his shoes—Troy is all good.) I know they're his. His shoes look empty, bereft, having lost their little child feet, having lost their purpose in life. Sad, empty Keds, abandoned or lost, can there be a difference between the two?

"Troy's," I say. Larissa picks them up and begins wiping dust off them in a fairly aggressive manner. We'd recognize Troy's shoes anywhere. They don't need his name in black marker. No other four-year-old keeps his shoes so clean.

"I'll take those," says Officer Loop, but Larissa hugs them to her chest in refusal. These are our shoes, her look tells him. We will not surrender them. The officer, with his request, has become our enemy, although again, I suspect our hostility is terribly misplaced. I couldn't touch the shoes, although I can feel them, their lightness, their soft shoelaces swinging in today's pleasant breeze, almost as if everything is normal. I love those shoes, their wholly optimistic red, their ridiculous cheerfulness and good arches. We will not give them up without a fight.

I walk hand-in-hand with Jake, who leads me carefully along the broken-up path, which appears murkier, as if my eyesight is failing, or maybe it's just the dust.

Did Troy have to walk through the dirt without his shoes? Was he carted, carried, bagged? I start to moan. Jake shakes my arm a little, the way you shake a jump rope that another person holds the other end of, making it go into waves and bounces. My arm has gone slack, numb, a mere leash attaching my body to Jake's.

"Stop," our police officer cries, and we all do, as if there's broken glass we might step on. (Oh, I so hope not, not without his little red shoes, please.)

"No!" I say.

"Stop," our law enforcement officer yells again, but he is not yelling at us.

I look up and I think I see the man, the one who has taken Troy, but it isn't a man at all. It's a woman wearing a bright, shapeless, yellow-and-orange blouse that seems like a costume, as if it is not really hers, with a contrasting purple headscarf, the word for which echoes in my mind in the voice of some ancient relative: babushka. The word evokes concepts, images—poverty, immigrant, despair—that perfectly match the expression on her face. Could Troy's kidnapper be a woman in a babushka who seems to have nothing more than that to her name? Might it even be a borrowed babushka, something she found along the ground here, abandoned or lost?

Then I see a man dressed in a peculiar green-and-brown checked shirt that hangs on him, a few sizes too big, not that this matters in the slightest, but it does get your attention.

Do they have Troy?

We see the pile—I think we all see it as a group, together, at once. Black trash bags, and I'm sickened to see them, really physically ill. Thank goodness you didn't eat breakfast, Patty, so you don't have to stop to throw up and can focus instead on this small hideous fragment of your imagination come true, the simple household item once known as a trash bag that you'll never see the same way again. Ever.

"Stop," says the officer guy, who grabs the trash bag and rips it open. Out pops not Troy (is that good or bad, Patty), but shards of other clothes, parkas, hoodies. Used clothing. Unloved used clothing, the kind a thrift store might reject. You can just tell.

The woman runs over to a shack, really a series of connected shacks, so abandoned looking that you would shield your eyes, if only you could. She reaches for the end of a leash tied to the shack—no, it's one of those children's harnesses (you saw them at the children's store, Patty, you just blocked out the image). At the other end of the harness is a child, a familiar child, a child that begins to take shape between my poor, poor eyes. It's Troy, alive Troy, looking, at first glance, almost all right. Almost at home.

"Troy," one or all of us yell. He looks confused, grabs his harness leash with his teeth, then spots me and stares. Then he stretches his right arm out toward me. The one with the hand that needs you the most, Patty.

Larissa is upon him first. She grabs the harness, tears at it so ferociously that the woman backs away, yelling something that may be Proggle speak or maybe another language, but regardless is a language I never wish to hear again. The woman screams at Larissa in swift, guttural, and possibly broken syntax. She pleads—whatever the language, that is the verb. Pleading. It's clear from her tone, and it stops me nearly dead.

She is begging for Troy, it seems. But who isn't?

Larissa growls back in a language mothers know everywhere, I suspect, which requires no articles, no structure, no end punctuation at all, unless it's an exclamation mark. One no one could argue with.

Larissa is pure animal-mother instinct.

Troy resembles the oddly dressed odd couple who seem so far from home. Troy could so easily be theirs, it's heart stopping.

Larissa rips orange flip-flops from Troy's feet while trying to tear him free of his harness. The green-and-brown checked man holds the other woman back as she yells and reaches for Troy.

Troy looks somehow past the point of being startled, as if nothing in this life surprises him anymore. I reach for him but he's beyond my grasp, but I feel him all the same—a warmth that starts at my fingers, though he is still several feet away as I move through what feels like Jell-O to get to him.

Philip helps Larissa disentangle Troy from the harness as I move in slow motion toward them, and then I've got him. I hug him. Larissa hugs his shoes, which she's managed to keep somehow during all this. I look at my boy. He's dirty, caked with a light layer of soot. (I think of the chimney sweep in *Mary Poppins,* although Troy's dirt is in all ways so much more real.) I reach into my pocket and take out the squashed cinnamon roll and put it in his left hand, which I do not bother to insist that he wash. Troy smells the roll thoroughly and takes a small bite of it. He burrows into me, revealing his bad right hand, dirty and caked with dried blood, and just really bad.

Larissa becomes human again, just like that, and gently strokes Troy's head.

"Cinnamon roll, your favorite," Larissa says quietly to Troy. I nod.

"Please," I whisper to the cinnamon roll, begging it for help.

We hear more of the guttural language, as a few more oddly dressed people appear, all of them seemingly covered with at least one layer of dust, but not in a way that would keep you warm or anything. Some of them scramble off with small children, some on harnesses, some free. The children wave at Troy before being dragged off, and he waves his hurt hand back at them, holding his cinnamon roll to his heart.

Jake wraps his arms around Troy, and therefore around me, and I feel that I could close my eyes now for quite some time and not let go, except that we're squishing Troy as he tries to take little bites of his roll. We all smell like cinnamon now, which may well be the most comforting smell in the world. It's almost enough to make you forget.

"Where are we?" I ask. Jake steps away from me and toward Philip, and we all look at the other people, the other kind of people, some of them fleeing, some of them looking right into our faces.

My eyes meet those of the oddly clothed woman, who has stopped yelling and now moans in her harsh language, which from the sound of it can only make her feel worse. My eyes sting from the way she looks at Troy with absolute longing: the very definition of bereft. I have nothing I can say to her. I can't yell at her; I can't comfort her. But we share something in our stare, for a brief moment, and I feel that I should be the one to apologize, but I couldn't explain why. I inhale Troy. She lowers her head to her checkered man's chest and makes a horrible, sick moose-like groan, inhuman and beyond the parameters of any known language, or at least any language you'd ever care to know.

The idiot police arrest the bereft woman and her checkered man. I can't help but feel they have the wrong person. The look on her foreign face seems to say the exact same thing.

"Illegals," the cop says with disgust, as most of the other people vanish. These cops are inept, which I realize now is probably best for everyone at this moment.

I look around at this makeshift camp or whatever it is. There are a series of aged wooden buildings, splintery, windowless. Long, thin structures that look no larger than a horse stall. The whole place resembles some sort of old stable more than anything else. The wild, wild West. An ancient wire fence surrounds the area, several parts of it broken down, maybe for some time, but there'd be no reason to fix the fence. No one would break into this desolate ghost town. No one would come here willingly, let alone stay. All indications are that this place is a last resort.

Officer Loop hits his walkie-talkie against his hand, as if trying to rouse it. "We need to question the boy," he says, suddenly accompanied by five or so police officers I do not remember seeing before, milling around aimlessly. Where did the police come from? And aren't they a little late?

"No," I say at the idea of someone asking Troy questions he would have no answers for. I feel Troy tapping me lightly with his bloodied hand against my chest, a Morse code of inexpressible need. He wraps his other hand encrusted with bits of sweet sugar and cinnamon around my hair. I am covered with sugar. I am sugar-coated Patty. I am the best Patty I can be.

Larissa thrusts herself upon the officers. "We're taking him home. He's had enough," she says.

"You can't!" they scream, almost childlike in their objection. A few actually say nuh-uh, as if this would have any effect on a day care provider.

But Larissa is a force, and they back up, and we find ourselves walking straight into reporters, cameras, vehicles, enveloped by the blasting surround-sound of generators. Police officers snatch at the misplaced people from the shacks, their children whooping as if this were no more than a game of chase. One officer begins knocking a shack down, and a woman screeches at him in an earsplitting language lacking any harmony, but then he deserves it. Sirens scream. Reporters' lights shine in our eyes—it's daylight, why are there extra lights? Troy shields his eyes with his sticky roll, getting some in his hair, which is dirty, too. But still blonde, for which we may be truly grateful.

Everyone talks at once, and someone I've recently seen on television shoves a microphone in my face. Larissa bats it away as we all try to move forward with giant steps, and I keep thinking the microphone's going to hit me in the eyes, blind me. (I should be wearing my glasses; I am not beyond needing protection.) Larissa smacks at it with Troy's shoes. The Keds have no comment.

We duck and push our way through the group of reporters who grab at Troy, reach for his hair, his fingers, his unutterable reaction. They pinch my arms and tickle my ribs maliciously, trying to get me to let go. Troy is mine, and anyone who thinks they can get past me at this moment really knows very little about anything. Holding Troy, I feel myself nearly double in size. I'm more than one person here. I'm his mother. I know what he needs. I might just know more than most people in this situation. I turn to Larissa, her teeth gritted. She looks as if she could kill someone right now, which I mean in the most complimentary way.

I carry Troy into the car, which Philip somehow has gotten halfway out here to us. I'd hold him in my lap all the way home if the law did not forbid it, if the law could only recognize that a child might need to be in someone's arms rather than in a five-point child seat. Another harness. Larissa locks him in the seat that Jake has quickly rearranged in the center of the car. I mentally check off each click you're supposed to listen for. I have read the manual, twice. I'm not as bad as you think.

I slip in beside Troy and hold onto his little grimy hand, the little hand I have missed. Larissa sits to Troy's right, keeping both of Troy's shoes on her fingers, making puppets out of them. Troy might like that, I think, but he stares straight ahead, his cinnamon roll hand in mine, his mouth gnawing on the other one.

Larissa wipes at Troy's hand with a baby wipe, cleaning around the spot he won't let go of. She makes no comment.

"You could sleep," I tell him. I want to tell him, You can be normal: Eat, sleep, ride in your car seat, be like other boys who may or may not ever have been stolen once or twice in their lifetime (so far?—unthinkable Patty, really, the things you think of).

Philip drives with Jake in the passenger seat.

We ride hand in hand. We could be anyone, but I know we're not just anyone, and we never will be (unless these things are way more common than you think Patty, and it's not like I'm an expert). I feel as if there's just more of me now; there has to be. Larissa leans forward to slide in a CD of a woman singing what sounds like Celtic lullabies, or maybe just plain Irish lullabies. Troy nods slightly to the music. All of us could stand to be gently sung to sleep at this moment, Philip the exception as he's driving. I've never really liked being sung to, but once again, it's so past being about me. I hold sticky fingers, glad for the gooiness. Troy and I are stuck together.

I look out the window to see the sun blink. Has a plane crossed its path? A large bird? Perhaps there's a scientific term for it. Perhaps it's an everyday occurrence that needs no name. I'm an English major, but I need to accept that some things are beyond words.

"The sun is winking at you," I tell Troy. He nods. My accepting child, who no doubt has come to understand too well that anything is possible.

I glance at his feet. The little Ked-less feet. The little Ked-less feet with little spots of blood you almost can't see, which when I scrape the dust off of, I see tiny bite marks, bruised spots, darkened dots. He seems not to feel them at all. Something has chewed on Troy's feet, and my stomach sours again. His hand and his feet. Some monster, demon, really abominable nightmare. I wouldn't be able to get my feet up to my mouth, I feel pretty sure. (I've tried yoga—and the answer is no.) Troy has been chewing on his feet, around the tops of his toes, in some necessary way that's almost comical to imagine, if it weren't for the nauseating imagined taste of dried blood and the nauseating pain that overwhelm you at the thought.

His feet. How could you not just cry?

* * *

Back at Larissa's, I unbuckle Troy and lift him from the car. I want him in my arms, I want to smell him, cinnamon and dirt, but Jake stops me and puts Troy down, placing both of his shoeless feet on the ground. Troy has no trouble standing (the bites are just around his toes, not all the way around the feet, which of course is unthinkable but there you go, I'm thinking of it), so I don't stop this. Jake looks at me with a sign of sureness on his face that makes me feel I am part of something larger, part of something I didn't know I could find. Jake takes my hand, and we let Troy walk into Larissa's house on his own, as he would any other day he might visit day care. I let him take a step away from me, sugar falling from my hands as he goes, no more than an arm's reach. A baby step.

Reporters surround the house again behind a yellow police tape someone has set up. (Is this now a crime scene, or has it always been?) The newspeople shriek things I can barely make out but that strike me as obscenities, the really bad ones, although I may not be processing language correctly at this moment.

Eva awaits us, all six feet whatever of her, taking up nearly the entire kitchen entryway, but in a good way. It's how you'd want to be greeted by family on a national holiday, a day where you've traveled hours and hours to reach this place, a day that brings you relief if not joy, not yet. It smells like Thanksgiving the minute we walk in. Eva is substantial and serious—everything about her says essential, especially right now. Eva lifts Troy up in a giant scoop that makes him head for the ceiling, and it's as if we all hold our breath as one, waiting to see if he'll laugh, cry, scream, or maybe throw up. Anything's possible. Troy grants us a small, almost absent-minded smile. Not a giant smile, more of a starter smile, a tester, to see how it feels, to see if it will hold. Dorothy watches him carefully, too. She doesn't smile, but her face shows some absolute form of understanding. A smile from her would be redundant at the moment anyhow.

Larissa and I lead Troy to the bathroom. She has one of those shower heads you can remove from the wall, then hold over your head as you sit in the tub or hold over someone else's head should this be a communal event. This is a communal event.

The thought floats by that we might be removing evidence, but it seems unthinkable that anything worse than being lost and tethered and living in a shack (again) has happened to Troy. Although I can tell both Larissa and I are thinking it. The badly dressed woman and man—with nicer clothes and cleaner faces, with a facility for the language, they'd be like any couple, wouldn't they? Were they just trying to complete their family? He looked just like them. Could they have felt what they did was right? Whether they took him or found him or felt he somehow had come to them? Is it their fault their lives have led them to live in shacks and have nothing left of their own but a language with too many G sounds? Or could I be misjudging: Could they have done something terrible or let's say worse than just keeping Troy, which after all, isn't all that foreign to him?

"A good warm bath is just what you need right now," Larissa says. We remove his clothes slowly, inspecting him slightly without letting on that his little boy body might be any different today than any other day, in case this hasn't occurred to him already. It is terrifying to take off his blue shirt. The earth decal has been almost completely picked off, but if it was at all useful, at all comforting, then it's okay with me—it has served its (unthinkable, Patty) purpose. Nothing too unusual on his torso, Patty. But you're nearsighted, don't forget.

Larissa removes his pants, chatting all the while, something about making his favorite foods, how she's got great bubble bath ready, never taking her eyes off of him. We see nothing that would make us scream or cry or be very, very quiet. No purple splotches, no indentations, no question marks. Larissa and I exchange glances, then look away from one another quickly.

We lather, rinse, and repeat.

Troy, who is not really one for the bathtub to any great extent, sits patiently as the grime of two days of who knows what slides off him and down the drain. He is hesitant to take his hand from his mouth, but he does. The skin is sore, red, ripped. It must sting if not ache. It makes me bring my own right hand to my mouth.

Breathe through your nose, Patty, I think, my mouth full of my own hand. I bite down hard. I want to share this pain with him. I bite down a couple times, hard.

I can almost hear the dirt releasing itself from his body, the warm water nearly hissing, attacking whatever has attached itself to Troy in the time he's been gone. Larissa babbles all the while, though I am immobilized by my own hand, which I've made a gash in and which feels oddly pleasant, calming. I suck the blood.

After he is clean, we fill the bath with bubbles. (Larissa has a giant size box of bath bubbles, Larissa is great.) We let the bubbles do their job. Troy catches a few that fly in the air with his left hand.

Just like a normal boy, Patty. Don't look at the other hand.

But I do look at it. Troy has begun to tear at himself along the side and palm, covering more area than before. And his cuticles are torn up. A manicurist would scream. You can actually see the bite marks around his knuckles, if you can't help yourself from looking. Troy holds his right hand up above the water, as if it were a small toy he doesn't want to get wet. As if it weren't part of him, or as if it's his favorite, most special part.

"I think it might be infected," Larissa whispers to me.

I can't think of anything to say. I only nod and point to his feet as well, although they are only slightly harmed. Larissa emits a sad hmm.

Troy has not said anything. He is silent, nonaccusatory. He is a kidnapper's dream.

If this incident leaves Troy even quieter, what will become of him? Doesn't he need words to run the thoughts through his mind, over and over again, like I would? Will it just be horrible black-and-white flashes of pictures he sees, like old-time newsreels? Would adding sound help, or like in those loud blockbuster end-of-the-world movies, would it only make things worse?

Larissa and I search for something in his eyes, just as we looked over his body. Our findings are so inconclusive. But our imaginations are limitless.

Larissa gently tosses bath toys into the tub from the laundry bag full of them hanging on the wall—Larissa is prepared. Troy sits quietly, a family of yellow duckies before him. We watch for odd behavior—will Troy attack one duckie with another? Will he bang the head of a duckie against the wall? Will he bring one to his mouth and bite down hard? It is a Rorschach test of yellow duckies, and we wait, Larissa and I, as she quietly hums a song from my childhood, One little, two little, three little something-or-others, but I cannot remember what they are, or whether anything bad befalls them. Children's tales do not always end well.

Troy does nothing but watch the ducks float. He barely moves at all. It could be so much worse.

When he is done, when we've washed away what we can for him, we take him from the tub and wrap him in a fresh sweatshirt and pants—Cecil's, which are too big but make Troy look even more adorable than usual, as baggy clothes will do on a small child. He looks tiny, sweet, fragile. We wrap his hand in gauze, not too tight, not too loose, just right. Larissa puts a sticker of a ladybug on top, and Troy remains mute. He goes out to the living room, hand to mouth but with his teeth far less vicelike, to find Dorothy and Cecil seated at blocks but not playing with them, I notice. Ella and Gretel are here, staring at him as well. He joins them, somehow impelling them to start building. Stacking, a child's attempt at making things right, or at least vertical.

Jake and Philip look at us, and no one can say it, but Philip tries.

"Anything?" he asks quietly.

"Just a nice bath," Larissa answers, positive childcare person that she is.

Do we all suspect that the non-English speaking migrants (vagabonds, gypsies, the words attack me with their political incorrectness), do we suspect them of doing something worse to Troy than whatever we can see that they've done? Do we suspect them of pure evil just because we find their language unattractive? If they'd spoken French, would we have embraced them, shared a bottle of wine and a brioche, and called it a day? (Two days, Patty, and you know you wouldn't have, but it's still a valid thought, somewhere in the universe.)

Weren't these people just another shade of desperate, Patty? You know what that's like. Does one crime make them guilty of another, especially one that would cause possible irreparable harm, whether you could bear to think about it or not?

Or are they now lost, missing, missing Troy? Was taking him from them right or just another in a series of wrongs?

Jake joins the kids to stack. He gathers Dorothy up next to him and manages to draw Troy over as well, the children's librarian assembling his audience. I find myself attracted to them, too, a part of them.

"Let's build," Jake says. Cecil sneezes. Can he still have a cold? Is it permanent? I suddenly feel a little guilty that we have not worried about Cecil today, but Troy is here, Troy is back, Troy fills us with worry. Troy begins to build, unable, I hope, to sense that all eyes are on him, or at least would like to be. I want to watch every move, every piece he chooses. Does it mean something if he goes for the green ones? The blue ones? Will he avoid purple altogether? I try not to evaluate every gesture. They're just building blocks, Patty. They can't possibly answer all of your questions.

Troy's tower falls over, and I hold my breath: Will he cry? Will he run and hide? Will he gnaw, either on himself or someone else?

"Oh," Troy says. We all exhale noticeably. It doesn't mean everything, an oh, but it must mean something. I don't think I can go on if it doesn't mean something. But is it enough? Couldn't even someone who has been treated in the worst possible way (imaginable or unimaginable, and I'm not sure the difference matters anymore), couldn't even that person come out with a little oh involuntarily, like a yawn or a hiccup? Jake looks in my eyes—it means something to him, too, but I don't know if it's the same something. I have only abstract words for such things. Specifics are unthinkable and could only lead to a lifetime of epic, violent, color-drenched dreams.

What will Troy dream? What has he dreamt?

We stack, we build, we topple, we rebuild. It's our way.

Chapter 9

The Best Possible World

I've been dreading it, but it's time. Larissa will come with me and bring Cecil, as another trip to the doctor's is routine for him. Larissa has taken him to a series of visits, his own mother claiming she has too much work, or not claiming anything, including her own son. I cannot understand it, although Cecil is no doubt better off where he is, with Larissa. She is a natural mother, a true mother, and basal charts mean absolutely nothing—they do not define her in the slightest. She is a substitute mother and a better one, although there may well be book after book, study after study, to suggest this isn't so. That the "real" mother is everything. Books can be short-sighted, unreliable, dead wrong. I never thought I'd think so, but maybe I've learned more than I ever thought possible.

We arrive at the doctor's office, which smells like bubble gum. Do they have bubble gum-scented antiseptic now? I'm not sure I want Troy smelling of bubble gum all day long, although he could smell so much worse.

Troy is sweet and clean beside me, and is all things good and perfect. His left hand rests on my knee, sometimes patting me with an irregular rhythm. His rebandaged right hand nearly hangs from his mouth, a light sucking noise coming from him now and then. I put my arm around him and pat his clean hair. I want to grab him and run.

It's hard to think of anything else. But go where, Patty? You owe this to Troy, Patty, you owe this to your little boy. This is what parents do, Patty. The impossible, the necessary. The admitting to mistakes.

There's truly no going back, Patty. Not once you're a parent.

Larissa watches me, continually rubbing Cecil's back—he's coughing hard today. We are a bundle of nervous energy, the four of us, quick movements and repetitions eating away at us. Cecil has begun to exhibit some kind of tremor in his body, a jolt that leaves him rocking, or maybe I just hadn't noticed it before. Cecil has never really been one to sit still in the time I've known him. He shifts his weight against the side of his seat and continually hits himself against the chair's metal arms. He looks as if he might be hurting himself. But either he doesn't notice the pain or doesn't care. Next to Cecil, Troy looks fine, unharmed, a small blondish boy who may never have suffered even the slightest trauma, just making the gentlest tapping with his index finger and sucking harmlessly on his hand (if you don't look too closely). If you had to guess which boy just underwent a kidnapping (again), well, you'd be wrong.

If you had the opportunity to choose which one to kidnap, however—don't think about it, Patty.

A young nurse in pink scrubs with matching pink braces on her teeth comes out from behind the desk. I try not to stare at her teeth, but Cecil's mouth hangs open at her, not that this is an unusual expression for him.

"Troy Grant?" She calls out. All eyes turn to us as we stand. I hear a few gasps, I see a mother grab her small daughter, who is in turn demonically yanking out the yarn mane of a toy horse. I put my arm around Troy, who would never do such a thing, who is sympathetic and kind to all creatures. I look back to Larissa.

"It'll be fine," Larissa says. Cecil nods, a generous gesture for him.

The nurse leads us to a small, cheerful room with sponge-painted walls. Blue with white sponged-on ponies. This is the room for little boys, little boys who may be sick (but don't need to be reminded of it), little boys who may have been hurt (but really don't need to be reminded of it). Troy sits on the long, padded table and runs one hand over the textured white pony on the wall (as if I need to describe where the other hand is). The nurse looks at me sympathetically and makes a note on her chart.

"The doctor will be right in," she says quietly, a look indicting that she knows why we're here, that she knows who I am. Or thinks she does. I am the girl in the paper, on the news, red hair maybe a little duller than she'd have thought. I'm older than she would have guessed and thinner, but not in the way you'd envy. Troy is the boy, that boy. I hate that he's thought of as that boy. I will never think of him that way. Depending on what the doctor says, Patty. Depending on what the doctor finds. How much can a small body tell when a child won't? I can't begin to know, but I feel sticky and sweaty and sick. Something in here buzzes, or maybe it's me. Troy just pats the ponies on the wall and makes little biting sounds around the bandage, little mouselike noises that hurt no one but himself.

"Nice ponies," I say. "We could paint your room with ponies," I suggest, kicking myself for not thinking of it before, for not lavishing attention on Troy's room, on our apartment, our home, which we've all but ignored. We spend more time at Larissa's, but somehow that has seemed right. I wanted Larissa to come into the examination room with us, but something in the waiting room, something in the way people looked at me, at Troy, made it clear that I have to deal with our situations alone, his and mine. His is worse, Patty—always remember, his is worse. We wait. We outline ponies with our fingers and minds. One is a unicorn, but just one, not far from where Troy sits, and when he finds it with his finger I feel thrilled for him. How badly can things go when you've located a unicorn with your left index finger? Such things don't happen every day.

The doctor comes in and it is suddenly, clearly, the best possible world. I almost hug him. I don't know what I expected—I always think doctors will be stern and white-haired (and male, you know you think it, Patty). But he is not old, he is not grayed. He is probably thirty-five, forty. His glasses are taped in the center where they've been broken for some time it seems (the tape is fraying). But best of all, the best possible of all, is that he has red hair. He is one of my kind.

"Hi, I'm Doctor Percy, but they call me Dr. P, although some kids laugh at that," he says. He and I look at Troy, who does not laugh. But he doesn't cry, either. He doesn't freeze up at a doctor in a white coat, although it is covered with cartoons of puppies.

I can only shake Dr. P's hand, speechless, hopeful. Whatever he has to say, I will take, but this one little coincidence, the red hair, readies me. I know that whatever he tells me about Troy, about what has happened over the last days, over the last years, I will believe. And I will take responsibility for it, just on the basis of hair color. Decisions have been made on worse grounds, especially mine. The secrets in this room humble me.

"I'm Patty, and this is Troy," I say. Dr. P picks up Troy's left hand and shakes it, wiggling Troy's fingers in a loose fish grip just for fun. Dr. P is a little silly, I think, goofy in his taped glasses, but the things Dr. P can tell us, well, we need all the silly we can get.

"How are you, Troy?" he asks.

Troy nods, loosening his bite on his hand, which comes away wet and red around the bandages. Troy hasn't said many words, but that's not out of character for my little boy. I want to tell the doctor this, but I refrain. Don't give too much away, Patty. Pace yourself.

"Well, let's get you a little checkup," the doctor says, glancing at the chart. Larissa filled out paperwork while we sat in the waiting room. She handed in the birth certificate. The words *accessory to the crime* shoot through my mind. I'm reminded of some line from an old play about the kindness of strangers, which makes my eyes sting with tears that feel like they rid me of something, some part of my life. I feel like I've cried out some part of being Patty that I don't want anymore.

"Four years old," Dr. P says. Neither of us responds, neither of us offers the slightest bit of information. Troy will never be a tattletale, I realize, although I don't know how good that is, in his case. The things he could tell, if only he could bring himself to. I wonder what he would indicate if language suddenly became easy for him and how he explains his life to himself.

"So, we'll take some measurements and just poke around," Dr. P continues, just kind of addressing the room at large, since he seems to have caught on that neither of us is the talky type.

"It says here you don't have his old medical records yet?" Dr. P asks, kind of a statement and happily with no trace of judgment in his voice.

"Not right now," I admit. There is enough truth in this, I feel. Besides, can't he just tell by looking at Troy? I look at my boy, blonde, tracing patterns of horsies on the wall. He looks like he should be in preschool right now, surrounded by Play-Doh, carefree, especially if you just ignore the right hand (and the toes, and has his knee healed from when he tore the skin off before? I have forgotten to check). But all little children have bumps and bruises, and get checkups, I remind myself, much as I reminded Troy on the way over. No one could need a checkup more than Troy.

"Okay," he says. "Let's just do this real quick." We remove Troy's clothes together. Troy doesn't really like having his clothes taken off (and rarely will take them off himself), but he doesn't say anything, just watches them float from his body with a grimace and gnaws on his hand. The doctor lays him down, Troy in his little boy underwear (it's fire trucks, although you can also get dinosaurs, but these are Cecil's clothes, so it's the trucks). Troy would probably have preferred the dinos, but again, he hasn't said anything.

The doctor starts examining, listening to Troy's heart with his stethoscope, listening to his lungs. Then he moves his eyes and hands downward. He has to look, I tell myself, he has to see. He passes over the knee fairly quickly. See, all kids get scrapes, Patty.

There are swabs, containers for samples, clear little slides ready to be slipped under a microscope. I've watched morbid TV shows (I can't bear to now—thank goodness there's no time when you're a parent). I hold Troy's left hand. Maybe you should sing, Patty, isn't that what Larissa would do? "This Old Man?" But I don't want to remind him of any men in particular, although I don't think the checkered man was old. I can't picture their faces at all—I would be a terrible witness, albeit a perfect suspect.

We are quiet, except for Dr. P who makes little encouraging noises that don't really indicate anything, kind of little uh-huhs and um-hmms, a happy clicking of his tongue. He really can't take it quiet, I guess, or he's just used to being a source of entertainment. He may really like his job, although not at the moment, I suspect.

He turns Troy over and looks around. I don't want to know exactly what he's examining, and to what extent and specifications. Larissa and I didn't look that hard—how could we? I listen for Dr. P's sounds, wondering what kind of thing would cause him to stop making the uh-huhs and what would provoke an uh-oh, for example, or worse, total scary silence?

We've only been here ten or so minutes, but a very, very long ten minutes. Dr. P finishes with his swabs and samples (I can't watch but swear I can hear what he's doing exactly), pulls the baggy underwear back up and reaches for Troy's hand. You know which hand.

He quickly unwraps our makeshift bandage and takes a look, reaches swiftly for an antiseptic swab, wipes around, hums a little *Chopsticks,* and rebandages. Dr. P is good.

"Troy," he says gently, putting his face at Troy's eye level. "We have to take care of your hand." He pats Troy's hand gently on the bandage, which is blue with zebras printed on it. The zebras all smile.

"We have to be very sweet to it—it's a good hand. Can you keep an eye on it for me?" I feel related to this man in a wholly new way.

"Oh," Troy says. Troy pats his own hand for a moment and tries to peek under the bandage. He strokes the bandage. It's not that Troy doesn't like this hand, of course. I think we all know that's not the problem, even those of us lacking in any training or advanced degrees.

"Change it once a day," Dr. P says lightly to me, as if giving me a recipe for making cookies, and nothing more. "I'll give you a prescription!" he adds, and I feel as if I've won something.

"Okay, Troy, let's see you hop like a bunny," Dr. P suggests, placing Troy's feet on the ground. (Yes, he saw the bite marks, moved his head from side to side, and kept humming.) Troy and I look at him in surprise. I don't know why the doctor would ask this, but I feel relieved, having taught Troy how to hop like a bunny myself once upon a time. It's amazing what comes in handy in this life, not to mention what you can disregard altogether.

Troy hops. I smile. My child can hop. Let us go now.

"Great!" says Dr. P. "How about touching your toes, bending over straight?" He guides Troy over, but Troy looks a little suspicious and comes back up. I give him a little nod, even though I don't understand the test, and worse maybe, Troy's reason for questioning it. I smile anyhow and bend over with him. I don't want him to think there might be anything wrong with him whatsoever.

"Nicely done," says Dr. P. He scoops up Troy and takes him to the scale and has him weighed and measured before Troy can object, not that he really would. Troy stands unnaturally still on the scale, perfect and so easily manipulated.

"Let's get dressed," says the doctor, patting Troy on the head. "Immunizations?" he whispers to me, but I don't know. Maybe he's had them. Even dogs get their shots, I think quickly, then banish the thought altogether.

"Yes," I say, although I'm sorry I can't offer more. I'm so sorry.

"It's time for boosters," he says. "To keep you healthy."

The nurse comes in to do her needle work, which I respect but do not like her for. How can you pick a career where you'll be sticking children with needles? Although clearly, I'm not seeing the bigger picture. After all, she's trained to hurt children as little as possible. What valuable training. Troy gets a series of shots, during which he says nothing, watching the needles enter his arm despite my telling him not to. Maybe watching closely as you're hurt by someone says something about Troy, something he can't say himself.

"You can say ow, or how about ouch," I encourage him, language instructor that I am. "I like to say ouch," I say. A needle goes in. I can't help myself.

"Ouch," I say for Troy. His eyes move to me each time there's a shot. I supply the ouch. It seems to work for him. And it's the least I can do.

I send Troy back out to Larissa and Cecil, who's playing in an area filled with toss pillows and rubber mats, kind of a children's padded cell. Cecil beats a pillow against the wall. It makes a deflated poof sound over and over. I look back to the doctor, who pulls me just inside the office area.

"I'll let you know if we get anything unusual back from tests, but so far, I don't see anything that you wouldn't, you know, want me to see," he says. I'm touched by his inability to express himself. He can't possibly mean by this everything I wish he did, and despite his red hair, I can't bring myself to tell him what role I've played here or what I know about Troy. Has he failed to see anything from long ago, from before my time? Is there nothing to see? I never found any signs of injury, except for some red scratches around the neck, but they've faded, haven't they? If he saw something, even something old, wouldn't he have to report it, by law or that moral oath taken by doctors on television but that you never actually see your own personal physician take?

Of course, he would, Patty. Of course, he would.

Is there nothing unusual about a child biting his own hand? Is this something he sees every week, or maybe once a month? I am not about to ask.

"Okay," I say.

"But there are cases," he stumbles, he's lost, his confidence is gone. "Incidents, specifics," he hesitates, he looks so disappointed at his own inability here. Doctors like facts, science—even goofy doctors with red hair and broken glasses want to be able to patch things up, apply an ointment, a bandage, a prescription. Make a conclusive diagnosis. "Not everything leaves a mark," he says, and I know what he means even if I don't know exactly what he's imagining, even if the felonious acts running through his mind don't quite match the felonious acts running through mine. Even if they do.

He is quiet for a long moment (try counting sixty seconds when waiting for bad news from your child's doctor—see how long your lifetime really is).

"But I don't think there's any more to deal with than there is to deal with," he says vaguely, but I know exactly what he means.

"He doesn't say much; it's not as if that's new for him," I offer. It's something I can give this doctor, me, the woman who has no medical history for her boy, the woman with a fake birth certificate and a felonious act or two of her own.

"Keep it down, everyone will want a child like him!" Dr. P tries to joke, then realizes he's done so badly. "Just keep treating him the way you do," he says quietly. "There are counselors he could see."

"At four years old?" I ask. What would they ask him, I wonder. Would they hand him dolls and ask him to do felonious things with them? Or wait to see if he did? Would they have a bungee cord handy? A dog collar? A dollhouse with a tiled bathroom? A purple but otherwise artificially lit mountain with paths that lead nowhere good?

"It's play therapy, not that I'm saying he has to, just if you don't notice a recovery, or the kind of turnaround you'd like. If the chewing doesn't clear up; if you don't like the direction he's going." I can see Troy now in the waiting room, looking on as Cecil throw pillows angrily against the wall. Troy just watches. He doesn't partake in the malevolent lobbing, and he's still the healthier of the two in nearly every way. Troy just pats his own hand gently. If anyone needs play therapy here, well, Troy wouldn't seem to be first in line. But looks can be deceiving.

"I'll keep it in mind," I say, nicely, since we've clearly spoiled the doctor's day of treating normal, healthy children. Children who have not been harmed, children who do not harm themselves.

As for the idea of therapy, I can file it away somewhere, under any of the twenty-six alphabetically assigned manila folders of my mind, where it will resurface easily if needed, under T for therapy. Quite a large file, as it turns out.

Dr. P shakes my hand. "You've done good here, Patty," he says, and although I think he means I've done *well* (*good* being something I've yet to do), my eyes fill with tears. It has been a long day, two days, maybe more. He hands me a pair of lollipops. I cannot begin to tell him that I don't deserve them, although his red hair makes me think I could tell him everything and he'd understand because he is different, too. He has been a child with red hair. But people don't like to hear that they're wrong, Patty, even redheads (especially redheads). I take the lollipops and walk back into the waiting room. I hand one to Troy and one to Cecil, who sticks it in his mouth without unwrapping it, but we don't criticize. Troy holds his to his nose and inhales, enjoying the sticky sweet smell.

"He looks fine to me," Larissa says.

"It's official, then," I tell her, tears still in my eyes. We take our boys home.

Chapter 10

Safe Passage

I'm wearing a groove into Larissa's gray, padded passenger seat, which I've begun to think of as an aging friend, and I haven't even tried to recline yet. We are spending some special time with our boys this morning, as the other playgroup kids have other things to do (parties, fun, regular kid stuff, nothing threatening, as if you can ever really be sure).

"What a beautiful morning, what a great day to be alive," Larissa says in the car, promise and conviction in her voice. I find myself filled with a vague hope that when I leave Troy behind me in day care to go back to work at the store this afternoon (you're a working mother, Patty, life isn't free, get back in the swing), maybe I won't be filled with anxious fear. Maybe this will be a day I'll actually want to remember.

Troy is safe when he's at Larissa's, I tell myself. Even a newborn would be safest there—tended, fed, loved if not out-and-out adored. And there will be other children for Troy to play with. *Play therapy.* Maybe we can move on, treat the kidnapping (this most recent one, anyway), as just another part of a road trip gone bad. Something we didn't quite plan on but that could happen every day. (Does it happen every day? Are there pictures on milk cartons of children who have strayed from Proggleland or been removed against their will, or even something in between? Is Troy's picture out there, too, next to someone's Fruit Loops?)

I look at the boys in the backseat. Troy rests his cheek against his car seat, his eyes unfocused, a calm semi zombie state he's adopted that's not hurting anyone. Cecil punches the inside of his car door rhythmically, saying uh, uh, uh. The term *at-risk child* comes to mind.

"Wow, look," Larissa says, calling us to attention. "It's really moving along." She nods at the new building site that I walked by not long ago near Bolts and Things on Main. The large store is now complete and all but open.

"I thought it took at least ten months to build a building," I say. I don't know why the number sticks in my mind. Ten months, longer than it takes to have a baby—grow an actual human being—but it's already a complete building, solid, permanent, nothing you could diaper, burp, kidnap, say.

"It's certainly coming along," Larissa replies. She frowns—people around here aren't happy with the new building. It's huge, for one thing.

"How did they get to build there if no one wants it?" I ask.

"Someone must want it," Larissa says, implying that it wouldn't be someone we'd want to know.

"It's not a very attractive structure," I say, although at least it isn't purple. I couldn't take a purple structure in our valley right now, and I'm not sure what effect it would have on Troy.

"Who's ready for a special brunch!" Larissa says, and I realize part of what I've been feeling is just plain hunger (somewhere in my stomach, just to the right of guilt).

I check the boys behind us.

"Good, ha-ha," Cecil says somewhat devilishly, and I can imagine the food flying now, as his manners aren't the best. Troy rubs at his soft car seat with his bandaged hand. He might be hungry. He hasn't said anything, but then, he wouldn't.

We lead our boys into the diner. We could be anyone, any two women with their kids, out for brunch. People look at us in ways that suggest otherwise, though. Customers stare at us, stare at Troy, then look away. I want to shield him with my body, and I could swear I hear Larissa growl.

Juliet skips over and leads us to a booth. We can be seen from the window, but I don't see why this should bother me anymore.

"I'm so glad you're here," Juliet says to us all, giving Troy no funny looks, which I think is wondrous of her. "Brunch is especially delicious today." She places little kids' placemats in front of the boys, along with mini packs of crayons. Troy smiles at Juliet, which I love about him.

"Are you hungry?" I ask Troy.

Troy looks at me as if he's searching his mind or maybe his stomach, trying to ascertain the exact answer, but it becomes difficult for us to focus on one another for long. Cecil begins acting up (all the child-rearing books call it that). He flips his fork around the table repeatedly, banging on the prongs, which seems a little dangerous.

"We're here to eat, Cecil," Larissa tells him. "But you have to behave correctly, or there will be consequences." Cecil stops the fork play but laughs, and not in a nice way. Juliet brings us a small bowl of chips. I think they're made from carrots, but I'm not about to point this out to Cecil.

"Can you draw for us, Cecil?" Juliet asks him. She smiles warmly at Troy, who most people will be gaping at with strange curiosity for a while, I realize. *He's that boy, the one who disappeared, the one they lost. The one those people took.* I can hear it whispered in the air. Juliet adjusts the kids' mats (they feature an outline of a rainbow ready to color in, ready to inspire, cure, heal, art therapy is a thing too, you know) and hands Troy the prettiest of the blue crayons. Cecil grabs for Troy's crayon for no good reason at all.

"Cecil, that's a second warning," Larissa says, but Juliet takes Cecil's hands in hers and directs them back to his own crayons, somehow propelling him to choose the orange crayon, although I don't believe orange is in the rainbow. I cannot remember ever seeing an actual rainbow, and I'm not sure what this means for my own happy ending.

I look to Larissa, who is clearly worried about Cecil. He has begun to eat the orange crayon.

"No, for drawing," Juliet says gently to Cecil, who I believe knows this but finds the crayon beyond temptation.

"Good," Juliet says, as Cecil begins to draw with one hand while banging a spoon head onto the table with his other. Larissa tries to remove the spoon from his hand, working to pry it from each of his five little fingers. She gives up. It's just a spoon.

Larissa and I exchange a look, and I feel relieved to think about someone else's child for a moment, for the first time in days. Troy sits quietly coloring. His rainbow is all blue, and I wonder what the play therapist would make of this. Would Troy be better off with a multicolor rainbow? Or is there something hopeful about a blue one? Something that says "I am okay; I love blue. Get over it." (At least it isn't purple, after all, or black, which could indicate something horrendous.) He colors mostly within the lines, which I never felt was necessary in life but somehow steadies me at this moment. Cecil takes his orange crayon and rips at his paper mat, and I have to think that a gouged rainbow is so much worse than a monochromatic one. In our particular situation.

Juliet quickly gives him another mat.

"You're good at this," Larissa tells Juliet, who helps Cecil. "Really good."

"Thanks," Juliet says. "I can bring you some food, too," she adds, ever cheerful. "What would you like?"

"I'm drawing a picture of a kid on fire," Cecil says. No one responds.

"Milk shakes?" I suggest to Troy.

"Oh," Troy says, interested, which makes both Larissa and I catch our breath with hope. You can hear us do it, but we pretend you couldn't. We're grown-ups. We're good at pretending.

"Vanilla milk shakes," I tell Juliet. "And avocado sandwiches."

"Goopy," Cecil says, but not in a way that indicates he won't eat one.

"All around," Larissa adds. "And fries?" she asks Troy. I know Larissa isn't big on serving fried food to the children, but we have so much to make up for and recognize that sprouts just won't do it. There is a time for grease. Realizing this makes me feel more and more like a mother.

Troy nods and continues to draw. Cecil leans down and bites the table, trying to tear a piece of it with his teeth. It's Formica, so there's no chance.

"No," I tell him a little too loudly, since for all I know children come in here and bite the table every day, although I doubt it. Larissa pulls him back lightly. She takes out a thin nylon strap, the kind she has at home to hold the child seats to their chairs, and she secures Cecil to his booster seat. She locks it with a snap, and although it's only holding him loosely, it seems to settle him. He bobs his head repeatedly and makes little popping noises with his mouth. Troy looks at him. (It feels like everyone is looking at Cecil now, although I wonder if he can feel it—he seems to be somewhere else at the moment.) I rub Troy's head, my perfect little boy, not noticeably damaged in any way, especially if you don't see the hand so much.

Larissa gives Cecil a longish rubber band, which he hooks onto his left hand, then stretches and unstretches with his right one, over and over again, hypnotically. This quiets him. I wonder if he's left-handed, although this may be the least of his problems.

"I didn't realize," I say to Larissa as I look at Cecil. I didn't realize what he's like, I tell her with a look. When did Cecil go from bad to worse? He was never adorable, lovable, or even very likable. But something has turned in him—he is no longer just an awkward, difficult child. He has gone one step further toward being the kind of child you might see in a horror movie, the kind of child who would play tricks on pets and scare babies, the kind of child who would come to some harm in the end. The kind of child who is so disturbing, you might not mind seeing him come to some harm in the end, if you were a certain age, say, eighteen and out at the movies with other eighteen-year-olds who have no real experience of the world. And aren't, of course, mothers themselves. Surely no mother could watch even the most disagreeable child suffer. Larissa nods at me slightly, reading my thoughts, which is also horror movie-like. We say nothing—another unspoken agreement between us. We watch our boys and wait for milk shakes, fried potatoes, comfort foods, comfort.

Like a bad joke, two short police officers walk into the diner. They carry nightsticks and, I can see, guns, and they come toward us, slowly. They're looking right at me. I cannot look them in the eye, and I wonder in this quick second if I will be hungry for a long time. *Fight or flight* comes to mind, especially the flight part, what with my history. But I don't flee. I let them come for me. I squeeze Troy's unbitten hand and try to remember this feeling in case I start to miss it, down the road.

"Patty Grant, right?" It's the bigger officer, although frankly, they both appear small. Small and young, with dark hair and matching mustaches, although I always think police shouldn't be allowed to have facial hair. I can't explain why.

I think they're the police from Proggleland, but I am so bad with faces.

Troy waves at them. Don't you just want to hug him?

"Hello, yes," I say.

"We need to speak with you," they say. I look at Larissa. I wouldn't know where to start explaining, what stories to make up, how they could possibly have happy endings. Wouldn't they all end like Grimm's fairytales?

"Do I have to go somewhere?" I ask. I can't let go of Troy. I look to Larissa to tell her this, but her eyes are wide with something like understanding, about this part, at least.

"Over here's fine," the shorter of the two (and really, they're both tiny) says. They gesture to the counter, behind which Juliet makes milk shakes without taking her eyes off of us.

I remove Troy's hand from mine. I need to make it across the room.

I've had this dream where I am pulling something like hair out of my mouth, Rapunzel-length hair, and it takes forever, and I'm horrified, and although I try in the dream to disguise just what I'm doing, everyone can see. Everyone is revolted, especially me. In the dream, I get a sickening feeling in my stomach throughout. Same deal, right now.

Sometimes in the dream, people throw stones at me, or what feel like stones. My face is always a blur of red that clashes badly with my hair, though it's not the worst thing people are saying about me. I never tell anyone about this because, well, isn't it just too disgusting to talk about? Would you?

I often don't sleep very well.

I make it across the small restaurant after what feels like several hours of this dream. I have almost nothing left to give, and my mouth is incredibly dry.

"The suspects are no longer in our possession," officer one tells me. He's my height, but twice my girth. Like a Weeble, I hear Dorothy's voice say, propelling me back to life. "He's just a Weeble," her little voice says in my ear, a four-year-old voice of encouragement. A Weeble with a painted-on police officer's suit. I hide a smile. I want to tip him over, watch him bounce back. Or not.

"Sorry?" I say, clasping my hands behind me, keeping them busy. The words *tilt him* cross my mind, but this isn't the time. It's not as if I've ever had a sense of humor before. I don't believe police do, either, although it's a generalization.

"Their whereabouts have yet to be determined," says officer two in police speak.

"There's a possibility of escape through a series of pathways from the abandoned area," says officer two, whose attention drifts toward the milk shakes in a way that seems stereotypical to me.

"The couple behind the amusement park who had Troy?" I ask.

"The suspects are momentarily at large," one of them says.

"Did you know these people?" the other officer says, glancing at my clothes for some reason I find offensive.

"No," I say. "Why?"

"It might seem that another parent would be more upset," a cop says cryptically. In my mind, little Gretel steps in to give him a giant push, and over he goes.

The children are with me in spirit on this one.

Cecil begins to have a fit, and I don't think it's from all of the passive voice the officers have used. I don't think Cecil's having a seizure, nothing medically frightening that would make you dial 911, but it's alarming, nonetheless. Troy leans away from Cecil. Cecil rocks, as if desperate to escape his chair, upturn the table, upturn our lives. He fights something we cannot see or hear, wailing unintelligible threats, spitting. His milk shake takes a tumble, but then Juliet has so carefully put a lid on the cup that it just bounces along the table. Troy rights it, but it falls again as Cecil grabs, hits, shrieks, then bangs the side of his head against the table.

"No, no," Juliet says, and she is there in seconds. I run to lift Troy from his seat. He reaches one last time to set the milk shake right and raises it and his own just as I lift him.

"What's wrong with him," officer one asks Larissa.

"Are you in charge of this boy?" asks number two. He actually goes for his nightstick, and Juliet gasps. Everyone must hear her.

"We'll go now," Larissa says calmly. "It's just hard for him, all the excitement," she says, although Cecil has made most of the excitement himself. We really have no idea what's going on in his head. Some things don't leave a mark.

Juliet bags up our sandwiches, and I hand her money.

"You're his mother?" a cop asks Larissa.

"I'm his day care provider," Larissa replies, in a way that indicates that she's even more than his mother. I'm sure they can't understand. None of us really can.

"Licensed?" one asks.

"Certainly," she says. "Daycare by Larissa, in the book, come by anytime," she tells them, although none of us ever wants to see them again. *Bad Weebles.*

"This is a public disturbance," says the shorter one, and now I really want to topple him.

Cecil reaches for the officer's nightstick and tries to bring it to his mouth.

"Cecil," says one or more of us. Together, Larissa and Juliet carry him to the van. They insert him through the door sideways. I try to help but do not let go of Troy the entire time. I'm certain to have squashed the avocado sandwiches under my arm, but it's the price you pay for being a parent. One of them.

Strapping down Cecil is not easy, not that child seats are ever as easy as advertised. Still, it's times like these when you could use a bungee cord or two, but I don't say anything. Once he's installed more or less within the legal requirements, we drive toward Larissa's house. Troy holds his and Cecil's milk shakes carefully. He will not put them down. (Both kids have cup holders, but I suspect Troy knows Cecil's milk shake would not stay long in a cup holder or within half a mile of Cecil, not that a young child should have such an understanding about distance, let alone the rest of these things.) Larissa reaches for the children's music but stops herself. Cecil quiets down anyhow, thankfully, who knows why. He makes the sound uh, uh, uh repeatedly, but not in the way that would make you hold your hands over your ears or call protective services.

Troy looks out the window dozily, the car smelling nicely of avocado sandwiches and fries. I'm fond of looking out windows myself, watching it all go by, so I find nothing to criticize in his behavior, not that I ever have. Larissa slows to a stop, but it's too soon to have reached her house, I know. It's still a half mile down the road—you can walk to it, not that we could have today, but in theory.

"Roadblock," Larissa says. Cecil shrieks from the backseat—I don't know why.

"Roadblock?" I repeat. Then it comes to me, all the movies I've seen. Roadblocks. Traffic stopped to check identification, look for criminals, thieves, child stealers. Could this roadblock be set for a new child stealer, or someone who has stolen in the past and not yet been apprehended? Are they looking for Troy's kidnapper, and if so, which one? Am I still in trouble? Hasn't becoming a parent changed everything like they say it does?

I feel the dream in the pit of my stomach again.

"Is it to find…the kidnappers?" I whisper to Larissa. It's the loudest I can get words out of my mouth.

"No, no," Larissa says, and actually pats my hand, which is gripping her front dashboard, my fingers turning white. "It's not like that," she says in an equally soft although not nearly as terrified whisper as my own. Then she raises her voice for us all:

"It's the frogs!" she says, a *Sesame Street* kind of wonder escaping as she turns back into the owner/operator of Daycare by Larissa. I don't know how she does it.

"The frogs! The frogs! The frogs!" Cecil exclaims, which does not make me like him better. He bounces in his car seat. (He's fast outgrowing it; it can barely contain him). He makes the entire car rock. I'm still feeling a little sick from the thought of being dragged from the car by whoever controls this roadblock, no doubt another Weeble in black, ready to expose me as a bad, bad person.

"Frogs?" I ask.

Larissa cuts the engine and waits behind a line of cars. She turns around to see the kids, keeping me in a corner of her eye for reasons maybe she doesn't even understand. "Every year the frogs come by. Traffic stops for safe passage. Let's go watch."

We get out of the car, Cecil extricating himself from his seat with remarkable ease, considering how long it took to strap him in. Larissa leads us to a crowd observing what appear to be hundreds of mud-colored frogs crossing the road. They have little spots but aren't nearly as green and Kermit-like as I would have thought. Maybe they're really toads. I lift Troy so he can see better and notice his eyes, wide and excited. My little boy is an animal lover. I'm so proud of him.

"Why are they here?" I ask.

"Why do the frogs cross the road every year, you mean?" Larissa says lightly.

"Well, okay, why do the frogs cross the road every year?" I ask her, feeling a little better. I like animals, too, after all.

"It's the same old story. They have to go where they have to go. Every year they migrate through town, right across the main road. They hook up with other frogs on their way, if you know what I mean," she says to me, raising a suggestive eyebrow. "It's an event around here, although we pretend not to stare," she says.

"How like life," I say.

"Hmm," she adds. We watch the frogs (I'm pretty sure now they're toads) cross the road. Troy giggles quietly. Cecil bounces up and down on his feet, as if he were attached to some kind of bungee jumping ride, ready to take a leap, and then he does. He breaks away from Larissa and runs into the path of frogs, an expression on his face clearly indicating that he is not an animal lover. His intentions are less than kind, less than humane, and so unchildlike that I find myself shocked. He begins to stomp.

We hear a roar of protest, calls of disgust from other kids, parents, day care providers (I assume), yelling "no, no" but somehow afraid to go after him, afraid to further endanger wildlife. The crowd restrains itself, but I can tell it doesn't want to, that if it could, it would reach for Cecil as one, grab him, and not wait till later to deliver his consequences. But this can't be—he's only a child. I find myself frozen in doubt and confusion, but then, I'm used to it.

"No!" Larissa yells, then daintily runs after Cecil on her tip toes. She struggles to hold him. (He is not a small child, not light like Troy, despite that I don't think he's over four or five. Could he be six?) Cecil kicks and tries to bite Larissa, which incites in me a real albeit brief stab of hatred. I run to her as the frogs disband (Troy is at my side now, don't think I'm not paying attention every single second), and I grab one of Cecil's legs, which (although you might have thought it would be a dangerous limb to grab) goes slack in my arms. We carry Cecil off, him laughing ha-ha all the way, the crowd murmuring threateningly. Cecil's body goes limp and seems almost dead. Troy holds a bit of Cecil's pant leg that droops. We drag Cecil from the scene. For the second time today.

Troy waves his bandaged hand at the frogs as we rescue Cecil.

Cecil is a bit easier to restrain in the car this time, but Troy begins to whine uncharacteristically, although without words.

"What's wrong?" I say, but I see.

The milk shakes have spilled all over the back seat floor. Troy begins to cry. Don't cry over spilt milk shakes I want to tell him, but this is no time for puns. The more he cries, the more my eyes begin to sting, as I realize that Troy has had many, many reasons to cry, yet I've never seen a tear. His little voice, which I seldom hear, makes croaking and gurgling sounds. I get into the backseat between the boys and put my arms around Troy, holding him. He looks right into my eyes with a question, and one I don't really think is about milk shakes at all, and he is overcome. He gurgles and grabs onto a clump of his hair using his better hand and tears it out from his head, making a small yelping sound.

We cry quietly, we hiccup, we take it all in. Troy grasps the clump of hair in his hand tightly, then holds it against his chest, a souvenir of sorts from another in a series of bad days. The clump is larger than you'd think. I tuck his head under my chin, hoping to protect it from further harm. His own chin rests against my right hand, and he begins to gnaw on me. I can feel it but for some reason wish he'd bite even harder.

* * *

We glide into Larissa's driveway, each in our own daze. We're greeted by a low silvery car, the kind I can imagine someone driving too fast in. The driver would have one of those headsets that you speak into, that make you look as if you're screaming at yourself. Maybe one on each ear.

"Mama!" Cecil yells too loudly for the inside of the van.

"Liv," Larissa says, in a way that makes it clear we're not happy to see her.

I rarely see her, and I like it that way. It's not that she's not friendly (she isn't, actually, but that's not it)—it's more that she's not here. I'm a working mom, too, so I'm not usually here during the day, although I feel like I am. Part of me is here. I don't get that sense with Liv, who after all, has left her sick and odd child with Larissa for weeks at a time. Larissa grimaces at the car, too. Liv has a presence, a posture that says she's important; she has a job in town (not like us over-the-river workers); she has places to be. I cannot envision her calming Cecil in a restaurant with fries, crayons, shakes. But I don't know. You never really know what goes on between a mother and child in private (do you now, Patty).

"Cecil!" Liv screams when she sees us. She's standing on the front porch, and although she's not smoking, for some reason she seems like she is. She resembles a movie star. She has a large mass of auburn hair—who does she look like? I want to ask Larissa, but I can see Larissa's mind is elsewhere, on Cecil, actually, and I'm glad someone's is.

Philip stands at the front door, looking at us with concern. I catch his eye, but I don't know what message to convey to him. Troy clings to me at the sight of Liv, his face still streaked with tears, his teeth still holding onto my hand tightly.

"Come to Mama," Liv says, her arms out wide, as if she hadn't seen Cecil in ages, which may be true. Cecil goes over to his mom and bumps into her somewhat meanly, which she seems not to appreciate and she gives him a little push back. I watch Larissa.

"Come inside," Philip says to everyone.

"What has happened to him?" Liv says loudly, and I look around, figuring that at least this is a quiet neighborhood and no one will notice. But one of the news vans is here. I can't imagine why, but a newsperson holding a camera approaches us. I believe the camera is on. It's pointed our way.

"It's been a tough day for him," Larissa says. Cecil's clothes are a bit torn in different places, maybe from us holding him down, maybe from something he's done to himself. I don't think blame is an issue here, but Liv might.

"What kind of care of him have you been taking?" Liv yells, although I think there's something seriously wrong with her verb construction. She turns to the news crew (now there are two of them, which I guess constitutes a crew, if not a story). Larissa's mouth is open. Philip comes out. Troy chews lightly.

"He's fine," I say.

"Isn't that the boy you let harm the endangered frogs?" The newsperson shoves the microphone in front of Larissa.

"That's horrible," says Liv.

"Yeah," agrees Cecil, although he's not helping himself any.

"Oh," says Troy beside me, although my hand nearly tries to stop the word from coming out of his mouth.

"And that boy—" Liv says, pointing at Troy, my quivering boy harming no one. I don't mind the light biting at all, pain is part of motherhood, I want to tell this woman. "What's wrong with him, anyway?" she asks. I feel the cameras swing my way again, my face going red, my hand going pale.

"Does he speak at all?" she asks us all meanly but in a way that clearly expresses she couldn't care less.

"I'm taking my boy home now," Liv says. "Away from these people."

She says people the way you might say monsters or predators or worse, were you the kind of parent who worried incessantly about such things. "How would you like to come home with Mama!" she says too loudly but in a way that might carry well on the six o'clock news.

Cecil begins to make a noise like yag, yag, yag, yag, repeatedly, excitedly. And we'd just calmed him down. Troy hiccups quietly, but I feel the pain of it inside my own chest.

"Let's all talk quietly," Larissa suggests, "inside," as she tries to swoop everyone into the house.

"Oh, no," says Liv. "I think we're done here." The news camera swings to a small sign on the house that says Daycare by Larissa.

"We're happy to care for Cecil," Philip says.

"It's no trouble, we've really got it down," Larissa adds, maternal instincts kicking in. She reaches Cecil's side and tries to get him to stop bouncing and saying yag, yag, yag. Both women stand on either side of Cecil now, Larissa trying to get him to stop moving, Liv shaking him as if to keep him going. One of his arms shoots upward, the other balances him and reaches for the ground. He's gone all Gumby, but not in a good way. It is painful to watch.

"He is not your child!" Liv says and wrenches her child from Larissa, who had been holding onto the downward arm, working her magic, but now Cecil just bounces to the car, hitting out at nothing in particular, at one point striking his mother. He is no doubt stronger than she thinks. I don't know if she's been around in a while.

"Ouch," says Liv. "Don't hit," she yells sharply. He quiets a little. A small moan comes from Larissa, who is breathing heavily. Philip holds her to the front porch as if a big windstorm had just come up and she might blow over or be ripped apart into little pieces. Troy hides his face in my chest.

They do not say good-bye, although Cecil waves frantically from the backseat. He doesn't seem to wave at any of us in particular or in a way you'd describe as cheerful, if you were watching him, or filming him. It's more like flailing. Philip leads Larissa inside and gestures for us to follow. We close the door hard in the camera man's face.

Chapter 11

Day Is Done

Inside Larissa's house we find Jake and Dorothy seated at the old upright piano, which is brown and a little crumbly but has an amazing sound. Larissa sits down on the couch, then rises quickly to go to the kitchen. She takes out a large quantity of frozen chicken nuggets, so I'm fairly concerned about her. I know she only eats breaded foods when she's feeling stressed. She zaps them in the microwave.

I place Troy next to Dorothy at the piano, where somehow there's just the right amount of room despite Jake's impressive size. Dorothy makes sure Troy fits, then takes one look at him and grabs a fuzzy book off the piano top for him to pat. He allows my hand to drop from his mouth at last, and more easily than I'd thought. How will I ever be able to thank this little girl.

"Can I help?" I ask Larissa because that's what you say at times like these. Larissa just looks at me, then at the kitchen, then back at me. She shakes her head no. We watch the microwave, listen to it buzz. We are probably standing too close to it. No one official will indicate what too close means, but I doubt Larissa cares at this moment. It's as if she feels that she deserves to stand too close, some sort of self-punishment, and I get it. When the timer rings, she takes out the batch, dumps them on a tray, and carries them out to the living room. She grabs a stack of napkins and dumps it beside the tray, then sits down. (There are always stacks of napkins just where you need them in Larissa's house, which I think may be what truly makes it a home. Kleenex, too.)

Jake is actually playing "Taps." I guess the day is done, or at least done for, even though I never used to end a sentence with a preposition.

"Why does anyone need that song?" Philip asks. Jake's eyes grow wide at the look of Larissa, who is staring at the nuggets maliciously, as if she might start hacking at them with a knife.

"It's easy to play," Jake says.

"Boy scout," Philip says critically. The children pick up nuggets from the coffee table and begin sucking on them, Troy tucking the fuzzy book under his arm. Something about the bite-size food appeals to kids—I read about it in one of the parenting books. There's half a chapter devoted to nuggets alone.

"I also know 'Jingle Bells,'" Jake says.

Philip shakes his head.

"Or not," Jake says. He gets up from the piano. Dorothy carefully wipes her hands on a napkin, so Troy does the same. She moves back to the piano and begins playing the really high keys so they sound like a soothing music box.

Larissa leans against Philip's shoulder.

"It's different without Cecil," she says, which is true in so many ways. It is quiet, for one thing, despite two four-year-olds, an ancient piano, a librarian, and fried foods. It's hard to understand her loss, but I know it's there. I almost know how she feels, losing a boy. My boy is still here, and I banish it from my mind when I think it just for a second: *My boy is so much better.*

A loss is a loss, Patty.

Larissa begins to cry quietly.

Philip turns on the TV, and we watch the silent picture. It shows a school bus that has turned onto its side and lays there like a sick animal, wheels slowly spinning. This goes on for some time, pictures of silent crises we don't really need to know about, the tinkling of piano keys. The kids come over now and then, taking nuggets. Philip changes the channel back and forth with their arrivals and departures: a harmless cooking show when they're near, the overturned bus when they're away. No one objects. No one tries to take the remote. Larissa sucks out the insides of a nugget while continuing to cry. She places the fried outsides in a napkin. No one's about to criticize her.

Philip changes to a channel with a newscaster from our past, standing in front of a place I will never forget. It's the abandoned area behind Proggleland, dust rising around the shacks, which appear deserted once again, if you don't count news crews as people (and we don't). Philip unmutes the TV, and some need, conscious or subconscious, makes me want to know what they're saying, and yet sort of not know. As a perennial student, such ambivalence about learning is new to me. Get used to it Patty.

"This is the site of the recent Proggleland kidnapping," says what's her name with the well-combed hair, "which has unveiled the location of one of Santa Vallejo's long-lost secrets," she says, adding unnecessary mystery to a story that makes me sick enough as it is.

"What is that place?" Larissa asks.

"Not so ancient history," Philip says quietly. Jake makes a noise of agreement.

The camera spans a lengthy patch of old barracks, or stalls, or what-have-yous. Small buildings that look uninhabitable, condemned, dangerous. I consider shielding Troy's eyes, but he stands right up against me, reaching out toward the screen with his favorite, most loved hand, palm up, as if making an offering. His face fills with recognition, wonder, confusion. I decide to let him watch.

"That's where you were," I say redundantly, judging by his gesture. Troy nods, mesmerized by the screen. Maybe they took the best care of him they could. Maybe they made dinner from scratch (Scraps, Patty? Don't think about that.) Maybe they thought they were saving him from something or that some higher force had brought him, wandering, lost, abandoned, to their home, such as it was. Maybe they did the best they could, making him feel as warm and wanted and at home as he's ever been. Maybe the harness was meant only for security, not for restraint. Troy emits a small sigh and pulls my hand close to his mouth. At the ready.

"As you can see, the barracks have been here for some time," the coiffed woman says, "dating back to the early days of the twentieth century, when this place was home to a fairground with a popular racetrack. These buildings housed the horses between races."

I'm sickened to know they really were horse stalls. People living in horse stalls.

"You knew this?" Larissa asks Philip.

"There's very little land in coastal California that hasn't been used for some purpose or other before," Philip says. "Nothing should surprise us. But yes," he says, "I know about the old fairground, if that's what they're calling it."

The camera shows the inside of a stall that's been turned into the best shelter it can, with colorful scarves hanging across the walls, hiding cracks and stains of unknown, unimaginable days. Soft but faded pieces of fabric lie on the dirty ground; broken, well-used pieces of furniture are strewn about. You could call it a pitifully narrow horse stall. Someone called it home.

"Built in the 1890s, the park, known as the Fairway Fairground and Racetrack, closed down in the 1930s. In the 1940s," our newscaster continues, "the federal government used the area as temporary housing for thousands of Americans of Japanese heritage, who were removed from their homes throughout the state and interned during World War II. Fairway Fairground served as a detainment center for those on their way to larger facilities in Idaho and Southern California."

"That place is pure bad vibes," Larissa says.

"No wonder we hate it," I add.

"So, was I absent that day in history class?" Larissa asks. No one answers. I think it's the history that was absent from the class, but I don't need to say anything.

"These are some of the photos of record from the era," the newsgirl says. The screen fills with black-and-white photos of people waiting in long lines, people who happened to have a Japanese ancestry: couples dressed warmly in well-designed coats, stylish hats. Women in dresses and low heels. Men in suits. Children in their best clothes. All of them standing, at a loss, in front of what's now known as the shacks beyond the old maintenance area of Proggleland. Some shade their eyes, as if looking just beyond, but I can't imagine at what. People here are not enjoying their day in the slightest, not amused at this park.

"About eight thousand citizens of Japanese and Japanese-American descent were rounded up from the cities and sent to Fairway, where they lived in what were known as 'the barracks' for up to several months at a time. The barracks had been adapted for human living," she says, and the photo changes to a bare stall that looks cold and in no way adapted for any kind of living. No scarves, no rug, no floor, only dirt. It's mostly dust and wood. The dust rises malevolently. It almost chokes me.

"It's a stall," I say. They look splintery, unstable, unsuitable in every way. I think of the stalls crowded with people, literally crawling with people. Something in the way they stand close together, hold onto their children: It says community. It says you can't take some things away. But you can try.

In this photo, their coats and shoes look way less stylish, frayed, fraying. Not warm enough at all.

"Cookie time," Larissa says, leading the kids away from the big screen, the black-and-white history of who we are, what we've done, what we've forgotten. Even Troy follows, I guess having seen enough, though not looking very upset at all. I breathe out.

"In recent days," the newsgirl continues, "the area has been used as maintenance facilities for the town's amusement park, Proggleland, which was built two years ago to attract families from around the world.

"If you like that sort of thing," Philip says.

"And have no knowledge of the past," Jake says.

"But unbeknownst to city management and spokespersons for Proggleland—" the newsgirl reads carefully now from some statement, and you can just tell someone who has legal authority (or thinks he does) has gotten involved—"in recent days, the area has been used in secret by immigrants who have come to this country without proper authority from the former Eastern European country called Hostainia, also known as Khaztanazia, or East Khaztanaziastan." She reads slowly now from her notes and stumbles over the pronunciation. "The country is currently without a name and is often referred to as the outlying area formerly known as Khaztania rather than Khaztania Proper."

"Again with the Proper, really?" Larissa says directly to the TV, having led the kids far from the big screen with a pack of organic oatmeal cookies. Desperate times call for prepackaged cookies, to say the least. Troy chews on his cookie a little more nervously than any given parent might like, especially me. Dorothy reads to him quietly, both with mouths full, which no one is about to criticize.

And then we're accosted by the color photos, and I feel so sorry for the woman who appears on our screen. The woman in the bright, odd shirt with the babushka, a look beyond misery on her face. It's a mug shot. She has obviously been apprehended after all. Her face stays on the screen for an unbearable length of time. Our eyes meet.

"I guess they captured her," Larissa says softly. The woman stares at us, profoundly sad, profoundly lost. Troy's other mother? I can't begin to think. Who is the real criminal here, Patty?

We see the dad, or whatever you want to call him, the checkered-shirt man. In his mug shot. He does not smile, either. Why should he? Just because someone points a camera at you, doesn't mean you should be happy about it.

I feel the tears in my eyes again. I don't remember my eyes stinging so much ever before. Something in the air, something in Santa Vallejo, something in me.

"Jeez," I say.

Jake puts an arm around me in the most wonderful way anyone ever has. Larissa touches my arm. Our family really feels for their family, our gestures say. We couldn't explain why, but in a perfect world, of course, we wouldn't have to.

"I'm so sorry," I say softly to no one, or everyone, but it doesn't do any good anyway.

"Those immigrants who have been apprehended, including the alleged kidnappers, will be deported as soon as our government can find a country who will take them," she says, too cheerfully, as if she's always had food, shelter, a complete family unit, a personal hairstylist, a country with its own history and a future ahead of it. As if she's never been the slightest bit displaced.

We see a map of somewhere in Europe, an arrow marking a country the size of an ant, and not just because Philip has a large TV.

"Those immigrants who have escaped our local law enforcement will be hunted down and imprisoned throughout the state," she says coldly, back to reading off her teleprompter, as if she's somebody we should listen to. "Anyone who has seen them should call the number on the screen."

I refuse to read the number. I shut my eyes.

"I certainly hope they send the Proggleland officers," Jake says. "They're incompetent." He touches my hair. I don't even mind.

We are not on the law's side. But the immigrants had Troy. Their mug shots reveal blondish hair, classic cheekbones: Troy looks just like them. He fits right in. How could they not take him, or save him, and is there a difference? Why should they have returned him? I didn't.

There but for the grace of god...goes through my mind. I read it somewhere.

A photo flashes on the screen of a child's ball in the dirt in front of a shack, right beside an old doggie dish. In living color.

I reach for the remote to change the channel. I have had enough.

* * *

Jake drives me from Larissa's to work in his pink car because this day is not over. We pass slow-moving Santa Vallejo patrol cars, the young officers inside peering out, driving stealthily. Prowling.

"Who do you think you're looking for," I say quietly to them. Jake looks at me as if he agrees, although he can have no real idea what he's agreeing with.

"Just go away," I tell them. I seem to be losing my fear of authority, and yet I feel incredibly sad. I think of Troy. Emphasize the positive, Patty. Breathe, count your blessings. Count them over and over.

The officer looks at me as if I'm familiar, as if I'm someone he should know. He rifles through some papers on his lap and looks at me again, and my heart stops beating. He looks directly at me, then his car takes him away. My heart skips several beats until I feel as if I've missed something, as if I've just awoken from something I should be able to remember but can't. As if I've lost part of my past.

He wasn't looking for me. But he thought he was.

We stop in front of the store. "Thank you," I tell Jake, although I don't feel it's enough to say. He runs his fingers along a strand of my hair again, as if it were actually appealing, and I feel something else fall away from me, something I no longer need or want, and probably never did.

"As long as Troy's home. Dorothy's home. We're very lucky," Jake says.

"I know," I say, and I mean it. We draw a little closer. I think of the immigrants, the children they had running around. Were those their own children or children they had found? Does it matter?

I finally know the answer to that.

We sit there for a few moments, visions of our children dancing in our heads, worries, concerns, hopes, and dreams, all things Hallmark Channel, and many that are so much worse. Jake takes my hand, and I transfer some of my worries through our hands, which hold each other's for more than a moment in a way that helps me breathe. Ambiguous but still large concerns float from his mind to mine, and vice versa, and for a minute they all wrestle then seem to quiet. We part slowly, with almost a handshake but something that's really so much more. It's new and different, scary and hopeful, like learning a foreign language, like finding it easier than you'd thought but knowing it's going to get to irregular verbs at some point. It's the start of something you know you will continue with, no matter what grade you get on your first draft.

We grown-ups go off for an afternoon of work, happy to be in our own land, where we can speak the language if we need to, where we're warmed by touching hands that have silently agreed on something to get us through the day.

* * *

When I return at day's end to Larissa's for Troy, he looks up at me with the sweetest possible look on his face, as if I've made his day.

"Hi," I say enthusiastically. I find I want to say it six or seven times, but I don't want to scare the boy.

Larissa, though, looks worn. She's at the table, folding Cecil's clothes, which smell clean in a not perfume-y or detergent-y way. They also don't smell at all like Cecil, who of course is no longer here.

Philip comes out from his office to say good-bye, carrying a stack of freshly printed papers. I can feel the stack's warmth rising in my direction. I so love printed paper. I want to touch the stack, embrace it, whatever it is. I reach out for it inadvertently then notice Philip looking almost guilty.

"So much paperwork, so little time," he says. I see official looking headings, snippets of legal phrases, large stamps of approval of one kind or another, although I don't know how many kinds of approval there need to be. There's something agreed upon in this stack, something verified, maybe even something above the law, Philip's expression indicates. Or below the law. And yes, I see words or parts of words. The Republic of Something. A bunch of words that end in -stan and -stia. People's names with lots of j's and z's.

There's something corrective about these papers, something official, something long overdue. Something illegal? Who am I to say? And then of course I wouldn't. We all deserve to be official in some way or another, accepted. Part of the community.

Something has been documented here between Philip and I, and Larissa passes by, looking at the stack and nodding. Documented by documents that Philip produces. Outside Santa Vallejo proper. In the valley.

And I'm not about to do one single thing to mess up the process.

"Good," I say. This valley rocks.

Jake and I meet again, as often happens at day's end, to gather our children, to inhale them, to count backwards as we look at their hair, their faces, their hands. We look at one another; we each touch our child's shoulders, but we share the touch. It feels as if we're touching one another, holding hands. We want to take our children home, our touches say, a feeling I never expected to have. We share looks, sensations, emotions I have no words for. There are only a few things I know: the five rules of commas, how to write a detailed descriptive paragraph, and that we want to take our children home and lock ourselves up safely for the night.

Tears fall in slender rows down Larissa's face as she continues to smooth out Cecil's clothes, running her hands against the cotton, the dark blue denim, the old corduroy. We back away silently.

Jake drives us to my apartment super slowly in his pink car. I have never driven with anyone who comes to such a complete stop. Who looks both ways. Who checks his mirrors. And probably not just for police cars.

We carry our sleeping children inside my little apartment, to Troy's bedroom. I place Troy at the head of the bed, Jake lays Dorothy, sleepy and mumbling the words *day is done, day is done,* at the foot of the bed. He pulls out the sheet and slides her inside, a little love letter of a girl slipped into a warm envelope. Jake pulls off his sweater and neatly folds it, a pillow for his child's head. I hug my boy good-night.

"I love you, Troy," I tell him. Is this the first time? What an idiot you are, Patty. How hard was it to say? What if you hadn't gotten the chance?

Troy sleepily pats me on the shoulder, forgiving, forgetting, and falling to sleep. He is a boy of actions, not words. Never underestimate the power of a sympathetic, loving pat on the back, especially from a child. Especially from your child. He wraps his fingers around his hair tightly, holding on as if to a treasured toy. Or maybe a loved one.

Jake and I are almost crying. Sappy, exhausted, worried, relieved. We would be cornball in someone else's novel.

We stare at one another, and this time he takes more than just my hand, touches me, and although certainly it has something to do with the children, this time it's also about us. He puts his hand behind my head and brings me in to a kiss. The children watch us, asleep but in absolute accord, I'm sure. I suspect Dorothy would say something in approval, and that Troy wouldn't say anything but would approve all the same, maybe with the smile Dorothy won't share. Then I forget about them, but in the best possible way. You bet I locked the doors.

"I feel like I've found you, like you've been missing," Jake says, and I feel that way, too, about both of us. "Where have you been?" he asks, hypothetically, I hope. He kisses me again silently, or maybe I've let go of my super strong need to hear at the moment, as not all senses are required at all times, Patty.

"You're here now," he says, and I answer him by ignoring how red my cheeks must look and kissing him back. It's almost funny when what's missing appears right in front of you. We continue to kiss, as actions can speak even louder than internal narration.

Still, just as easily as I always start a letter with Dear and end it with Sincerely, just as instinctively as I will always use the serial comma even when everyone else stops, I lead Jake to the other bedroom. Some things require little study, and I've had scarcely any about this sort of thing.

Jake kisses me with a protectiveness and strength, a warmth that comes not just from the unquestionable largeness of his body, which is twice the girth of mine or more and taller by about the length of two good dictionaries. I find safety in his size. His neck is big, his chest is wide, his arms reach all the way around me and have room for more. His grip is just right.

I'm left with my mind blank and between kisses can only say, "Hi." Troy's the smart one, feeling the need to say little. I let my words go.

Jake smiles and kisses me more, then gets into my bed with me, removing clothes as he does so. I always admire how men undress haphazardly, unselfconsciously, and even with one hand. The other is on me at all times, when not removing my clothes, after which it returns to me every time. Our clothes get dumped together in the pile to spend the night co-mingling in warmth and affection, safe. I love our clothes at this moment in a way that is irrational, but I don't care. Reason is overrated. We kiss the whole time. I am one of those people who cannot be kissed enough, although you wouldn't guess this about me from a photo or news clipping, say. And yet I resist it somewhat, someone that close, touching. But I can only argue with myself for so long. Jake seems to know this as he keeps his face close to mine while our bodies do the things they have learned over the years to do, as they move along in a wholly intense way that requires amazingly little thought, even from me.

Jake returns his glasses to his face—I think he dumped them on the ground earlier but I'm not sure when or why, and how is beyond my caring. He is not one of those people who look naked and mole-like without glasses. In fact, he looks exactly the same with or without them, and I don't know how this is possible, except that I'm fairly nearsighted and maybe I can't really tell the difference. It is such a nice face, either way, the beard a new thing for me but something I'm suddenly all in favor of. I had no idea. You learn something new every day, Patty. Sometimes more than one thing, depending on the seeming length of the day and state of undress.

"What a day," is all I can think to say.

"It's a great and terrible day," Jake says. I look up at him, and at least he's smiling in an ever-hopeful way. "What more could you ask of a day?"

"I might have asked for a little less terrible," I say. Jake nods.

"I try not to ask for anything," he says.

"You librarians," I say. "You wait for others to ask. You have all the answers."

"It's true," Jake says. "I'm full of information only of use to others."

"Hmm," I say, although I'm not sure it's out loud. We are quiet for a bit.

Our children lie sleeping in the next room. All is well under this roof. How often can you say that? How often do you stop to think it? I think it over and over, trying to drive it into Jake's mind as well: Think it, too, I tell him. I feel it working. I am suddenly capable of conveying positive helpful thoughts and placing them inside the mind of a large, warm person. I have never communicated so well.

Jake is still looking at me as if I'm someone special.

"This is the part where we talk or sleep?" I say, not so much a question as a see-saw of a statement.

"Yes," he says, both groggily and almost happily, for Jake, who does not usually exude a great amount of joy. It always seems sort of curtained off, the joy of Jake.

"Okay, so tell me things, anything," I begin, but stop myself. What if he asked me the same? At this moment, would you tell, Patty? You would, wouldn't you. Kisses and all that, and you'd tell it all, as maybe you should. When would be a better time? But I don't. Not right now, anyway.

"Tell me something you wish you could tell me but are afraid to," I say instead, in what I suspect may be a startlingly unintelligible grammatical construction, were anyone grading here. "Tell me something with a happy ending." I'm not sure I said the last part out loud. It's late.

"There's not so much to tell," Jake says. "But there is a little. I guess we all have a little."

"Hmm," I say noncommittally. There's just a little felony to tell. Worse things have happened (and this week, too).

"You don't have to," I say.

"I want to tell you about Dorothy," Jake says. It wakes me up a little.

"Is Dorothy your daughter or...not your daughter?" I ask redundantly. It's not even something I need to know, is it? It may be the unaccustomed warmth of the bed, the surroundings. "It doesn't matter," I say quickly. "It doesn't."

"I'm not sure if it matters," Jake says. "She's mine, though," he says, and I believe him. Troy is mine, after all. Cecil was Larissa's, but briefly. Jake rubs a hand across my head, reparting my hair from the middle to the side. I don't look great that way, but I don't say anything.

"I killed Dorothy's mother," Jake says.

"Oh," I say. Oh, I think.

"Car crash," he says.

"Oh," I say again.

"I was driving. Dorothy was in back, asleep. I don't think she could possibly remember. She wasn't injured. I was only hurt a little. But her mother died. I'm responsible. I actually had no business driving," he says. "I drank back then."

I don't ask for details. It's not like he's writing an essay and I need supporting facts, five details per topic sentence. His thesis is clear.

"I didn't end up in jail. The police said it was the other driver's fault."

"But that's different," I say.

"I believe I was responsible either way. I was driving and had had a drink, even if my alcohol level was still technically ok; I was endangering lives. I could have caused the accident. Just because the other guy was drinking, too, does that mean I wasn't in the wrong?"

I'm no one to answer this question, and I suspect I couldn't talk him out of this feeling no matter what, though maybe I'll try. It feels like someone should try.

"I wasn't a good anything," Jake says. "Driver, parent, person. I should have fixed that."

"Maybe it was just an accident and you can't admit it," I say, because I need to say something, and because the truth can be hard to decipher for yourself, especially when you've done something wrong or suspect you did. I know.

"It was an accident that shouldn't have been," Jake says. "Which makes it not accidental at all. I shouldn't have been driving that car, not there and then. I'm responsible."

"So now you go around saving people?"

Jake looks as if he's been caught at something and his secret is out, a look that, for example, would be unbecoming on me but that is overdue nonetheless.

"You jumped into that cold river after Cecil," I say. "Bravely and with abandon."

"That's easy," Jake says.

"You helped save Troy," I say.

"Also easy," he says.

"No, not easy. If that's easy, then what would be hard?" I ask. "Do you have something in mind, some superhuman trick you're going to try to perform? For repentance or whatever?" I know so little about religion. Maybe repentance isn't the right word, but Jake seems to understand.

"No, I don't plan it anymore. It's not one thing I want to do," Jake says. "It's daily, it's every minute, it's owing every minute," he says.

"That's a lot," I say.

"I owe a lot," he says.

"I couldn't do that," I say. "Think about it every minute." Or do I? I think about things plenty, but I still think there are moments where even my biggest worry (and we all know what that is) gets pushed aside in my mind, into a small, cramped corner reserved for such things. I could be fooling myself, though.

"I can't do it every minute, either," he says, clearly disappointed in himself.

"You can take the rest of the night off," I suggest. Jake smiles, and we're quiet.

"I really love Dorothy," I say. "I don't care if she doesn't smile and if she never wants to," I say.

"It's her right," Jake says. "But I'm hopeful. And Troy?" he says, a two-word question that's too huge for my small bed and for my small life.

"Troy," I say. I smile. "Troy is mine, my responsibility." Does the rest matter? How I came by Troy? The boy looks nothing like me, after all. The truth couldn't be a gigantic surprise. Maybe except for the details, the late-night drive, the French fries, the bungee cord, the constant fear of being followed.

I think for a moment as Jake watches me, completely nonjudgmentally, which is especially nice when you're naked. "Troy is my little boy," I say, nursery rhyme style. I run it through my head a few times. I don't know what Dr. Seuss would have to say about such a simplistic understatement. I suspect he wouldn't approve, and not just of the rhyme scheme. But he's outdated now, right?

"Whatever you've been through," Jake says, "it's working out. Troy's here, he's okay. He'll speak more, if it's right for him," Jake says. "Quiet isn't so bad."

"It's the librarian in you talking," I say.

"I wasn't always a librarian," he says.

"Back in the days of bad driving?" I ask.

"I was unhelpful in every way," he says. "I was a dynamic negative force, which isn't a good thing in a person my size," he admits.

"I like your sizableness," I say, despite that I suspect any computer's spellchecker would place a squiggle under such a word. "You're the most positive large physical force I know. I guess you've shifted your magnetism entirely," I say, even though I'm not sure the term is scientifically correct. It's late in a long day to be making metaphors.

Jake parts my hair back to center, slowly brushing it with his fingers, a gesture I find soothing in the sleepiest of ways.

"It's good to be home," I say. Jake takes a piece of my hair in his fingers and kisses it. You're holding a redhead, I want to tell him, despite that he can see as much. We are not always what we seem, I want to say. But I don't think it matters to him, or maybe, possessor of all knowledge that he is, he already knows.

Chapter 12

Visual Disturbances

It could be any day, in any person's life, a workday where you find yourself lulled by routine. I thrive on routine; it's what makes me feel both most useful and most normal. The most Patty I can be is at work, often doing something menial, fixing commas, noting misplaced modifiers, sorting nuts and bolts. I'm the to-do list type, whatever's on it. It's all the same, and for better or worse (and why judge it, Patty), it's what makes me who I am.

I clean off our electric fans on display, which is intricate work, pushing the dust cloth between the hard wires of the fans just so. I'm wearing one of those thin dust masks (we sell a package of four for six-ninety-nine, a bargain). I adore the anonymity I feel behind my mask, even if there really aren't any customers in the store. No one to spot me and maybe no one trying.

I am back to work; I'm a normal working mom. My child is okay. So, he has an unusual relationship with his hand. I change the bandage daily. I am good at following instructions, directions, rules and regulations, normally at least. Troy seems to treat his hand as if it's a dear long-lost friend, or at least less of an enemy. He whispers to it. Sucks on it a little. Lets it play with his hair. You'd barely notice, especially if you didn't watch him constantly every minute you're together. Especially if you weren't terrified he'd start biting at any minute, ripping hair, bleeding. Okay, so he gnaws a little around the edges of the bandage. He pulls out a few hairs a day and leaves them for me on the table. It is still nothing you couldn't bear to see, as Dr. P might say (and has). It could be worse. It could get worse. It's not as if you can ever stop worrying anyway, Patty.

Still, a quiet child is so underrated, as Larissa might say (and has).

"Where's everybody today?" I ask Walter through my mask as he passes by, carrying a box filled with something metallic, small objects that clank against one another like jingle bells, although 'tis far from the season now.

"Everyone's checking out the new store," Walter says softly, and Eva lets out a huff of disapproval as she polishes the front counter with our all-natural lemon and oil polish (it smells like freshly baked lemon meringue pie baked by someone who loves you, just loves everything he or she knows about you). Our store smells wonderful, like a beloved family home, even from behind my mask.

Eva puts down the polish. "Well then let's just check this out," she says, and Walter places his box on the counter with a crash of jingles, which cry out their objections to this idea. We all grab our coats. I remove my mask, although for a quick minute I long to keep it on. Ours is not the kind of town where people walk around wearing protective masks, although I have been to that type of town. Those people have their reasons.

Outside, we follow a small crowd to the new store, which opens this morning. We can see the sign for the building all the way from Walter's store, several blocks away. The new store is called J. Means, & Company. I'm annoyed and not just because I think a comma before an ampersand is grammatically incorrect. It's that J. Means sounds like an alias to me.

"J. Means?" I ask Walter. "Is it a person?"

"It sounds like a person," Walter says.

"A person afraid to admit to his first name," Eva says.

"His or her first name," says Philip, who has joined us and managed to echo my thoughts exactly. He and Walter shake hands, more a silent agreement than greeting. Walter ambles along with the crowd somewhat gaily, with no animosity toward anyone headed to the new store, as opposed to, say, his own store.

I stroll with Philip. We could be brother and sister, it strikes me again, misplaced at birth. Our red hair and paleness take years off of us—I look about twelve today; Philip could be my older brother at fifteen, although I know he's thirty. We redheads just always look young, innocent, at first.

"J. Means is a conglomerate," Philip tells us.

"What a horrible, horrible way to go through life," Eva answers him.

"Poor J.," Philip agrees. "He has a number of stores to keep him company, apparently."

"And an ampersand," I say critically. "Actually, he has quite a lot of unnecessary punctuation." It's the English teacher in me.

"There are worse things," Walter says as we enter the store.

"It's Bed, Bath & Beyond all over again," I mutter to no one in particular, remembering the store in San Diego. That store had a lot of punctuation, too. Maybe with this much square footage you feel entitled to overly punctuate. J. Means is huge. You could add an exclamation mark, and no one would probably object. Besides me.

"It's big," Eva says, not exactly a compliment. Our store is small, sweet, quaint, perfect. Our store smells of lemon meringue. This store smells of, well, nothing, or at least nothing good. There's a smell I can't name, a pervasive almost odorless scent, something blowing through the fans above us. It smells like mindless shopping.

"Big box," Walter says.

"What?" I ask.

"These stores are called big boxes," he says. "That's what they're like."

"Big, nondescript," Philip says.

"Cold," I say.

"Bright," Eva answers. None of these is a positive adjective. Nothing here would remind you of lemon meringue, although if you spent enough time here, I imagine you'd long for lemon meringue. After a while, though, your mind might be so numbed that you wouldn't be able to identify the craving (so you'd keep shopping, searching, longing). You might think you want slipcovers instead, in your confusion. The bright lights hurt my eyes, as little migraine forewarning spots appear here and there, little surprises, little old friends dropping by without calling first. I had a lot of migraines in San Diego. These are not happy memories.

Despite the spots (and the darkening that lies ahead, some things you can count on), I notice that no one's buying anything.

"Everyone is just wandering," I say.

"It's too much," Walter answers. We pass by five aisles of throw pillows, every color under the rainbow and a few that were never meant to be, although it could be my disturbed vision getting going. I don't trust myself here.

We wander, amazed. There are seven aisles of cleaning supplies, two alone for dust removers (they must not know about the cotton cloths we sell—they're really all you need). Two rows of glass cleaners, and we're not talking all-natural, either. The labels begin to swim in front of me. I'm fairly sure some are in French. I swear there's one in Greek. I cannot pronounce the ingredients. Philip lightly takes my arm and pulls me along. I've become somewhat disabled, small child-like, the little sister tagalong. I could use a child harness—I wouldn't mind being led at all, especially if someone were to take me outside. I cannot see the outside world at all from in here.

We work our way back to the front of the store, passing by hardware, vacuums, baking supplies, toasters (there were twenty-six different models, which is impressive), air cleaners, sheets, comforters, feather beds, hypoallergenic feather beds (how is this possible?), soaps, creams, bath beads, towels, more bath beads, mirrors, shower curtains, picture frames, clocks (not one was ticking, which I don't think is a good sign), specialty foods wrapped in cellophane that you buy to give as gifts, Easter decorations, and finally, some small appliances I do not recognize but that look like they'd be painful if you got your fingers caught in them. I close my eyes and follow our group. You cannot hear footsteps despite the fact that the place isn't carpeted. The floor is that soft, I guess, or I'm losing audiovisual. It happens.

We stop at the checkout area, which is eerily quiet. No dinging, clanging cash registers here (and again, no one really buying anything, anyway). There are five rows with five registers per row. Ours is a relatively small town, so I think the store has overprepared at twenty-five cash registers. I think I see more over in the customer service area. Come to think of it, they do hum very softly. And smell a little funny.

"Nobody's buying," I whine, bumping slightly into Philip as we stop. Young people guard the registers, poised, bored, some of them looking very much like my old students from San Diego, but they can't be, can they? Could they be the ones I failed or wanted to fail? Is this where failed students end up? It doesn't seem fair despite their inability to write a thesis sentence, let alone a proper conclusion.

Granted I work in a hardware store, but it is so much more than this. So much more alive and real. And necessary. Though I'm biased and am not feeling especially well.

People just mill about. Juliet stops by us, wearing pink and green leggings beneath a white sweater and resembling a little fairy doll in the best sort of way. If she were a doll for sale here, someone might snap her up.

"There's nothing to buy," Juliet says, "even though there's everything to buy. Does that make any sense?"

"I know just what you mean," Walter tells her. He looks very sad.

"My head hurts," I say.

"My throat hurts," Juliet replies.

"The back of my throat hurts," Philip says, "but not the front."

"Mine hurts right in the center," Juliet says, "but not on the sides."

Eva sort of puffs herself up, rising to her entire six-point-whatever feet in height. It's as if she extends her arms all the way around each of us, though again, my imagination has gone bonkers. "Let's go home," she says, leading, gathering, offering hope or at least a quick escape. I follow them out. It feels as if we're all holding hands, but I don't think we are. I stay close. My head hurts right through the center, in one spot in front, and in one spot in back. I can't feel my throat at all. The world appears two shades darker, which may or may not reflect reality.

I know I can walk with a migraine coming on and pretend it isn't. I doubt I look much more stunned than usual.

Several people accompany us back to Walter's store, where the customers pick up hand baskets they hug to themselves. I know how they feel. Our baskets are old friends. Sure, they're metal, not actual woven baskets, but they're a cheerful red. Candy apple red (they don't smell like apples or anything, but wouldn't that be nice?). Our baskets, our whole store welcomes customers who happily collect items they really need. Paint, nails, Comet. How I loved the smell of Comet as a kid. Walter and Eva become busy, checking out, clanging away, chatting with friends, people who live here. There's laughter. Eva even hugs a few customers who look like they need it. Someone brings in a freshly baked pie in an oversized pan. Coffee brews. I take my headache out of here, dragging some unused cartons out the back door to the recycle bins. I'm not sure the clang of our register is what my head needs right now despite the alluring scents, which are becoming a little too strong for me. I even smell candy apples now.

I love to recycle. I inhale the fresh winter air and rip apart the corrugated boxes as if I were Supergirl (I wouldn't mind a cape right now; it is chilly) although it doesn't really take that much strength, I suspect. Still, in my semi-hallucinatory state, I feel caped and stronger than anyone else, a redheaded girl of wonder in a world that values recyclable goods and neatly stacked cardboard. It is a good world. I am the type of migraine sufferer who feels euphoric after the spots clear up and the headache arrives, so why fight it? I'm fairly sure I've gotten some of my best thinking done in this state of mind, though I do tend to forget the details later. My vision begins to normalize a little, and I feel like I could eat an entire pie. It occurs to me that I've never really liked lemon meringue, that I despised it as a child, the foamy meringue making me feel a bit sick. But I've changed. I'm SuperPatty. I can do anything, especially if I don't have to focus too hard.

I follow some faint hammering sounds coming from beyond the courtyard, out to where the shack used to be, before a storm did away with it, imagining that only I can hear these sounds. (Because I'm SuperPatty, stronger, better, maybe even taller with hair that doesn't tangle so much.) I find Will there and wrap my cape around my shoulders. He's working on the building, no longer a shack but a sturdy structure, the size of a guesthouse maybe. An ADU, though I don't know what that stands for despite my superior mind at the moment. I could imagine living in it, or working in it, or eating pie in it. It wouldn't be so bad.

"Are you going to live here?" I ask him.

"No, it's not for me," Will says.

"But you're building it," I say.

"I designed it," Will says.

"Architect," I say under my breath, the way some old people used to say "Communist." Will gives me a funny look. I'm probably slurring my words in my superstate. Migraines giveth but also taketh a lot away.

"But you don't live anywhere," I say. "Do you?" It's not just a question. It's a superpowerful inquisition.

"I guess," he says.

"But then again everyone lives somewhere, it's the very definition of living," I say. "Unless you're dead."

He just looks at me funny. I don't blame him. I suspect he can't see the cape, let alone the migraine.

"Thank you for finding Troy," I say.

"No, no," he says, shaking off my thanks.

"Yes, yes," I tell him. "Are we not even allowed to thank you?" I ask, mixing up my superhero slogans. Although I think the Lone Ranger predates superheroes, which is unfair to him. I don't think you can tease Will, though. That much I can sense, what with my super powerful intuition.

"No, you're not allowed to thank me," he says.

"Oh my, you are the Lone Ranger," I tell him. I don't tell him I'm Supergirl. As if it weren't obvious anyhow. I don't think I've ever really spoken to him before. I suddenly feel bad for him. He's broken down; something about him has failed and failed badly. His completed graduate degree aside (yes of course it matters to me), he seems so at a loss. Even worse off than you, Patty, because you have a home and a job and a boy, and sometimes an omniscient sense of power and accomplishment.

"So, you designed it," I say. I get it now that I'm my best me, my whole me, sharp pains in my head notwithstanding. "You gave us Proggleland. Why?" The need for at least three details (per paragraph) overtakes me.

"Student debt," he says succinctly.

"Oh," I say. Student debt? Are those two words enough? It certainly explains it all but seems pathetic anyhow. Everyone's got student debt these days. Well, nearly everyone: the advantage of a state college education was that even I could afford it. I, Superpatty or regular Patty, take me or leave me, do not have outstanding student loans. I am a rarity in so many ways.

"I built the park they wanted, where they wanted." I've never met anyone I'd describe as less of an amusement park kind of guy. He's so pale he could have red hair. He looks as if he hasn't enjoyed himself on a roller-coaster or eaten a hot dog in some time, maybe never.

"Fond of eerie dusty paths leading to dilapidated buildings?" I ask. I have never used the word dilapidated in a sentence before. Dilapidated, Patty. Super use of an adjective.

"I followed the parameters," Will says quietly. "I didn't say anything."

"What?" A laugh escapes me, which isn't nice, of course. I thought superheroes had better manners. I toss my hair back onto my cape.

"Proggleland," he says. "I set it right on top of a piece of land where people were taken from their homes, held hostage for no reason. People died there."

"Jeez," I say. I can't think of what else to say that wouldn't just be rubbing Will's life in his face.

The happiest place on Earth shoots through my supermind.

"So now what, you refuse any human kindness and live in the street?"

"Basically," he says.

"Did you at least pay off your loans?"

"Yeah," he admits.

I watch him hammer for a minute. I don't think the building really needs any more nails. I know busy work when I see it.

"And you're the only one to have ever done something bad?" I say.

"I don't think that matters," he answers.

"Perhaps," I say majestically. He's not the only one who's done something bad, I happen to know, but I don't feel the need to get into it.

"This structure seems just right," I say, patting the store/shack/house/additional something or other, trying to get him to stop hitting nails, which he seems to do compulsively, a little like Troy biting his hands, it occurs to me. I really need Will to stop, though.

We stare at one another, he in faded clothes, me in my cape. I examine the building—a strong albeit smallish structure that fits in well with Walter's store, fits in well with the architecture, the community, our town. A building meant to hold something, nuts, bolts, guilt, maybe hopes and dreams. He surrenders his hammer to me and walks away—he never stood a chance against my powers. We have reached an understanding, even though once again, I don't really know what's going on. I walk back to the store, becoming more and more normal with each step, losing my superpowers. I even trip. I had hoped it would all last longer.

* * *

After work I return to Larissa's to get my boy. I greet Larissa at the door carefully but not too carefully, the way we've been treating her since Cecil's mother took him away. It is an entirely different world for Larissa without Cecil, quiet, easy, but not in a way she would have hoped for. Still, my boy is here. My head can throb all it wants—my boy is here.

"Hi, Troy," I say, giving him a hug, kissing him on the top of his head, away from the tugged raw patch of scalp that is healing. He smiles goofily when I do. I'm probably smiling goofily myself, but then parenthood requires absolutely no vanity.

Troy smiles. He is seated before a Play-Doh cookie cutter that I'm fairly sure is shaped like the state of Texas. He raises his hurt hand for me to pat, which I do, gently.

"Hi, Patty," Dorothy says, emphasizing the proper greeting. Ella and Gretel wave Play-Doh encrusted hands. Troy's are completely clean, which I respect him for, although I hope he didn't catch Play-Doh phobia from me.

"Nice shapes," I tell him. He has seven Play-Doh Texases in front of him. I try not to think that this means anything at all.

"Oh," Troy says, not exactly a subject-verb construction, but we are so grading on the curve here. Exclamations have a value all their own. Dorothy nods approvingly. Troy is happy and safe if not conversationally oriented. His right hand is clean if a little red from need and history. That's my boy.

I find Larissa in the kitchen, where she has just baked cookies the shapes of several states of the Union, although I'm never entirely sure what some of the little ones on the Eastern Seaboard are. She hands me a small burnt one, as we agree that our authoritarian roles require us to eat the crispiest cookies, thank goodness. I hold it up and give it a look.

"Rhode Island," she answers, "blackened."

"Crispy," I say, and eat it.

"I think crispy is a euphemism when we're talking about burnt cookies," she says.

"I don't have a problem with euphemisms or burnt cookies."

"Good," she says. "I've had to disconnect the fire alarm twice."

"I'll keep your secrets if you keep mine," I say.

Larissa looks toward Cecil's abandoned chair, which is all scratched up from fingernails. Cecil's idea of creativity, or maybe just nerves. None of the other children wants to sit in it.

"How's it going?" I ask, hidden agenda language for how is she feeling about losing Cecil.

"Hmm," Larissa says. She eats a cookie (isn't that Massachusetts?), and I grab an Oklahoma (in my mind someone sings: *You're doing fine, Oklahoma, Oklahoma, OK*—but who?). Larissa picks up a laundry basket and leads me to the spare room. My music stops abruptly.

"You've redecorated," I say, then wonder if I've said too much. It's the kind of day where words pop out of my mouth. I may even have been singing out loud.

The room, former basal chart room, more recently Cecil's makeshift bedroom, is now lined with photographs of children, some in black-and-white shots, some in color. It looks a little like a lineup of missing children's photos, I can't help but think. Could they be stolen, missing children, Patty? All the children smile, but there's something wrong in their expressions, and I'm frightened by them all together like this. They begin to swirl a little around my already challenged vision. (Should you really be eating sugar, Patty?) The pictures seem to come toward me, accusingly. I turn to Larissa in my discomfort. She's perfectly at home here.

"They're from different countries," she says. "For adoption," she says quietly.

"Oh," I say, relieved, sort of. They're not missing. They're not missing at all. They're extra children. In abundance.

"How would you choose?" I ask softly, partly to myself. How would you choose, Patty, or would you leave it up to fate, impulse, a late-night whim in a panic, an irrational, possibly unreasonable if not immoral act, and your head felt just fine that day.

"I don't know," Larissa says.

"Do you get to pick?" I ask.

"No," Larissa says, "there's a lot of applying to do, a lot of evaluation, a lot of judging. We're not all as perfect on paper as we seem in person," she says.

"Or vice versa," I suggest. I'm a little better on paper, I think, depending on what you've read, whether the photos were in color, and who has printed up the document, of course.

"Maybe it works both ways."

"How does Philip feel?" I ask.

"Philip works on his computer," she says. "He downloads the pictures for me, the forms, but that's just a starting point. We would have to admit to a lot after the starting point. Phillip helps people solve their information needs. He helps people find their place. It's his way of changing the world."

"One piece of paper at a time," I say.

"What he's doing is important," she says proudly. "It's just hard to express on an adoption form."

I look at the children. "They'd be lucky to have him and you," I say, turning my head from child to child. "We all are. You're the best mother of any of us. No contest."

"It feels like a contest, though," she adds.

We examine the faces. I wonder if someone touches up the photos. Can every unwanted child really be this attractive? I think of Cecil (and I think of him as unwanted, I really do, even though his mother has taken him home). I can see his less-than-attractive features, his giddiness, his tics and all-around oddness. Who would put his photo on their wall? He's not the Hall of Fame of Unwanted Children type, let alone wanted.

"It's so complicated," Larissa says.

"Red tape?" (Not everyone comes by a child as easily as you, Patty.)

"Tape of every color, every language, every conceivable detail. It may even be too much for Philip." Larissa leads me from the room. It is not a happy place, despite the border of smiling faces. I can hear them screaming beneath their smiles. I think Larissa hears it, too, and I don't think she even gets migraines.

We return to the living room, where the smell of Play-Doh begins to bother me, so I bring a burnt crisp to my nose and inhale deeply. I think it's Baja. Smells bother me when I'm like this, and even the burnt sugar seems less soothing than usual. The screaming has dulled in my ears, but I feel as if I still hear it, then recognize it as something else. I look toward the front of the house.

Jake and Philip stand by the front door—Jake takes up much of the frame in a way that leaves no room for doubt and is utterly reassuring and heart-warming, for a moment at least. There's no one I'd rather have at my doorway, or someone else's. They turn toward the sound too, as do the kids, who have become quiet. Larissa steps toward it. It's the screaming of sirens.

"Fire trucks?" Dorothy suggests.

"No," Ella says. "Those go whew, whew, whew."

"Police cars go roar-roar-roar," Gretel says.

This is neither.

"Ambulance," Larissa says. "Oh, God." She looks at Philip. It's not that small a town; it's not as if we know everyone. But something pulls at Larissa, some intuition. Her face leads us outside—there's nothing we could say to stop her, her glance insists. We get in the van so well-equipped with just the right number of seats. (There are always enough car seats in Larissa's van, like magic.) Philip drives. I'm in the way back with Troy. Jake follows behind in his pink car, although we have Dorothy in our center row with Ella and Gretel. We follow the siren; I don't know why, but to question it seems wrong, although it crosses my mind that there's some issue with legality, and not for the first time. I don't think you're supposed to follow an ambulance, although I don't particularly think it's one of my bigger crimes. The ambulance whines pitifully, then howls. It seems only right to either follow it or get as far away as possible, and though I know which I'd prefer, there's an importance to this I can't deny. Larissa moans in the front seat, and Gretel begins to whimper. I look at Troy. I don't know what to tell him. He taps his hand repeatedly against his growing-back hair spot on his head.

A few lost sparkles pass by my eyes.

"How can you catch it?" Larissa asks Philip.

"Shortcuts," Philip says. He drives carefully, turning this way and that. Not like a roller coaster ride, more like a carefully developed plan. Maybe they've done some practice escape routes for emergencies. Maybe that's not a bad idea, Patty.

The ambulance takes us over the river.

"Don't they have their own ambulances in town?" I ask.

"No," Philip says. "We have them all in the valley."

"Why?" I ask, but I assume the answer is too long or too dull to tell a carful of people following a siren to what couldn't possibly be a happy ending. I turn around and watch Jake drive, a serious look on his face. He follows the correct car lengths behind us. I would wave, but it doesn't seem appropriate, and I know he wouldn't take his hands off the wheel to wave back. I love this about him now. I love to watch him take care. It's all so new to me.

We follow the siren's wail to a beautiful house, large and architecturally just-so in a lifestyle magazine kind of way. Windows stretch four times my height, four times Jake's height, for that matter. You could never reach all the way up to clean these windows, but then you would have someone else to do that, Patty. You'd pay them lavishly. The driveway sparkles as if someone just polished it (you would have someone to do that, too). Maybe it's just my eyes.

The ambulance people have run in through a side gate made of black metal molded into an intricate peacock shape. Jake, somehow in front of us now, follows them in. Larissa's out of the car and with him before I think we've come to a full stop, but I don't mention it. Philip corrals the rest of us beside the van at first, but then it's as if our group is magnetized and we cannot do anything but follow the others in. We all are drawn forward, perhaps from the ring of the siren that echoes in our heads, despite that it's been turned off. I suspect I'll be hearing it for some time.

"Where are we?" I ask, although I feel I should know. Perhaps if my head were clearer rather than mostly numb, I would know. But I haven't been here, and I realize I don't want to be here for any reason, especially whatever reason I'm about to discover. I feel a little nauseous and am fairly sure I can hear the words before he says them.

"Cecil's house," Philip says.

"It's Cecil's house," Ella repeats sharply, clearly having been here before, implying I'm a little bit stupid not to have known or at least to have guessed. Liv's home. Who couldn't have guessed?

We hover by the backyard, where there's a swimming pool of dark blue water and a small waterfall that almost mystically attracts us with its wind-chime-like dribbling sound. Maybe there's a wind chime. There are things I should notice, my sore head tells me, details, background, characters. The setting: It is too cold to swim—the wind ripples the navy blue water. There is no fence around the pool (and it looks as if they can afford one). The clues are all here. The fluffy white towel lying on the ground. Beside it, the long, stretched-out rubber band the boy uses for some purpose only he can understand. It's not a happy trail that leads us here.

The ambulance workers surround someone laid out, dripping; Jake kneels on the ground with them. Larissa stands back, one hand on Gretel, one hand on Ella, although I'm not sure all of a sudden which girl is which. Liv, Cecil's mother, holds a cellphone to her ear, although I don't see her talking to anyone. But I can't be sure. She doesn't look wet, I notice, a detail, just a detail, but still. If someone were to ask me later. She looks dry, pressed, and ironed.

"It's Cecil," Dorothy says, a finality in her voice that I hate to hear from a four-year-old.

We all huddle toward Larissa, Liv standing somewhat apart. Philip leads the children away quickly, into the house with a giant swoop of his arms, although I hate to feel the tug as Troy lets go of me and leaves my side. I should go in with them, but I have to watch, even though I can't really see what they're doing. But I know what they're doing. We all know what they're doing.

"He's drowned, hasn't he?" Liv asks the ambulance workers, although it's not much of a question.

"He can't swim?" I ask.

"He forgets," Liv says. "He doesn't act right."

"It's winter," I say. A detail.

"It's heated," she says. She's wearing a neat heavy down vest and Uggs. Dry ones.

Larissa looks over to us. She looks as if she may bite Liv.

"You didn't jump in?" I ask, stating the obvious but using a question mark anyway, as if I could be wrong, as if I wouldn't mind being wrong. Or maybe it's just the English major in me using punctuation correctly. It's utterly beside the point.

"I'm not a good swimmer," Liv says, and Larissa's eyes and mouth widen. She has lost her sound, though.

I hear Jake calling Cecil's name, not angrily, but with authority, force, a quiet insistence, as if it's absolutely the correct word to say and should be enough. Philip returns and drags Larissa inside, her mouth still open but not working in any way at all. I watch as Jake helps the men lift Cecil onto a stretcher, his body not as limp as I expect him to be. I've never seen a dead body before and am shocked to be seeing one now. It's not the day I'd thought it would be at all. A dead child. Even dead, Cecil seems as if he is flailing, one leg going the wrong way, his mouth open oddly, pathetically. I find myself moving along the glass windows as they carry him, shielding those inside from seeing the body, although it's that tinted glass and I can't really see if anyone's watching. I can't see the small eyes, the small O shapes on their faces. The live children's faces. I hope to God they're watching TV instead, sitting too close with the sound up far too loud.

The men carry the dead body past the fancy gate, and Cecil's swimsuit catches on the peacock form, so they have to tug a little, which makes me cringe. They move toward the ambulance, which now seems to be humming. I hadn't noticed before, but it must have been humming this whole time, waiting, revving. I look at Liv, who acts a little insulted, taken off guard, as if she hadn't planned for a party of people by the pool at all. This wasn't how she saw her day going, either, her angry look tells me. I wonder if she has a headache. She looks at her phone and I can see her begin to press buttons. It's a fancy phone. I should have one for emergencies, although I still think they emit rays, and it's not as if Liv's having a phone has prevented this emergency, although perhaps that's asking too much of personal electronics. The ambulance buzzes softly into the distance, taking Cecil's life with it. Liv continues pushing buttons frantically, as if that does anything.

I grab Liv's phone from her, and she looks relieved, but when I throw it into the pool I see her nearly jump in after it. She stops herself. She does not look at me but watches the phone sink. I'm awash with disgust and nausea, and I'm not unhappy to vomit on her Uggs. It may be the best I've felt all day, under the circumstances.

"Ugg," I say. I do not mean it as any sort of compliment, let alone apology.

When I walk out to the driveway, I find Jake standing still, watching where the ambulance must have gone. (It's a circular driveway, a spacious perfect O dotted with purple flowers and fruit trees with petite oranges on them, as if that's helped anyone here). We look at each other. I can't think of anything to say. Jake sits down on a rock and cries, as if he'd just fallen off of something and hurt himself badly, as if part of his body just broke, an entirely involuntary crying that is altogether required by circumstances, both past and present. I find I can't cry. I didn't really even like Cecil, if you can not like a child, which I think is possible. He was a terrible example of child, I want to tell Jake, but this is awful of me. And of course, Jake must know it, too. Jake who saved the awful child from drowning once (once that you know of, Patty). Jake who was too late this time.

"We were all too late," I say, and then I'm overcome, too, gasping for air as my cries begin to double me over, until Jake pulls me close to him on the warm rock. I think it's synthetic. A fake rock. We're crying as the dead child rolls off in the buzzing ambulance, back to the valley, back where he belonged. Jake stops crying and puts a hand on each of my shoulders, not shaking me but pressing, making me stop, as he says, "the kids." We take deep breaths. We silently count to ten. Then to twenty. We go back inside to get our children, try to figure out what we will say, how we will surmount it, how we will keep them out of therapy for years, how we will love them enough and keep them safe from too-blue pools of water, from darkened amusement parks, mysterious structures with harmful intentions. From rivers, drownings, disasters, natural and manmade, although once again I remember the English department's handbook against the term "manmade," which suggested "developed" or "technologically built," as if no one were responsible at all.

I just want to hug my boy, and I wouldn't mind at all if he were to hug me back for a long while.

Once inside, I do not know how we'll get across the room we find ourselves in—this room in Cecil's house, the dead boy's house, clearly what designers mean by a great room, with one of those giant-screen TVs that seems a little distorted and has served no one well. The kids watch a cartoon where the girls are drawn with sharp features that make them look unnerving and dangerous, but wise beyond their years. I suspect Larissa doesn't let them watch such shows under normal circumstances, but maybe they're watching the sheer size of the screen as much as the show itself, if they're watching anything at all and are not just stunned by the death of a child. The death of a child they knew, a child they did not love.

Except for Larissa, who did. She's the only one who could have. Larissa didn't care that Cecil was disturbed and disturbing, and becoming more so with each day. He was real and alive, he was in need, and he was hers, even if only part of the time. She and Philip hold hands, sitting on a hearth that appears to have been made of pearl. Larissa cries silently. She has not located her sound, or maybe the giant TV drowns her out.

I reach for Troy, who sucks his hand and stares at nothing at all. His volume is on mute, too.

We return to the van, the warmth of it making me exhale for what feels like the first time in an hour, making me feel that I'd forgotten what warmth felt like and had lost all hope of ever feeling it again. One or more of us are crying. Troy sucks his hand, spreading the little sucking gestures around, going from bandaged knuckle to knuckle, then palm, then back, his face unexpressive. Maybe he's not registering Cecil's drowning, maybe he's troubled by the Japanese cartoon (I don't think they were speaking English, come to think of it), the sudden quiet, the coldly sparse house. One of the girls in the middle seats cries softly. (I suspect Gretel and/or Dorothy, as Ella never hid her animosity for Cecil.) Maybe it is Ella, as she's lost her foil, and what good is even the best novel's heroine without a foil, I think, my mind reeling through fictions I have known. Because they're easier to analyze than actual life, Patty.

Focus on what you know, despite that you can't focus at all, and hold onto your boy. A character who loses his or her foil signals something, the end of an era, maybe, or at least the end of a chapter. A denouement, a plot point. That you have made your way through a significant portion of the story. There's no turning around, no going back, now. You're almost there. Which can be a scary thought when you don't know where things are going at all.

Larissa slips in a CD I've seen in her car before of women chanting, which might have struck me as annoying in a previous life. Now I find it lulling, not interfering with my thoughts in the slightest, not that I'd mind all that much if it did. It almost settles my stomach.

Philip stops the van at one of those drive-thru doughnut shops—the kind with a giant doughnut on top, brown and faded by the sun. He orders a dozen mixed. I turn behind me and see that Jake has followed us in his car right into the drive-thru, then stops to order something as well. The men pick up their orders with us listening to the chanting (are the words in Old English, and are they even words?) and we continue on our sweet but funereal caravan home. We sit in the warm van filled with baked goods and the ever-trying-to-be-cheerful pink donut box, riding home, eating chocolate crullers, bear claws, French twists. Glazed, plain, apple cruller. I do not know which one was Cecil's favorite, which makes my eyes burn with tears. Or would Cecil have just chewed on the box? Troy, perfect Troy, has picked a donut with little colorful sprinkles that fall all over his clothes and the car, but I don't say anything. I watch instead as Dorothy licks the chocolate off a donut, then puts the plain part in a napkin and tucks it in her sweater. Maybe she'll give it to her father, to Jake. Maybe he'll accept it as precious because even without the frosting, the intention is good and pure. Maybe Dorothy even has Jake's best interests at heart. (Chocolate frosting isn't all that good for you, and it probably isn't real chocolate anyway.) We will go home and make real food for our children, who have been tempted but not filled by their sweets and sit waiting, sticky in their sprinkles and confusion. Troy's sprinkles have gotten into his hair and eyelashes, and when he blinks at me they go flying, which makes us both giggle. I put both of my arms around him, picking the sprinkles out of his hair with my teeth, which makes us both giggle even more. The warm chanting women do not seem to mind, and the sprinkles are melt-in-my-mouth sweet. I crave them; I can't get enough of them. I try to savor each one because these are the things you need to do each day, each moment you can, each day you can, if you can only remember to.

Chapter 13

Purple Mountain's Majesty (Redux)

"Just a little off the sides and top," Dorothy says.

"Oh," replies Troy a little fearfully.

"Now, now," says Larissa, who hovers over Troy with scissors that look incapable of cutting so much as a sheet of paper, what with the ducky beak coverings on each blade's end.

"A little haircut to take us toward springtime," she says, as if she goes through a winter like this one every year. As if our lives are even the slightest bit normal. I nod at Larissa: I want us to have some normalcy, too. She blinks the sadness from her eyes.

Larissa has set up a play barber shop (or perhaps beauty salon, or stylist, depending on your income tax level). Troy sits on a tall stool beneath a sheet, awaiting his turn. His ripped-out patch of hair still grows in slowly, but a little trim, Larissa insists, will help him feel better about it. We have examined texts that say so. Right next to the grief books with their overwhelmingly vivid covers that show people embracing or heads together, or people extending meaningless gifts. One just shows two empty hands and is so heartbreaking that I have covered it in brown-paper-bag wrapping. That book is the worst sort of gift imaginable, worse than no gift at all.

I sit on a nearby stool, awaiting my turn. I'm nothing but split ends on a good day. After barbershop, we will play paint store and select colors to repaint the dining chairs, especially Cecil's, which no one will sit in anymore. See chapter three of the brown-bag-wrapped tome for more details on why we repaint, donate, read hopeless self-help books, and both try to remember and try to forget.

Juliet, clearly not on duty at the diner, sits just inside the door at a table, wearing fuchsia and green leggings that make me feel a bit nauseated. She reads to Gretel and Ella from an Easter Bunny-type nursery rhyme book as the girls fingerpaint. Jake is at work. Philip wanders from room to room, lost, lingering here and there, claiming he's waiting for his computer to do something. Away from his computer, he is always slightly panicky.

"Just a few snips," Larissa says, as she begins on Troy. It's Troy's first hair cut that I know of, and maybe that's what's making me so teary eyed. I'm overwhelmed with emotion, but I couldn't explain why and am not in the mood for self-help anyway. My eyes feel as if they're filling up with something that isn't entirely good news.

"Your mom's having sympathy pains," Larissa says of me.

"Parents get sentimental," Dorothy tells Troy. She hands me a snippet of his hair, and I sob a few times.

"I don't know what's wrong with me," I say, shaking my head till I feel clearer. "I guess I just love this hair!" I try to make light of it and kiss the hair repeatedly.

Dorothy giggles and nudges Troy lightly under his cape-like sheet that holds the trimmings, a few blonde curls. I make what I hope is a funny face, and Troy giggles as well. He picks up a curl and chews on it a little nervously.

"Patty's next!" Larissa says, trying to remove the cloak from Troy. When he resists, she lets him take it. As Dorothy applauds, Troy takes a little bow in his cape. Then he explores the still jagged hair spot with his hand, patting at it repeatedly, a hypnotized look coming over his face that I've seen before but have not yet looked up in a parenting book index. I don't want details, psychological terms. He's not hurting anyone.

I walk over to the taller stool but stop. We all hear something, feel it, experience it at the same time. A lengthy magnificent jolt. I look at Troy, who has his mouth open in that all-alert way. We all have our mouths open. My heart is beating like mad. Philip runs back out from his computer room.

"Earthquake," Larissa says.

"Sonic boom," I say.

"Tree fell on the house!" Philip cries.

"Wow," Dorothy says.

Larissa herds us all just inside the kitchen.

"Should we get under a doorway?" Juliet asks, closing the Easter books, preparing for something, although I'm not sure disaster preparedness requires you to close your books or that this is a disaster. Then the lights go out.

"Power out," I say.

Larissa grabs the kids. "Earthquake." She herds them under the kitchen archway, although I don't think it's all that structurally sound. It's a nice arch, though.

"Earthquakes roll," I say. I'm from California, I must know something.

"Roll or shake," Philip says, a helpful correction. He doesn't mean anything by it, so I nod. "That was a bang."

"Pow," Ella says. Ella watches too much TV.

Philip runs out of the house.

"You're supposed to stay inside," Larissa says.

"Tree," Philip says. "It sounded like a tree."

"We don't have big trees," Larissa says to me.

"Sonic boom," I say. "We had them in San Diego." And Los Angeles. The noise of my childhood, an unexplained boom you'd hear from time to time that would make you stop suddenly, look around, then go on with what you were doing. Were they planes going overhead too quickly? Stealth bombers testing something over our fair skies? Incidences that if we knew what to actually call them, we'd be terrified? Something with no name at all?

"I don't think so," Larissa says. She's grabbing the kids. Gretel and Ella raise their water painted hands straight in the air, as if they're under arrest.

Larissa's waiting, and I realize what she's waiting for, because we all live here, helplessly anticipating that day, that final quake. She moves the kids quickly to the front doorway, which is supposed to be the best place to be (as long as you're away from power lines, falling trees, and your house was built before a certain year when they stopped making strong doorways. They keep changing this date—whoever they are—so that basically, we don't know where to stand anymore). There's no real place to be, except outside of California. This is earthquake country, and there may well be a sizable fault right under us. There was one under me in San Diego (and Los Angeles). They're everywhere. They make us the nervous wrecks that we are or at least add further anxiety to those of us with natural tendencies.

"This isn't it," I say.

"This is it," she says.

"I'm turning on the TV," Juliet says. "Oh, no power."

Philip comes running back in. "Nothing hit the house," he says. Larissa gives him an I-told-you-so glance. "But not an earthquake."

"We have an emergency radio," Larissa says, "under the sink with the first aid kit and extra water and plastic bags, and the water purification tablets."

"Is this an emergency?" Philip asks.

"I think it was just a big noise," I say. Troy giggles. He's not biting his hand, I note to myself. How bad a day could it be?

"Just a noise and a shake," Juliet says with a hip wiggle, trying to encourage the kids. Gretel and Ella push one another out of the way to come join her. Some days, competition is everything, even today.

"Oh!" Troy says, excitedly. Is it his first earthquake? Maybe. I don't remember a big one in San Diego, but there were frequent minor ones. Would he have felt them outside, chained to a doghouse? You may feel them less outside (chained by a cord that tended to sway anyhow, no doubt—yuck, sickening, Patty). Could he have been safer outside than in? Don't think about it, Patty.

We remain inside the house, door open, when we hear the next sound. It's another boom, less boomy though. More like the most thorough thud imaginable. It doesn't jolt so much as vibrate. It resonates, to use a word from our Rhetoric and Writing course, where they tried to teach us to be teachers. Ask your students to make their words resonate. This sound, though, resonates unlike any freshman I've encountered. It may not be the right verb at all.

"Earthquake," Larissa says again even more nervously.

"Big thud," I reply. "No shaking or rolling. It does not qualify."

"Earth something," Juliet says. "Anyhow." We stay by the door, but Philip closes it. I like the idea of this, too.

"The big one," Larissa whispers in my ear. A picture falls from the wall in the living room with a crash, although I don't think it had a glass panel in it. This is a fairly childproofed place—I don't think there's much glass at all. It's a good place to be in an earthquake, come to think of it.

"So, are you telling me these are just big thuds?" I ask. "Is this a thing?" I'm getting a little impatient. It doesn't feel like an earthquake, but we are poised, waiting for something more, something scientists tell us most homes are not prepared for. And we're all becoming a little irritable, waiting, wondering, counting the seconds till the one we've been waiting for hits or not. I'm beginning to feel a little disappointed, and I'm not the only one.

"Maybe we should get in the van," I suggest. I find I want to be there.

"The van," Larissa says. "Yes."

"Just stay put," Philip yells, bringing over the transistor radio every family is supposed to have. Larissa's is in a giant zippered baggie along with about a five-year supply of extra batteries. I admire her for this. I'd gladly trust any child of mine with her. I've never seen such a large baggie.

The radio is bright yellow, boxy, and tough-looking, with a flashlight attachment. Troy is safe because of this radio, I tell myself. You know how untrue that is, Patty. The radio will not keep you safe. It still isn't a bad idea to have one, although I don't know why my mind is so argumentative today.

"Yellow," Ella says, showing off.

"Oh," Troy comments. See, he likes it, too.

"Like a canary," Juliet tells him.

"Canaries are noisy," Dorothy informs us. I don't know if she's read it in a book or if it's a personal observation. I don't think I've ever seen a real canary. I've never really understood the appeal of having noisy little birds in your home.

It occurs to me: Didn't someone used to use canaries to test for dangerous smells? Uninhabitable areas? Disaster zones?

"Do you smell something?" I ask everyone. Am I always asking this question?

"I smell something," Larissa says. "Is the kitchen okay? Um, anything burning?"

Philip looks back in toward the kitchen. "It's fine." It's a little messy, but not too bad. I mean this is a day care location. The kitchen's entirely visible from the front door. We can all see perfectly well—it's the smelling that's troubling us.

"I think you can get out of the doorway," Philip says. "There's nothing on the radio."

Larissa raises her arms in the air. "Wait." We wait. We are quiet. Juliet and I make little sniffing sounds and movements with our noses, still in search of the proper metaphors and similes for the scent of whatever's going on around here.

"It smells artificial," I say. "Manmade," I say on purpose, in defiance of the English department guidelines because nothing feels quite real today.

"It smells like the amusement park," Dorothy says softly, and she's right.

"Let's get in the van," Larissa says. She lowers her voice. "The doorway isn't working," she whispers to me.

Philip nods at her, and we get ready to go for a ride. We exit the premises, as an emergency manual might say, in case of an emergency.

* * *

In the car, Larissa tries to call Jake on her cellphone but can't get through to him at the library or on his cellphone.

"Why would his cellphone be down?" she asks.

"Can a cellphone be down?" I wonder.

"It's out of order," Dorothy says knowledgeably albeit incorrectly.

"Bathrooms are out of order," Juliet tells her, and they giggle. Troy looks confused. I don't take him into a lot of public bathrooms, as I find something semantically incorrect about taking him in the ladies' room. And I can't even picture the day when I'll let Troy go into the men's room alone. Something horror-movie terrible happened to a boy in the men's room at the beach in San Diego when I lived there, something that I can see in my mind over and over again. The ladies' room wins by far.

We begin driving around, looking for signs of what may have happened here in our current hometown, searching for whatever we couldn't see. Signs of what we fear most. I'm not sure if you're supposed to be driving around in a disaster or of course if this even is one. But we see plenty of other people out driving in their cars. It's a good day for a ride, if you take away the sonic thuds or what-have-yous, but at least these have given us a reason to go out, to forget the laundry and the dishes in the sink, chairs that need painting, children we have lost. Forget about our real life and search for other dangers, real or imagined.

We go over the river. I see the Saturday bustling of primary color vans, just like the ones in the presentation about Santa Vallejo. They are much nicer than Larissa's somewhat commercial van, brighter, newer, but they seem just as directionless and confused.

We wave at children in other cars. It's just an outing, that's all. An outing that follows an odd, too-loud thud. Something hit us, but what?

Then I recognize our route, and I start to feel queasy. I want the car to turn around, but I'm in the way-back seat. With Troy.

"Um," I suggest, hoping someone will read my mind, make a sudden turn, take us out of here.

"It's okay," Juliet says, "everyone's going." I hear my mother's voice, asking me, "If everyone were jumping off a bridge, would you do it, too?" Not that we've seen anyone jumping off the bridge, thank goodness.

"We'll just drive by," Philip says. "Okay?"

I look at Troy and envy him for not having a sense of direction. He does not know where he's headed. He does not realize what lies in front of the line of cheery vans. He's on his way back to Proggleland, but then aren't we all. Except that the destination isn't what it once was, not a place of excited trepidation. Not for us. Never again for us.

Shades of trepidation remain, of course.

Our van stops. Other vans stop. Our mouths open, our doors open.

Dust rises. When it settles, it will reveal even more clearly what we see now, maybe the result of the first thud, maybe the conclusion of the second. Proggleland's purple mountain shape has been given a giant push and leans significantly and precariously to the right. A giant purple warning of sorts. Not that any of us needed one.

Philip laughs. The rest of us make very little noise.

"It's leaning," Dorothy says.

"It's like a cake that got jostled in the oven," Juliet says, waitress-like, or maybe as if it were a good thing. It may be.

Dorothy holds her nose. "It doesn't smell like cake."

"That's the smell," Larissa says.

Troy massages the sore spot on his head in a way that makes me think of patting one's head while rubbing one's stomach. It makes me a little dizzy—rubbing my stomach might help a little. Or maybe it's the leaning, oddly smelling mountain that's making me feel queasy.

"You have to admit," Philip says, "it adds a little something."

"The leaning tower of Proggleland," Larissa says.

"People will come for miles," her husband responds.

I shake my head. "I hope not."

We listen to the crowd around us. Murmurs of earthquake, landslide, act of god, just plain dumb luck.

Then we move together as a crowd, as if something's luring us, as if history calls our names, as if it won't let us forget. We continue down a familiar path to see what history has preserved for us or what Mother Nature may have reduced to ashes.

And there are the barracks, the once-upon-a-time horse stalls, still standing. Impenetrable, unforgiving. Groaning slightly on a cold day. Nightmares that just won't go away. Dust settles around the place, but it's all still here, staring us down.

"You'd think the old boards would just fall down," Philip says. It's all still standing, yet it looks uninhabitable, not all that different than it did before.

"How could the new structure have been knocked off its foundation, or whatever, and the barracks still stand?" I ask.

"It's Disasterland," Larissa says. "It's not going away."

Troy claps his hands as if a magic trick has been performed, one with good intentions.

Off in the not-too-far distance, we can see the purple mountain amusement area, leaning as if ready to keel over and die, not that you'd ever confuse it with a living thing. Over here, the abandoned shacks moan slightly as if they've been harmed by whatever it was we couldn't see, as if they can't put that harm into words, either.

Will appears and looks at the deserted squeaking ghost land, then to the inauthentic mountain not-so-fun land. He turns his head to lean with the structure. Not his proudest moment.

"It was built to rock a little in an earthquake, but it was supposed to right itself," he says.

"How could someone have built an amusement park or whatever this place is on a site once used for—imprisoning people?" I ask.

Will says nothing.

"Were people tortured here?" I ask. I hear roller-coaster type screaming all around me. It may be the wind, but maybe not.

Philip holds the yellow transistor radio to his ear. We hear murmuring from it, a low frequency. I like the soft sounds of muffled radio. I always have. If your hearing weren't so acute, you might take it for the sounds of a ballgame, if you were lucky and didn't hear every little pin drop, even the imaginary ones.

At least the awful Proggleland music has stopped.

"They're saying not an earthquake," Philip says, ear to radio. "They're saying it's an earth jolt."

"There's no such thing," Larissa says. "Can they just make this up?"

"If they don't have the science, then yes, they can just make it up," Philip says.

"I don't buy it," I say.

"It's NPR," Philip says, and I see his frustration. If they're wrong, who's left to believe?

"What's the difference between an earthquake and an earth jolt?" I ask, although it sounds like the opening of a joke. I wonder if earth jolt is one word or will become one word in a future edition of Webster's, where this event might be referenced. *An earthjolt in Northern California in the beginning of the century caused a local amusement park to lean to one side, although onlookers found it somewhat hypnotic in effect. The earthjolt remains a mystery, though common usage now allows one word.* The thought of it makes me want to get out a red pen and separate the words earth and jolt. I can't help it.

"It sounds less scary," Juliet says. "Earth jolt!" she says, with a friendly voice, moving her hips in a dance style once known as the twist.

"Earth jolt, earth jolt," Ella repeats.

"What's next, earth shake?" I ask. I find it redundant to have so many terms. Earthquake, earth jolt. Something needs revising.

"Earth shake!" Gretel echoes. "Like milk shake!"

"Oh!" my boy says. He does love a milk shake. See, milk shake is two words.

"Earthquake has become such a frightening term," Juliet says.

"You just have to whisper it," Larissa says, "and people get nervous. I know I do."

"They're saying it's some kind of movement, but not enough to measure on the Richter scale. But something," Philip translates from the radio murmurings.

"Clearly," I say, nodding toward the structure.

"Where were you in the big earth jolt?" Larissa asks me facetiously. "It lacks seriousness."

"The earth jolt has nearly toppled the amusement park," I say reporter-style. "Thousands of proggles remain trapped within." Ella laughs meanly.

"Who says there's no such thing as a happy ending?" Larissa adds. She doesn't exactly have fond memories of the place, either.

Then we hear sirens.

"Oh!" Troy says fearfully. He tugs at his bandage. I wish I had a pocketful of cinnamon rolls, something to tempt him, to tempt his teeth, or his hand, or just the biting demon. I picture it bright red, devilish, enormous. When it opens its mouth, all you hear are screaming sirens.

We listen to the sirens moving slowly through Santa Vallejo. They don't sound like they're in a hurry. What's the point of a slow-moving sirened vehicle? It's an oxymoron in a town built on someone's worst history. I can't make sense of any of it.

We look to Will. Larissa asks simply, "Will?"

Will shakes his head, but I think he knows something. Philip leads him to our van, and we all get in and head through town, following the siren that moans so slowly, it sounds as if it knows there's really nothing it can do.

We follow at a respectable distance, quiet taking hold of the van. When I realize our direction, I'm stricken. I hear Dorothy whine. I want to grab Will and shake him. Ask him why we can't trust this town to keep us safe, as if he could answer such things, this thin person who hangs his head nearly out the window. He looks as if he could use a car seat, a bolster. A protective harness. But he doesn't look like he deserves one.

"The library," Dorothy whispers. She rolls down her window and sticks her nose up and out, inhaling, questioning. It smells like the library now, a bit like the amusement park, but newer. That highly questionable smell. And we're still half a mile away.

"What's happening?" I say.

Troy rips off a piece of bandage with his teeth, then seems to offer his hand to Will to gnaw on. But I might be imagining it.

We approach the library. Could it have tilted, too, tossing Jake to one side, across the room at the dizzying windows? Will he have gone down with his library? He's the type to do something like that, especially if there were children in the kids' area to protect. I envision tumbling encyclopedias, the domino effect of stacks falling upon stacks. I remember seeing this in a movie, a slow-motion shot of one huge shelf banging into the next, no hope for any poor patron—or librarian—foolish enough to be interested in the biography section, Ancient Egypt, car repair, pop-psychology. Where is Jake? Is he in the 800s? The 900s? Fiction A-J? Local history, where he thought he was safe?

I love a library, even this strange one. So, it is only natural to love the librarian. It's my most natural tendency in years. I try to stifle my own moaning, or maybe it's all in my head.

The siren roars, sounding its call: *Where is Jake? Where is Jake?* Slowly, steadily.

We arrive at the library and stop the car, all silent. The sirens finally quiet down; the ambulances sound like they're panting, exhausted from their journey. There's a small billow of black smoke shooting straight out the top of the purple library. The smoke also seems in no particular hurry, nor truly dangerous. Which shows what I know.

"Our library," says Juliet sadly.

"It's melting," says Dorothy.

"It can't melt," I say, but I look at Philip, who like all of us is slightly stunned. He looks to Will.

"Not exactly," says Will, who I realize knows exactly what it can or can't do. Of course he built the bad library too, designed it to look all cutesy but put it on another piece of hopeless if not contemptable land. Or landfill. So much of Southern California is built on it, why shouldn't it be the same up here, too?

We see Jake coming out with a tall stack of books. We run to hug him, to help him with the load he carries. To scream and jump, the things we need to do in life, right this minute, impending ridiculous earth jolts or not.

"Dad!" Dorothy says, then stops hugging him. "You smell funny," she says. She takes one giant step back.

"There's something on fire underneath," Jake says.

"You have to stay out," Will says.

"We need to save the books," Jake says.

Philip nearly traps Jake in his arms. "You really have to stay out. It's built on old transformers."

"Isn't a transformer one of those large robot toys, from the movies?" I ask. The last thing I need is a giant robot around here.

"No, old electric transformers. They're from the structure that used to be here," Will says.

We stare at him.

"They should have been removed," he says, dismally. "They'll let off elements you can't be near in a fire."

I feel furious, my stomach in knots. "Is nothing built right around here?" I ask. Will looks at the ground, so I guess it was a rhetorical question.

"I need to get the books," Jake says, heading back to the library.

"Dad," says Dorothy, and Larissa grabs her, as we are not about to let her go into that library. The potentially chemical-spewing library. Philip and Will run after Jake, into the library. I don't want Jake in there, but I feel glued to my spot. Troy makes a fearful sound by my side, his hand at his mouth, a strip of bandage dangling from his fingers. He opens wide.

"No, no, Troy," I say. Not the hand. Not because of some earth shake, one word or two. Not after being rescued from a doghouse, after being kidnapped twice, after having his friend drown in a too beautiful pool, after whatever it is we're seeing today. Not the hand. Patty, stop him. I take his hand, I kiss it.

"We love this hand, Troy, remember? We have to take care. This is just a funny purple building, another one."

I pat him on the hand, then smooth his hair, not because it needs it, but because I need to. "This is what matters," I say. "Troy."

Troy brings his teeth back together. He watches as I kiss his hand, his other hand patting at the side of his head I so hope he won't tug hard at. I offer him my own hand. It's an easy gesture to make.

"If you need it," I tell him.

He chews on my hand lightly, then looks up at me. I nod through the slight piercing and say, "We're together in this—" but what can only be described as a truly disturbing sense of smell overtakes me, and I run to the geraniums by the library's windows and throw up.

"Eew," Dorothy says.

Juliet comes over and rubs me on the back. She holds my hair. I throw up again. I feel dizzy.

"I don't think those are real geraniums," I tell Juliet. We look at them. They're fake. I never noticed this before. Maybe nothing will grow around here but fake flowers and giant purple structures that can't handle a little shaking and may be endangering both human life and world literature.

"Yuck," I say, feeling another wave of funny smell. Are the fake geraniums scented, too? I barf again, barf being my choice of vomit words from childhood.

"Oh," Juliet says, then as with any perfect domino effect—or what they used to call chain reaction, but domino effect is more warlike so it's gained in popularity in times like these—anyway, Juliet throws up as well.

"Aim for the geraniums," I say. "They already smell bad." And we can look somewhat inconspicuous if we face the side wall, as if we're admiring the landscaping, real or artificial, not barfing repeatedly. I was never that fond of geraniums anyway.

"Oh!" exclaims Dorothy, then breaks free from Larissa and runs over to another geranium area. Dorothy throws up.

"Uhh," Larissa says, holding her own stomach, but she maintains her equilibrium, so to speak. Maybe she didn't have any breakfast. I notice other people standing around, beginning to wretch as well. I have never considered myself a trendsetter before.

"This has got to stop," I say. Juliet leads us all back toward the van. We take turns patting one another's backs.

"Oh," Troy says, trying to make some point. He waves his wonderful hand in the air, conductor style, as if trying to bring our performance to a halt. My child doesn't understand the difference between performance art and sudden illness, but that's okay. Maybe that's not a terrible character flaw to have when you're four. Maybe it's all a performance, maybe we just think we feel sick. Maybe that's what the chemical compounds do to you. Fool you into a false sense of illness when what you should really feel is just plain appalled.

Jake and Philip come out with more books and lay them on the ground. Will follows them, jumping around madly.

"Don't touch them anymore," Will screams as Larissa approaches one little step. I just stand by, sick. "Just leave them—they're contaminated with PCBs. The whole inside is contaminated."

"It's one little stream of smoke," Jake says, looking at the books with great sadness, as if he has failed them.

"That's more than enough," Will says with a seriousness that makes my stomach drop, as if it could feel any worse.

The men step away from the books they've rescued, backing up slowly. I can hear Jake let out a low but quiet groan. Books should not be on the ground. They should be in someone's arms, but these books are, at least potentially, hazardous to your health.

"We could hose them down," Will says, "but I don't think it would help."

"Books don't respond well to water," Jake says.

"I didn't mean with water," Will says. Jake's eyes widen. We hear a smallish boom, if a boom can be smallish, from somewhere in the depths of the library.

"We need to go," Will says. He turns to the crowd around us, which now includes what are often referred to as bystanders, along with people dressed in padded gear and protective helmets, everyone standing there watching the single stream of dark smoke from the library's top, as if it were coming from a fireplace, although the fireplace inside is fake. This is not a fake flame, though the dangers here may well be manmade.

The library's walls creak with the latest boom. A wall settles slightly, a long break forming before our eyes from top to bottom, creating a new entrance. A little as if it has been unzipped. Even a purple library deserves better than this.

"Wow," Larissa says.

"Oh!" Troy screams unusually loudly, with fear in his voice. The shriek feels like it grabs at each one of us, or maybe just at me: It rips at my limbs and heart malevolently. Troy runs toward the unzipped library entrance, trying with all he has to get through it, and I feel myself scream in a kind of pain my mind has no memory of.

"Troy!"

But the crowd replies with its own sense of purpose, and a large group of people rushes after him. It almost looks like a joke, a trick, an act, as if ten or twelve or more people are trying to see if they can get through the door at once, and I fear for his safety—will he get doused by chemicals inside? Will he be trampled by the crowd? Do scenes of blood and gore await?

Is there nowhere this boy can be safe?

Somehow moving as one giant set of arms and legs, five or ten or fifteen people grab Troy before he can get through the break. They raise him up; they roar in victory. The moment feels like a scene in a gladiator movie, a prolonged, well-needed moment of rejoicing, a success of historical proportions. The crowd rescues Troy, they embrace him, they place him upon their shoulders and gently wave him in the air. He is their triumph. There is a long moment of hip-hip-hurrah, whether anyone needs to say it or not. He is theirs; he is all of ours. Troy raises both arms in the air, the bandage strip waiving breezily like a flag of conquest, and he smiles; he beams. It's the best ride of his life.

We all respond as one, we rally, we rejoice, and the crowd returns my boy to me.

I wrap my arms around Troy. He breathes through his mouth quietly, and we can both feel his breath as it warms his hand so close to his lips.

Will begins to corral us, forcing us to retreat, back to our cars, back to our homes. What were we thinking staying here so long, anyway? I hear whispers of short syllables, dangerous-sounding chemical compound abbreviations made from the most innocent of letters. ABCs gone truly evil.

"Just leave it," Will says, as the hazmat figures take over, looking fake, plastic, rounded by their suits, walking without moving their arms—almost like proggles. We get in the van. I see Jake hop into his car alone, no doubt smelling of disintegrating books and unpronounceable toxins. I want to join him, but I know he won't have me there now. We catch each other's eye, though, and I put my arms around Dorothy too. We will go home, clean off the funny smells, place the books we own around us on our beds, hold one another close, use literature wisely.

"We'll rebuild," Will says, standing straight, a tiny spark of confidence in his voice, as if he's trying it out. He looks me straight in the eye. "It's what we do."

* * *

Back at Larissa's, Jake has showered and sits off to the side, as if he doesn't want to subject us to what his body has taken in, although even I can't smell anything bad on him anymore. He smells like Irish Spring, although it doesn't seem like a natural enough soap for Larissa to have around. Maybe it has a clandestine use, removing chemicals of unknown effect from your body. Her disaster supplies are vast.

"Cookies," Larissa says, as if they are the answer, and they might well be. She brings us soft, warm sugar cookies frosted in pink, and you just want to kiss them, cradle them in your arms. They're that cute. I've never felt such longing for pink icing before. Troy and Dorothy devour them, the last two children left with us in Larissa's home, if you don't count the photos of (starving? freezing? abandoned?) children lining

Larissa's spare room walls. Who could need a cookie more than any one of those faces?

Don't think about it, Patty. Larissa brings me a plate of cookies as I sit here in my place on the couch again, as I watch Jake who will not sit with me. For some reason, I cannot bring myself to eat a cookie. They suddenly look sickening.

"It'll help get that taste out of your mouth," says Larissa, sucking on her own cookie. I look at the beautiful cookies. I want one, I know I do, but I am repelled. I look up at Larissa, confused at my own ambivalence.

"I just can't," I tell her. Could it be the chemicals, the fire, the groaning of the shacks in a way that makes you want to run, move away, rewrite history? What has made me spurn an innocent frosted cookie?

Larissa looks me over, head to toe. She waves a cookie in front of my nose, and I grab at my stomach.

"Oh, Patty," Larissa says, and I feel like I can read her mind right now, which is so clear, so single in its thought, so positive an indication. I wonder if she'll be angry, if she has a right to be, but she's happy, she's beaming. That she suspects before I do should hardly surprise me.

Larissa takes my hand and leads me to the bathroom quietly, and I go. I feel much younger than I really am.

Larissa has an array of long thin boxes under her bathroom sink, ranging from the brightly cheerful to the deathly serious, all neatly lined up. Pink, blue, digital, two-minute, three-minute. Early response (no package admits it gives you a late response, if you're stupid enough to still be wondering at that point). Plus/minus signs vs. Yes/No. Can it be maybe? I would be so happy with maybe. Maybe would let me eat the cookie in peace, wouldn't it? I close my eyes and pick a kit, thinking this is the most unusual impulse item I've ever selected. A simple store-bought kit, with results easier to read than a report card.

"A baby," Larissa says, beaming. She doesn't even wait for the results.

Chapter 14

Family, a Noun

It's the kind of day you want to stay safely indoors, in bed maybe, or hunker down at work, hang out in the local diner, wherever you feel safest. The air is chilly, the wind sharp with a warning that what lies ahead isn't going to be enjoyable. But you have to go through it just the same. To get to the other side, wherever that is.

At lunchtime, Walter closes the store, flipping over one of those old open/closed signs you see in movies. (We sell them for $1.99, and I admit I've always wanted one for my life in general. Sometimes I'd like to wear one around my neck.) I slip a dark sweater over my Bolts and Everything work shirt, something more appropriate for where we're going. We all head out together, Walter, Eva, and I, each of us having added a layer, making us a slightly more dressed-up yet muted version of ourselves—us but less so. I follow behind them, elders in the front, Eva taking the lead, head held high, though not one of us smiles or looks in the slightest bit hopeful. We pick up Juliet from the restaurant. (She's also wearing a dark sweater—it is today's uniform— and her leggings are a subdued gray, which makes me sad for her.) We journey on toward the local park. It isn't far from Larissa's house: She often takes the kids there when the backyard seems too small, when the world closes in uncomfortably. It's a place where they are safe to run, she believes. It's all fenced in with green chain link (not as ugly as you might think if you're a mother or caregiver and realize the need for a safe boundary). You can see people approaching from any side, which I've come to appreciate, now that my eyes tend to wander to who might be passing nearby, at the ready. Who stands in the shadows, who lurks, who bides his (or her, don't forget) time? Maybe no one. But who knows better than I what can happen when you forget to focus for a moment? They say eyes on the prize for a reason, though this has never occurred to me before.

Valley Park is a rectangular green space, like the green shape you'd find on a board game, a space intended to be park-like according to someone's design at least. Only six trees surround the periphery, but they're six good trees, tall and somehow leafy. They're real trees. Such things have begun to impress themselves on me. I find the smell of trees particularly appealing today. I'm not the tree-hugging type (I'm a little more afraid of ants than I should be), but I can see the appeal of it. The scent alone could make me try it, although not today. It would be less than appropriate today.

A small crowd, both children and adults, gathers by the children's area, which has been decorated modestly with a few balloons, as if what we're headed for were just a birthday party that no one is too happy about attending, if such a thing exists. That party would still be a happier occasion than this. We encircle a single brand-new swing—its leather seat awaits, uncracked, undamaged by wind, rain, or small hands, a swing for all those children who will play here. *Dedicated to Cecil,* says the plaque on it, *who loved to play.* Did Cecil love to play? Did Cecil play once upon a time in any normal sense of the word? Did he lose his love of play as he developed each tic, each cough, each disturbing characteristic? Was he doomed from the start? Was he always Cecil-like, slightly different and never in the best of ways?

I hug my boy, who has come with his group of preschool friends, Dorothy, Gretel, and Ella the terrible. Ella brushes a few specs of sand off the swing, perhaps in apology for her constant harassment of Cecil.

Does she feel guilty at such a young age? Should she? Will she change her ways now that her rival is dead, drowned, gone but memorialized in a small, one-person-at-a-time swing set? What happens to a character after she loses her rival? Will her next chapter be a happy one? I search my mind for literature I know. The results don't look good.

I hug my child as we look at the swing dedicated to a dead child. Cecil's mother is not among us.

"Where is Liv?" I ask Larissa. And not for the first time.

"She's moved on," Philip says for Larissa, who knows better than to answer. "They're not pressing charges against her," Philip adds quietly.

Tears begin to fall down Larissa's face. She just shakes her head, and I wonder if we wanted them to press charges against Liv. The term "press charges" makes my heart race a little, and I bring Troy closer to me. Liv endangered her child—shouldn't there be charges? Or is his drowning enough punishment, if punishment is the issue? What does all this mean to her? For surely, even with a child such as Cecil, the loss must mean something. But I can't know, and I'm glad not to. My child is warm. I scrunch down to place my lips on his head; he raises his hand to his own lips, looking almost like he's about to blow a kiss good-bye, especially if you didn't know the other options he keeps in mind for that hand.

I blow a kiss with my hand to show him. "Cecil," I whisper. Show and tell. Troy repeats the gesture and maybe even the sentiment, if not the word.

Cecil. Who names a child Cecil?

Jake joins me with Dorothy, and I rise and lean into him in a way I don't remember ever doing. He is my tree to hug. (I have become very emotional these days—I never would have considered the "man as tree" metaphor appropriate in life before, for example.) Have I ever felt close enough to someone to allow him to support some if not all of my weight? Jake puts his arm around me, his other tapping his coat pocket, where I know he keeps the early response test. Jake carries the test with the blue line everywhere. He taps it and smiles. We've talked about it, about where the color blue can take you, about how we will go there together. How we will revise the nuclear family (surely there must be a less militaristic word than nuclear, besides non-nuclear). The new family; the family for our times. Not your mother's family, something newly devised, invented, re-created—something we've given a whole lot of thought to. Something that fits us, our lives, our community. Community, I hear, smelling something sweet. I'm so sappy these days.

We've discussed it all, long nights of making pro/con lists/, outlines of possibilities, jot lists, always reaching the same conclusion: We will give our baby to Larissa. We feel he or she is as much hers anyway—and that it is the best answer to all of our questions, worries, and obligations. It's the very least we can do, the thing that's most right. Who deserves a baby most? Who could deserve a baby more?

Though I'd usually say it's not up to me to decide (though I've been wrong before), it actually is up to me to decide—me and Jake. Our choice is a little out of the ordinary, sure, though this should surprise no one. Jake and I need to do this—we agree 100 percent. Still, we will never be far away from Larissa, Philip, the baby. Dorothy and Troy.

Family has fifteen meanings in Webster's, and the new me, the new Patty, is suddenly all in favor of making up a few more—or maybe giving up the dictionary altogether. Time to stop being so literal, Patty, and maybe give up the parenting books well. Or maybe we'll add our chapter (if not a whole book) on how to raise your child—or someone else's—unlike any Larissa has read so far. Or just let her write it. No one has been outlining it longer. No one deserves it more. I am in awe of her research. For Jake and I, this is the essay answer to our mistakes, our lives so far, and will only take us nine months to write. It's not multiple choice. More like a final exam or maybe a complete dissertation.

"Things in life have rarely made this much sense," I told Jake, who said the same words to Larissa for both of us. For all of us. We watched the idea dawn on her, the notion, the meaning, the very definition of family, a noun. This is the something that's right we've been wanting to do, a thing that makes up for a different thing, a mistake (or two). A joyful thing—one look at Larissa's face that day told us that.

Larissa stood there radiant with expectation, and of course I, with all my paleness and continuous nausea, was not radiant. But I'm not going anywhere, either.

At the park today, Ella reaches forward to clean the swing again, although I don't think it needs it. I hope this isn't the start of a compulsive disorder for her. Will there be post-traumatic stress? Will Ella, not to mention Gretel, begin to chew on something or someone, or take on any of a myriad of PTSD characteristics?

Who will need therapy the most?

"Should four-year-olds even be at a funeral?" I ask Jake.

"It's a memorial service," he says.

"And that makes it okay?" I ask.

Jake shakes his head. "Nothing makes it okay. They shouldn't be here. No one should be here. It's a question without an answer," he says librarian-like but not meanly, upset that he doesn't have the right response, that it doesn't appear in his reference book of a mind. I'm sure there's advice in some of the childrearing books: Chapter Fourteen, Taking Your Child to a Funeral/Memorial Service/Swing Dedication. Or maybe not. Maybe it's too awful to write about. Surely no parenting expert would want to picture us here today, standing before a sad-looking swing, attempting to endure a memorial service for a disturbed child allowed to drown in an overly expensive albeit unfenced swimming pool on a cold, cold day. I can't imagine a Chapter Fourteen that could offer any help at all or that any reader wouldn't just skip.

We all stand around, looking at the swing, which moves back and forth of its own volition in the chilly breeze. It's cold. The children should be running, jumping, sliding, propelling themselves through the plastic tubes, generating heat, drinking from little juice cartons, then repeating the process.

Instead, we stand before the swing, no doubt each of us making a secret wish. A small community of onlookers surrounds us. Maybe they came for Cecil or just for some boy they heard had died. Maybe they've lost children of their own. Maybe they thought this was just any day and came to let their children enjoy the playground. Maybe a memorial service was the last thing they expected, but they're too polite to leave, or maybe too stunned. I see families, moms, assorted solemn faces, some marked with pity, some with mouths agape. All your worst fears, gathered here this morning, staring right at you.

I scan the faces in the crowd, faces that blur, faces I don't recognize exactly, or do I? They begin to take on more clarity. If that man over there had a checkered shirt, if he and his wife were dressed in more of a gypsy style (instead of her wearing cotton clothes that look as if they may once have belonged to Larissa, and he an old denim shirt like Jake would wear)—if the woman were wearing a babushka and orange-and-yellow blouse, and if she were standing in front of a shack? Who would she be? The woman staring at us—if she looked displaced, homeless, without a country to her name—wouldn't I recognize her? Haven't we met before? Just because you're wearing rescued hand-me-downs and look familiar from having your mug shot on the TV, does that make you a bad person? Or just one of us?

Aren't we all immigrants? Can't illegal in some way describe any and all of us at this point? You know the answer to that one, Patty.

She's the woman who lived behind the amusement park, and she meets my eyes, a look of pure kindness on her face, a face that seems afraid to show too much happiness, too much expression, as if it weren't safe, yet. Hers is a face full of relief, belonging, community. A face that was no doubt brought to some semblance of legality by reams of computer printouts, courtesy of Phillip, who creates fresh lives digitally and with feeling. With a name, real or imagined. She has been documented, her face tells me. She has a child by her side, a little girl. A little girl she has found? A little girl who was always meant to be by her side but who had once been lost, between homes, between countries? It is so clearly her daughter, despite different hair color, not quite the same nose, lips that turn up at the sides. Anyone, no matter how nearsighted, would know this, even if you couldn't quite see their faces clearly, from the mother's stance, her attention. You'd just know that's her child, whatever the origination.

Troy waves at the woman; she gives a little wave back, then nods at me. She mouths a word in our direction in a language I don't know but feel like I understand just the same. It doesn't matter whose language it is.

I look at Larissa, who nods, too. This is our community. It's a big valley: We've got room. We can extend our arms, at the very least metaphorically.

"Is anyone going to speak?" Juliet asks softly, returning my thoughts to why we are here, to Cecil. But we are all stricken. What is there to say?

"We're gathered here for Cecil," says Walter, who no doubt has said something similar before, although not for a four-year-old, I can only hope. And not for such a four-year-old. Walter is the eldest and most commanding of us, the most like whatever religious personage might officiate something such as a swing dedication, memorial service, moment of silence for a disturbed and disturbing boy. Eva stands strong beside him generating a necessary warmth.

"We come to dedicate this place to Cecil, to his memory, for the happiness of all who come after him," Walter says. Eva nods, exuding strength. Troy bites at his thumb but not too hard. Dorothy keeps her face stoic. We watch the swing. It doesn't seem right. The swing stands a little away from the other swings, a solitary swing. Something about it screams Cecil in a way that makes me think I'm going to be sick, but I keep it together. It's not about you, Patty, don't go throwing up. No

Chapter Fourteen would find it appropriate adult behavior, even for someone in your condition (that means a mother, Patty, someone who should know better, maybe have brought a few crackers along to settle her stomach, not to mention a few to pass around to the children). I am empty handed. I stuff my hands in Jake's coat pockets for all they're worth.

I think about what Walter didn't say: that we've lost a child we love, that we will miss him every day, think of him every day, mourn him every day. These things are all untrue. The children will forget him. We will forget him in almost no time at all, and we'll be relieved to forget him. The swing will forget him—it never had to know him, to sit and eat with him, to try to bring him under some kind of control, keep him calm and from hurting himself or someone else. Cecil would have destroyed this swing, kicked it, sunk his teeth into it, scratched the heck out of it. In time, the memorial plaque will come unglued, fall into the shredded bark below it, be trodden upon, disappear. Only Larissa will remember, but even her memory will fade, and in her mind, he will become a normal boy, a beloved boy, a wonderful little boy who came to a tragic end. One who was loved by all and memorialized on a chilly day by those who adored him. Surely no boy deserves less, even Cecil, who is not the boy she will remember.

Thank god it wasn't Troy, Patty. Not my child. That's what you're really thinking. That's what everyone is thinking.

Larissa clears her throat, Larissa, the true mother among us, who has the most reason to not come to our aid today but who does anyway. "Okay, kids, who'll be first?" The usually brave bunch stays in place a moment, the reformed Ella even taking a step back. I let go of Troy, and he goes happily, my Troy, skipping, practically jumping into the swing. Who wouldn't want such a boy? Dorothy heads over and gives him a push, and Troy beams. He glows.

"Good," he says softly, his voice gruff and squeaky. You could miss it if you weren't listening closely for any little sound, and you might think you'd imagined it if you had your hopes up too high, but I hear it. Those of us who need to, we hear it.

"Good," Dorothy replies to him.

* * *

Back at my apartment, I fill brand-new packing boxes that I fully intend to label this time. I use a pregnancy-approved scent-free marker. Troy's Room, I handwrite messily, not teacher-like at all. Dorothy's Room and Our Room, somewhat vague, but I know just what it means. I add an exclamation mark to Kitchen! for no reason at all. I give each box a pat.

I have recycled all traces of old boxes.

We are moving to a rental house two doors down from Larissa's. It's a small house, the same blueprint as Larissa's but reversed, so that it feels familiar, yet I keep walking into walls. This will be my first "our home," a place I choose to live in with others I love. My eyes start to water, a clear indication I'm just too hormonal for words, one reason I prefer to pack alone. You can be as mushy as you like with a marker and stack of cartons as your companions. They keep your secrets, as I already know.

Packing becomes a joyous event, and I don't stop smiling till I find the old brochure, the one from the presentation about Santa Vallejo, the promotional materials that led me to where I am today. Welcome to Santa Vallejo, it says, although not one of the photos seems to be the right color—the sky is too dark, the river too blue. The brochure seems more a suggestion of what they hoped the town would become. I've found myself not in Santa Vallejo proper, too expensive to live in and toxic in so many meanings of the word. I am safer in the valley, happier. *Community,* the brochure says in a handsome twenty-four-point font. It doesn't refer to the valley at all, as if it didn't deserve mention. It doesn't talk about a leaning amusement park that wasn't any fun to begin with or a library that has trapped its own books inside, a library that has forgotten its history. It doesn't mention that Santa Vallejo is falling down, falling down, falling down.

In the back of a drawer I find my glasses. When I put them on, the brochure appears too bright. It's clear now that there's been something wrong from the beginning.

I glance at the fine print on the brochure, a sentence marked with an asterisk. I could swear it's as if a TV announcer reads it to me: *Your Actual Life May Vary.* Your actual life may vary, Patty. You forgot to read the fine print.

I push up my glasses and see that the actual asterisked remark says something entirely different. The brochure says only: *Your Life Awaits You at Santa Vallejo, a Development in Progress.* I'm unsure what they mean by "a development in progress." Do they mean the town? Are they referring to my life? Isn't a development in progress just a simple redundancy, and one that doesn't warrant an asterisk in the first place?

I put the brochure into the basket that we use to transport our paper, glass, and plastic to the large recycle bin outside the apartment. Troy likes to carry it and will be thrilled to find something to recycle. I'm making sure no one accidentally reads it to him, grabs it accidentally like a bedtime story. It's the worst kind of make-believe, with its heart in the wrong place.

It's late afternoon in the store, where I find myself nesting in a way, laying new shelf paper, dusting (with my face mask on), scaring customers with my masked efficiency, not that I'm malevolent about it.

I take some old, ripped shelf paper and a few empty cartons out behind the store, and spot Will with his lowered head. "Hey," I yell at him, although I certainly know his name. He speeds away.

"Hey," I say, more aggressively. Surprising even myself, I throw an empty cardboard box in his direction and beam him in the shoulder. Nice girls don't throw packing boxes, Patty. But he brings out the worst in me, what can I tell you?

I'll be watching him. He can be my rival, the Cecil to my Ella. "I will keep you honest," my very good shot says.

He silently heads for the new building, the new mini house-like structure behind the store that has replaced his old habitat.

"Okay, what's in the shack?" I ask.

"It's not a shack," he says.

"Don't talk to me about semantics," I say, as if he were a freshman (not that I ever used this tone of voice, but it might have helped if I did). I grab a key out of his hand. He's so weak. Why doesn't this boy eat something? This boy who is my age.

I unlock the new shelter. Am I about to find another one of Will's houses of horrors?

Inside, the place is warm, with a soothing natural light enhanced by the slightly familiar buzz of a personal computer, along with the warmth generated by the redheaded man tending it, who could not look more like a brother of mine if he tried, and whom I know as Philip. Then of course there's the man just to his left surrounded by books, stroking them as he reads the titles to the man who is now my brother. There are books everywhere in the cramped but cozy building. It is not a shack. Will's right. Jake looks up and holds the volume to his heart.

I open my mouth, but nothing comes out. Philip waves. Jake caresses his book. Will slinks in behind me and starts shelving. I cannot ask my question, and Jake cannot answer it. With all the words tucked away in the volumes lining these walls, you'd think we could borrow a few.

"Hi, Patty," Philip says.

"Welcome to Santa Vallejo Library *temporarius*," Jake says softly. "May we help you?"

I just stand there, not sure what brought me, why I'm here, what I thought I wanted. I'm also feeling a sense of déjà vu.

"It smells nice in here," I tell them.

"We were just saying that," Philip says. Jake pats a book, then adds it to a pile.

"People think books smell musty," Jake says, "but they're wrong."

"Whose books are these?" I ask. "These nice smelling books?" I pick one up. It is called *History of the Santa Vallejo Valley.* It is Volume One. It's not real leather, and it's not very heavy, but it feels like a survivor.

"Ours," Jake says.

"Ours in the utilitarian sense of books belonging to the masses stuff?" I ask. "Ours as in yours and Philip's? Yours?" I say, turning to Will, who can't quite manage to stare me down.

"Ours." Jake says. "They belonged to the valley. There was a library here."

"Here?" I ask, as in here in a shack?

"No, where the new store went in, but not so big," Jake says. "Old, unstylish, not architecturally correct."

"No comment," says Will.

"Cozy. No blinding fluorescent lighting," Jake says. "No fireplace, no learning center, no amphitheater," he adds.

"Books and shelves," Philip says. "And librarians."

"These were valley books," Jake says. "They took them all when the new library was being built."

"How did these books get here?" I ask. "Not that it's any of my business." Maybe I should just go. It's just books. Stolen books. It's not high up on the food chain of crimes. Worse things have been taken. Who do I think I'm kidding anymore?

"We rescued them, before the building became uninhabitable," Jake says. "These books are untainted by chemical obscenities."

"Oh, I like the sound of that," Philip adds, jotting something down.

"Philip made them disappear from the system," Jake says. Philip waves a hand over his PC, *Let's Make a Deal* style. I repeat the gesture, which is a fun one to make.

Philip pats his computer. "The information age. Watch the information disappear, watch it reappear. That kind of thing."

"We brought the books back to the valley," Jake says.

"And the fire that started in the library, did you—" I stop, not sure where exactly my question is going, whether I'm headed toward an accusation or running away from one, fast.

Philip and Jake look at me, eyes widening in their innocence. Then we all turn to Will.

"No, that just happened," Will said. "No one had to start that fire. You could argue it was bound to happen someday. I should have argued it, anyway."

"We've been bringing these to Philip's garage for a while. The Santa Vallejo people wanted to hide them in boxes if not toss them altogether. So, we took them. We're restoring our own library," Jake says. "It may not have been right," he starts, then stops for a minute. We let all of our thoughts catch up. Then Jake goes on. "But these are the ones that are left, now, so it's something. It's something between right and wrong."

Proper runs through my mind, but in a good way.

"You guys," Philip says. "They're books and they're here now. They would have been destroyed. Does the rest really matter?" Jake and Philip look at me, waiting. As if it were up to me, Patty Grant, fugitive, liar, thief, really bad English teacher, child endangerer, box thrower.

"I love books," I say. The room lets out its breath. Jake nods. Philip goes back to his computer screen.

Weren't library books intended to be borrowed, anyhow?

Jake holds up the local history volume. "I'm not sure this one is quite up to date."

"It is slim," Philip says.

"I think I may need to work on a revised edition," Jake says. "Put it into words. Rewrite history."

Philip nods. We all consider this.

I'll want to read the local history book that Jake writes for us. I want to know it all, commit it to memory, happily turn the page to each new chapter, look forward to the next volume, and the next. I won't even mind if my name appears. I want to rebuild; I want to nest. I live here now.

Epilogue:
My Actual Life May Vary

We turn our attention to holidays, just as Larissa once suggested. Before we know it, it is time for that scariest of nights, when parents' fears are often spoken if not realized, at least if you read small town newspapers and listen to suburban myths, both of which I have given up following. It's not that I want to be ignorant, just less terrified every day. After all, we still listen to NPR on the emergency radio for the big picture of our lives.

No need to throw the baby out with the bathwater, one of the most horrid expressions ever, comes through my mind. Where could that even have come from? I will not look up the derivation. Instead, I turn my attention back to where it belongs.

Like to the child who curtsies in front of me. "See, I am Dorothy," says my little girl. She has the full Dorothy regalia on, her light brown hair in braids, the blue-and-white checked dress, the basket with a petite toy dog. (Why Larissa had a Todo-like stuffed dog in the closet remains a mystery, though not exactly a shock.) Our Dorothy has ruby slippers. I wait for her to click her heels. I may try this myself. I've never had an occasion to before.

"You certainly are Dorothy," I say. I don't need to know more than that, and neither does she.

Jake takes Dorothy's picture. He does not say "smile," he does not prompt. We will wait for Dorothy to decide for herself what she wants her face to reveal. Dorothy raises her basket and clicks her shoes together. Three times. She doesn't say the words, but that's okay. They speak for themselves.

Troy is a small brown bear tonight, no deep meaning, nothing psychological in the slightest. Just a happy, bouncing little bear of a boy, who has been saying *roar* in every possible inflection, meaning "hello," "I would like an apple now," and "please hurry and finish dinner," although my translations may be a little off. My boy is a happy little bear, right now at least, and there are worse things to be in life, as he and I both know. He has several Winnie the Pooh Band-Aids across his hand in carefully selected places, but accessorizing is not the worst thing. Trust me, you would barely notice. Don't all bears need Band-Aids? Don't we all?

Tonight, we trick and treat like any family, strolling along the well-organized streets of our valley at dusk, flashlights in hand just in case, to ward off the sense of danger that comes with nightfall, although daytime can be plenty scary. We have a special Halloween plush pumpkin rattle (stuffed with organic cotton by fair-trade workers in Nepal) to bring to baby Joshua at Larissa's.

I also have extra batteries for the flashlights, extra bags for candy, extra shoes in case Dorothy's ruby slippers cause blisters. We probably won't need any of it. We may need something I'd never have thought of. We are sure to get way too much candy. We probably will drop the pieces we covet most. I have no way of knowing for sure, no guide to tell me what to do, and I know enough not to believe one anyway. My actual life will vary.

My thoughts bring me back to the moment, the holiday, when I trip on a crack, and a cruel sense of déjà vu overtakes me. For a minute, I'm not sure where I am, though I'm afraid, and as I look up, I see a dull green house with a fence, and behind the fence I could swear I see a doghouse, and maybe something hanging from it, a cord, a piece of twine. But I've been up since very early, working on the costumes, engaging in my new life, and I don't have to check out everything anymore, do I? I don't need to research every little thing. I mean, I'm not even wearing my glasses. Should I be more careful or ignore my imagination completely, put one foot in front of the other?

Jake stands behind us. I take Troy's hand, I take Dorothy's hand, I look both ways, and I prepare to step off the curb toward the houses I hope will give us the best and most tightly sealed treats.

"Ready," I say. It doesn't require a question mark at all. But one still lingers. There's always going to be at least one to any story you might live through, don't you think?

The End

Acknowledgments

This book has taken a kind of persistence that often feels like a giant vat of strawberry ice cream has landed on my head: delicious but a bit painful. I'm thrilled to be able to thank a few of the really good people who shared the flavors with me along the way.

Top of the page thanks to everyone at Santa Fe Writers Project that I've hounded for a good long time now, especially Andrew Gifford for every yes along the way plus a couple of maybes; Nicole Schmidt for finding my manuscript in the first place; Adam Ferguson for a lovely edit; Rachel Weber for her careful copy edit; and Adam al-Sirgany and Monica Prince for their truly sweet support and encouragement.

Thank you to my writer friends for listening to me talk about this story and looking it over from time to time. That's you, Jane Rosenberg LaForge, Jill Yesko, Christina Pitcher, and Beverly Ball.

Thank you for general support and well-being to: Cindy Lambert, Vicky Norton, Dave Smith, Monica Summers (and Ellie and Luca and Lyric), Linda Childers, Susan Louie, Keri Northcott, Ron Salazar, and Lynn Muradian.

Many thanks to Scott Baldwin for his inspiring artwork and longtime friendship. And to Jackie Garcia for her savvy PR and website skills.

Thank you to the San Fernando Valley for raising me then letting me go.

I've dedicated this book to my late mother-in-law, Patricia Everitt, who was such a steadfast champion of my work (and nothing at all like Patty btw). Thanks and love to all the Everitts, especially Michael and Casey. Ice cream's on me!

About the Author

Linda Lenhoff lives in the San Francisco Bay Area and writes for a variety of publications when she's not completely covered by cats. *Your Actual Life May Vary* is her fourth novel and was a finalist for the 2019 SFWP Publication prize, the Galileo Prize from Free State Review, and the Orison Prize. The first chapter, "Your Actual Life May Vary," was published in *This Side of the Divide* by Baobab Press in 2019 and also appeared in The Tishman Review and Embark. Linda's story "Joie to the World" recently won second place in *Lilith Magazine*'s fiction contest and was published in the Fall 2023 issue. Her earlier novels include *The Girl in the '67 Beetle*, *Latte Lessons*, and *Life a la Mode*, which was translated into four languages. She earned an MFA in Creative Writing from SDSU but is a UCLA Bruin through and through. Follow her on Instagram at lindalattelessons or at lindalattelessons.wordpress.com.

Also from Santa Fe Writers Project

Magic For Unlucky Girls by A.A. Balaskovits

The fourteen fantastical stories in *Magic For Unlucky Girls* take the familiar tropes of fairy tales and twist them into new and surprising shapes. These unlucky girls, struggling against a society that all too often oppresses them, are forced to navigate strange worlds as they try to survive.

> "A wonderful, truly original work."
> — Emily St. John Mandel, author of *Station Eleven*

Mona at Sea by Elizabeth Gonzalez James

This sharp, witty debut introduces us to Mona Mireles — observant to a fault, unflinching in her opinions, and uncompromisingly confident in her professional abilities. Mona is a Millennial perfectionist who fails upwards in the midst of the 2008 economic crisis.

> "*Mona at Sea* is sharply written Millennial malaise that dares to be hopeful."
> — Georgia Clark, San Francisco Chronicle

If the Ice Had Held by Wendy J. Fox

Melanie Henderson's life is a lie. The scandal of her birth and the identity of her true parents is kept from her family's small, conservative Colorado town. Not even she knows the truth: that her birth mother was just 14 and unmarried to her father, a local boy who drowned when he tried to take a shortcut across an icy river.

> "Razor-sharp...written with incredible grace and assurance."
> — Benjamin Percy, author of *The Dark Net*

About Santa Fe Writers Project

SFWP is an independent press founded in 1998 that embraces a mission of artistic preservation, recognizing exciting new authors, and bringing out of print work back to the shelves.

  @santafewritersproject | @SFWP | sfwp.com